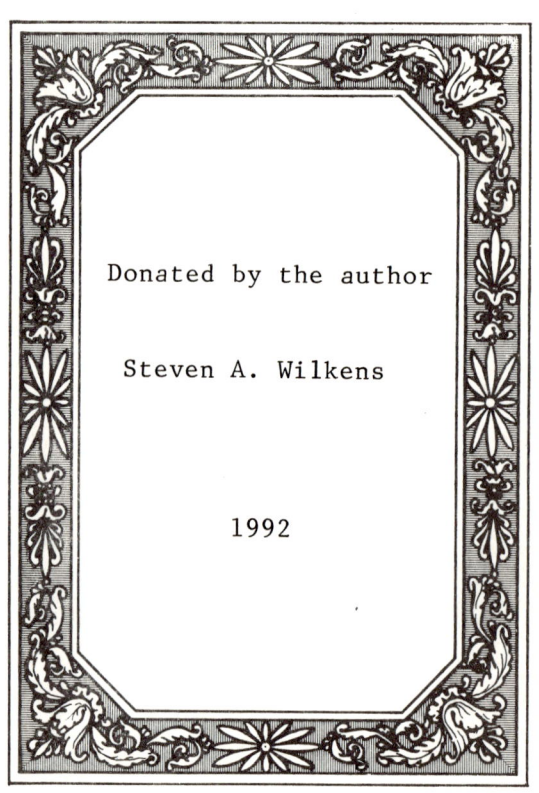

Transport
A Novel
by
Steven A. Wilkens

Dorrance Publishing Co., Inc.
Pittsburgh, Pennsylvania 15222

Copyright (c) 1991 by Steven A. Wilkens
All Rights Reserved
ISBN # 0-8059-3237-2
Printed in the United States of America
First Printing

To my wife Becky Ann, and all my friends that offered the support to see it through.

*This novel is a work of fiction. Although based on historical fact, the names, characters, places and events are either the product of the author's imagination or are used fictitiously.

ACKNOWLEDGMENTS

The author wishes to acknowledge the following people for their help and support for seeing this project through. Without them TRANSPORT could not have happened. Clive Cussler, Eugene P. Wilkens Sr., Nancy Michiels, Joe Fierke, James Austin, Paul and Eve Germain, Sharon Bredice, Margaret Ketchmark, Margaret Hybarger, Judy L. Rogers, Norman and Katherine Kinney, Rick and Marcie Bonney.

. . . there are times when things are not what they seem. When the difference between right and wrong is not black or white, just shades of gray . . .

CHAPTER ONE
December 6, 1941
23:00
11:00 PM

The 2180-ton Japanese I-18 had finally arrived eight miles off the entrance to Pearl Harbor. It had been a trying eighteen days since she had left Japan with a two-man midget submarine attached to her back. The I-18 was one of five I class boats carrying the midgets for the impending attack on America's mighty Pacific Fleet's home.

Twice the boat had almost sunk to the bottom during routine diving drills. Both times the cause was found to be debris left over from the building yard.

Since neither the boat nor her crew had any real combat experience, her commander, Captain Tanaka, thought it prudent to drill, drill, drill, all the way to Pearl. It was during one of the diving drills that the boat nearly dropped to the bottom like a stone. The dive started off alright, the alarm rang, and the lookouts dropped down through the hatch, followed closely by the Captain. The hatch was securely dogged down just as the water washed over the coaming.

The drill was to take the boat to ninety feet and level off. Ninety feet came and went, the bow grew heavier, and the angle of the deck made standing erect difficult.

The navigator instantly shouted for the forward trimming tanks to be blown and all forward discharge pumps to be engaged. This failed to have the desired affect, and the boat kept sinking. Captain Tanaka ordered all ahead speed, trying to shift the momentum. The Torpedo Officer rushed forward to the torpedo room to do whatever possible to save himself and his boat. Torpedo Officer Yuko Shoji found two men already attacking the problem for all they were worth, but to no avail. A foreign object was jammed in the forward trimming tank valve, and nothing could be done to open the valve. They had already put everything they had into forcing the valve with the wheel spanner.

By now the boat was sinking faster and faster; it wouldn't be much longer before the intense pressure of the ocean depths crushed the pressure hull and sent the wreckage and the ninety-seven lives it housed plummeting down into the dark abyss. The boat had already passed the designed depth of 325 feet and was still sinking. Yuko grabbed a nearby wrench and started beating the side of the valve in a desperate attempt to dislodge whatever was jammed. Suddenly the valve started to turn, high pressure air started hissing into the tank. But was it too late? The boat continued to sink, reaching 375 feet. It was believed that the boat could stand the pressure at 400 feet, but no one was sure. They had done all they could, now they stood silently and watched the depth needle slow. Is this how they would die before they had a chance to fight the enemy?

At 385 feet the needle of the depth gauge finally stopped and the boat leveled off for a moment, then started to shoot back towards the surface, like a frolicking whale, the I-18 broached the surface nearly out of control. Luckily there were no enemy patrols around to witness the spectacle.

The near death experience only served to heighten Captain Tanaka's demands for more drills, which commenced forthwith and continued constantly until reaching their destination. The only time not used for drills was the time needed for charging the batteries. This time was also used for preparation of the midget. Most of the crew was relieved to see the neon lights of Waikiki beach; it meant relief from the riggers of constant drills. The time had finally come to stop training and start doing.

Strains of music could be heard coming from the beach, and the colored lights of the runway at the airfield were clearly visible, as were the headlamps of the occasional passing motor car. There were no visible signs that the Americans knew they were there. As the I-18 wallowed in the swells of a roughening sea, last minute preparations were underway on the midget. At twenty mile intervals the same rituals were happening on the other five midgets strapped to the backs of the mother-subs. At various other points around the island, twenty other Japanese submarines were taking up their assigned positions waiting for the hostilities to commence.

At last the appointed moment had come for the launching of the midget. The midget's Captain Hideyo Fujita stepped into the control room and bowed to Captain Tanaka, then turned towards Yuko and smiled. Hideyo and Yuko had grown up together, played together as children, and now had gone to war together. But somehow they both sensed that this would be the last time they would see each other. Before taking his place in the midget, Hideyo placed a letter into his friend's hand, bowed one last time, and was gone.

The mother sub released the clamps and dived, freeing the midget and sending it on its way. The midget reached the entrance to the bay just before the air attack began. Luckily an American vessel was entering the harbor and the nets had been pulled back for it. As Hideyo guided his small craft ahead and slightly to port of the incoming U.S.S. ANTRARES, another midget fell in behind ANTRARES hoping to sneak into the bay in her wake.

The midget bringing up the rear of the ANTRARES was sighted by a U.S. mine sweeper, and the four-stack American destroyer WARD rushed in on the attack sinking the midget. Hideyo pressed on with his attack. The enemy's battleships loomed large in his periscope; he quickly picked his target and focused his total being on the ARIZONA.

Explosions were bursting all around him; his knuckles had turned white from the pressure he exerted on the controls. Any thought of escape had left his mind, the target was nearing, he was about to fell a major American capitol ship with his little two-man craft. Suddenly the target rose in the water and took an instant list. Flames and flying debris, mixed with steam and smoke, partially blocked his view of the enemy.

Then a jarring concussion knocked Hideyo against the steel sides of the cramped confines of the control room of the midget. He quickly recovered and swung the periscope to starboard. An enemy destroyer was racing towards him with forward guns blazing. Hideyo took one final look at the ARIZONA; the battleship was settling into the mud. It was already doomed, so there was no point in his pressing on with his own attack. The time had come for him to escape this other fellow.

Hideyo quickly altered course to port and hoped to find safety amongst the towering hulls of the American battleships anchored in a row. His plan was for the destroyer to lose sight of his periscope and not risk firing on him so close to other U.S. ships. A daring plan by any standards. With all the chaos coming out of the sky, he was counting on the battleships not seeing him at their sides. Then, when the destroyer had lost his scent, Hideyo would move out and attack one of the ships that had just been his safe haven.

Hideyo had nearly made it when a four inch shell ripped into the port ballast tank blowing the thin skin wide open. The explosion allowed all the compressed air to escape, removing any buoyancy the craft had. The midget plummeted to the muddy bottom of the bay. Hideyo realized that there was little hope of survival, the surface was only fifty feet above, certainly shallow enough for a free ascend. But even if they could reach the surface, what then? Prisoner of war?

Hideyo decided that he would rather die than surrender to the enemy, but he would allow his only crew member to decide for himself. For either of them to try an escape would mean flooding the midget to open the hatch. Not that it mattered, a hairline crack in the pressure hull on the port side was slowly allowing water to seep in anyway.

The other officer decided to make an effort to escape, reasoning that he might be able to get clear of the bay and swim out towards the waiting mother subs. Hideyo agreed to let him try, although he didn't even loosen his own safety harness. As the seal of the hatch was loosened, water quickly flooded the interior. While his partner wiggled through the hatch and made for the surface, Hideyo didn't fight it. He took a deep breath and filled his lungs with water and lost consciousness. The war for him was over.

CHAPTER TWO
April 23, 1945
03:00
3:00 AM

The telephone rang several times before Beckler was able to shake loose the cobwebs that entombed his brain. Turning over in his bed, he reached out into the total darkness, feeling for, then lifting the receiver. A far away sounding voice began talking before he could get the phone to his ear.

"Captain Andrew Beckler? You there?" The voice asked.

"Yeah, this is Beckler. Who the hell are you?"

"This is Lieutenant Delair, at Naval Operations, Alameda."

"Naval Operations? What do you want? What time is it, anyway?" Beckler demanded.

"Sorry to wake you, sir, but I have my orders too," Delair defended.

"Orders? Orders from who?"

"I'm not at liberty to say, at this time, who gave the order. But I've been instructed to inform you, that you are to report to this office at 0600 this date."

There was a short silence before Beckler responded.

"Report to Alameda? What the hell for?"

"As I said before. . . ," Delair started to say.

"Yeah, I know, you're not at liberty to say!" Beckler finished it for him. "What does the Navy want with a Merchant Seaman?"

"That I don't know as yet, sir. All I do know, is that it's imperative that you're prompt. So, please be here at 06:00."

Beckler started to argue, but gave it up as a lost cause, and agreed. Returning the receiver to its cradle, he turned on the light next to the bed, and looked at the alarm clock that sat between the telephone and a rather large ashtray, that had overflowed with spent Camels. It was 03:04. Beckler cursed silently.

Why, he'd bet a month's wages that that Lieutenant Delair was some pimple faced kid that had brown-nosed his way up the ladder. He'd also bet that Delair had placed the call at this time of the morning, more out of intention than need. So either he wouldn't get any more sleep, or he would go back to sleep and not show up at Alameda at 06:00. Well, no matter what the motive had been, the punk had won. It was too early to get up, but too late to try and get any more sleep.

Beckler threw back the sheet, and swiveled his feet to the floor. The booze from the night before made his head pound the moment he was in an upright position. His mouth tasted as though he had been chewing on an old sock. After a moment's stretch, he screwed the knuckle of each index finger into his eyes, as if to adjust their focus and yawned. The air was stale and laden with odors indicative of what his life had become.

There was the smell of dampness, mildew and the scent of slowly rotting wood, that bore witness to the long, painful decline of the structure that housed his spacious, unkempt apartment. Intertwined was the odor of soiled laundry, empty beer bottles, and cheap perfume.

He glanced back over his shoulder at the mass of blonde hair with dark roots covering the face of a woman he didn't know. He sadly shook his head, and wondered. What had he been doing to himself? This was not his style. His body ached as he lifted his six-foot, two hundred and twenty pound frame. At forty-eight, Beckler had been in top shape. But since his last command, which had fallen victim to one of the Fuehrer's U-Boats, he had spent far too much time in dockside bars, feeling sorry for himself.

He had been pulled from the water, with what remained of his crew, by a British destroyer. Just the thought of it brought back vivid memories. He could still smell the stench of burnt flesh and taste the bunker oil that had coated his mouth and throat as he gasped for breath amongst the wreckage and the dying.

The British had taken the survivors to Liverpool, where those that were able to travel could take the next returning ship to the States.

After trying to find another ship along the East coast, and failing, Beckler had taken a bus to San Francisco in hopes of having better luck. For reasons he didn't understand, he couldn't sign on any vessel, even as a cabin-boy. Now the Navy wanted him. Something didn't feel right. He wasn't sure what, but it didn't make any sense.

"What the hell," he figured. Maybe he was reading too much into it. He should at least listen to what they had to offer. It just might be the ride he had been looking for. Anything would be better than the last six months.

By the time he had showered, shaved and dressed, it was almost 04:00. He grabbed his overcoat, laid money for cab fare on the night table next to the sleeping stranger, and stepped out into the crisp morning air. The eastern sky was just beginning to show signs of the impending sun rise, still some hour and a half away.

Beckler always ate at the same dingy little cafe, for reasons he never really thought of. It wasn't the food. That was always over-cooked, under-cooked, or cold enough to make you wonder whether it had ever been cooked at all. The waiter was always the same; distant, uncaring, and for the most part, down-right rude. The cafe itself was old, poorly lit, and seemed to cater to the down-and-out crowd.

But it was in the neighborhood, so to speak. About seven blocks from the dump Beckler presently called home. Besides, Beckler didn't care to be friendly himself. He went there simply to get something to eat. At least there someone wasn't sticking their nose into his business. They took his order, threw it together, banged the plate down in front of him, then left him alone, with the exception of the occasional passing of the coffee pot for refills.

Beckler buttoned his light jacket about half the way up, the morning air was cool and damp. The early morning streets were deserted as he made his way down the worn cement sidewalk. A crumpled empty paper bag skidded down the middle of the empty street, driven by the morning breeze. Somewhere off in the distance, a startled dog began to bark, which soon had a whole chorus of other canines responding.

All of this seemed to work in unison to make Beckler feel more alone than he had ever felt before in his life. He was walking down a street in the middle of a big city, and yet had the sensation of being the only living soul. This feeling was not something new to him.

Since he had arrived in San Francisco, he hadn't met anyone who's name he could remember, not even the bimbo asleep in his bed.

He had grown up in a small town, knew everyone in it, and they knew him. Here he knew no one, and was known by none. The saddest part of all was that it didn't matter. He didn't want to know anyone, it was as though he was about to slip through the crack in humanity and no one cared, not even himself. Then some stranger calls in the middle of the night, and like a rope thrown into the pit of despair Beckler has something to cling to. He didn't have a clue as to what the Navy wanted with him, but it didn't really matter so long as he had something to focus his attention on other than a bottle of cheap booze.

The front windows of the cafe seemed bathed in a soft light as he rounded the corner about a block away. The old sign with its peeling paint creaked as it swung in the light breeze. The front steps were made of concrete and had several large cracks in them, and the corners were broken away by years of use. The large, old, wooden front door, with its many layers of peeling paint, always stuck a bit, unless one pulled on it hard, and then it banged loudly behind you once you entered the cafe, propelled by an over-sized rusty spring.

Beckler made his way over to a corner booth and slid onto the worn wooden bench, just as the grumpy waiter, with a cigarette hanging out the corner of his mouth, stepped up. The waiter looked as though he slept in the storeroom when they didn't have any customers, then quickly got up to wait on tables when he heard the front door bang. His hair was unkempt, he needed a shave, and his clothes bore witness to the menu of the last two weeks.

After a greasy breakfast that sat in his stomach like a rock, Beckler took a cab across the San Francisco-Oakland Bay Bridge. Once in Oakland, the cab turned south and followed Route 17. As the cab slowed to a stop, just outside the main gate to Alameda Base, Beckler could feel the anxiety building in the pit of his stomach.

Stepping back after paying the cabbie, he stood and watched as the yellow Checker Cab slowly pulled away. Beckler felt as though with it, his security went also. Only when the cab could no longer be seen did he turn and walk up to the guard, who upon the appearance of the cab, had left his shack, and had been standing on the other side of the gate watching Beckler.

"I'm Captain Andrew Beckler. I'm to report here at 06:00."

"Just one moment." The guard replied, as he turned towards the shack, and called out Beckler's name to another guard inside. In a couple of seconds, the other guard inside nodded, and the gate swung open.

Once on the base, Beckler made his way over to the tin Quonset building marked 'Base Command'. At a desk, just inside the doorway, was a cigar-chomping runt of a man with two gold bars on his collar. The Lieutenant was busy reading a newspaper, and didn't bother to put it down as Beckler came up to the desk.

"You must be Beckler." He said out of the corner of his mouth, while still reading the paper.

"Are you Delair?"

"That I am." Delair replied, as he lowered the paper and rose to his feet, which made him not much taller than he had been while seated. The Lieutenant stood only about five foot tall, and looked completely the part of an ape in a people suit. He had large hands, at the end of long arms, arms that were much too long for the size of his body. He had dark black hair that was well-groomed, except for a crook in the part, about half the way back. He appeared to be in his mid-thirties, a good one hundred and seventy pounds, which for his height, made him barrel-chested. A smile came across his face, and he extended his hand towards Beckler.

Delair's size, as well as his actions, had caused a moment of pause in Beckler, but he quickly recovered and took the extended hand. Delair gripped Beckler's hand like a vise. Beckler couldn't help but wonder if Delair was squeezing so hard, as if to show strength, despite his size. Or if it was due to the Lieutenant's muscular build.

"Where's this big-wig that I'm supposed to meet?" Beckler asked in hopes of freeing his hand from the beartrap that encased it.

"You're a punctual man." Delair smiled smugly, as he released Beckler's hand and stepped from behind the desk, motioning with one hand toward another door. "Please, follow me."

The lieutenant led Beckler down a long corridor, before opening a door to a blackened office, and flipping the light switch. The lieutenant then stepped back, and motioned for Beckler to enter. Following Beckler, the lieutenant then closed and locked the door behind him.

"Have a seat, Captain." The lieutenant offered, while he stepped around the steel desk. "I want to thank you for making it here on such short notice."

"The phone call I received from you left me little choice." Becker replied flatly, as he sunk into a nearby chair.

"Yes, I know. And I'm sorry that a more advance notice couldn't be given. But to answer your question, as to whom the 'big-wig' is, you're looking at him."

"You're it!" Beckler bellowed in shocked surprise.

"Expecting someone else?" Delair questioned, with a tinge of that same smugness. "Not that it matters. I'm from Naval Intelligence, and we have an important assignment for you, Captain Beckler."

"Go suck an egg. No Lieutenant is going to wake me in the middle of the night, and then play games with my head."

"Back off, Captain. You're already here, why not hear me out?"

"Naval Intelligence? Important assignment?"

"Very important." Delair replied, with an air of intrigue.

Beckler sat silent for several seconds in order to size this Delair up. He wasn't sure what to make of him. What did Naval Intelligence want with him? Beckler knew he would have to move cautiously. On one hand, this could get him the ship he'd been looking for. But at what price? From what he had seen so far, he was reasonably sure that he didn't want to become Delair's bedfellow. For the moment he would have to play along. He simply didn't have enough information on which to base a decision.

"Naval Intelligence, huh?" Beckler questioned again.

"That's right."

"What the hell do you guys want with an old sea-dog like me?"

"Oh, you're our man all right. We've had you in mind for some time, Captain. If the time came, we always knew where to find you." Delair said, "But don't worry Captain, we're not going to ask you to infiltrate the enemy, or anything like that."

Suddenly it all started to fall into place, the reason he wasn't able to find work. This bastard had been standing in his way all along! The Navy had kept him right where they had wanted him for the past six months.

"Evidently, that time has come."

"It has, and here you are."

"Time for what? Just what is it that you want from me?" Beckler demanded to know, not at all liking this Delair or his attitude. For five bucks, he'd like to have a go at showing this little s.o.b. some manners.

"You, my dear Captain, are going to work for us," Delair said calmly, as he watched for Beckler's response from across the large steel desk. He was beginning to sense that he had better soften his approach.

"Go to work for you? That doesn't answer a thing that you haven't already told me. I want to know just what kind of work it is that I'll be doing for Naval Intelligence."

"You'll be in command of a supply-support vessel." Delair replied, choosing his words carefully, trying not to disclose any more than need be.

Beckler was beginning to like the message, if not the messenger. It was what he had been yearning to hear for months. But there were several fine points yet, that didn't make any sense.

"Just what exactly is a supply-support vessel? And why are you using a Merchant Seaman instead of regular Navy? Why, too, is Naval Intelligence involved?"

"Whoa, wait a minute," Delair replied. "let's take one thing at a time."

"Okay. What's a supply-support vessel?"

"A supply-support vessel is just what it sounds like, a merchant vessel transporting supplies to troops and/or ships in combat." Delair explained, "That, too, explains why we are using you instead of regular Navy personnel. Your expertise is in shipping freight, and that's all we want."

"That's only two out of three."

Delair rose from his chair again and walked over to the window silently. Beckler could tell that the Lieutenant was having trouble answering that one . . . Why Naval Intelligence? That made the answer all the more important.

For his part, Delair was fighting for an answer that would appease Beckler. He knew all too well that Beckler could tell him to go screw himself, and walk out. He couldn't let that happen; he needed Beckler, if this plan was to have any chance of succeeding. But how much would he have to disclose to satisfy the Captain? There was no way of knowing.

"I'm not at liberty to say." Delair answered, praying that it would be enough.

"Not at liberty to say?" Beckler repeated, as he rose from the chair not believing the gall of this man. "Then to hell with you and your ship."

Delair didn't respond. He had somewhat expected the reaction Beckler displayed. Instead, he stood there watching dust gently blowing across the compound, in the growing light of dawn. He hated being on the spot like this.

Then Beckler did just what Delair knew, deep down, he would do . . . he started to leave. Delair had to think fast. Beckler would have to go along with him on this one. Finding someone else, at this stage of the game, was out of the question, there wasn't time. What had made Beckler so right for the job, also made him a hard case to sell on it.

"Wait a minute, Captain." Delair said, not knowing what to say next. "We want you, no, we need you. I'll tell you what, I'll try and get security clearance for you, and once you have that, I'll tell all."

"Not good enough, Lieutenant." Beckler replied, at last comfortable to be in control of things. "You want me? If so, then you had better come clean, and I mean right now. Or else, I'm out of here!"

"Okay," Delair resigned, "We chose you because of your expertise. We know that you spent many of your years at sea, sailing between the west coast and the Orient. Also you know more about this type of vessel than anyone else we have. For you see, most of your peers find themselves, these days, at the helm of some Liberty ship. Just as you were, until your misfortune. I wish I could tell you that the ship we're giving you is one of those new vessels, but it's not to be. The U.S.S. URSHEL KING is of somewhat older vintage."

"How old, is 'somewhat older'?" Beckler questioned. "And why not a Liberty? I heard that they built one in less than a week."

"The URSHEL KING was laid in nineteen-ought-seven. Built of steel, she is of the same basic design as the new Liberties."

"But why her, and not a Liberty?"

"The reason for the use of the old vessel, is the same reason Naval Intelligence is involved." Delair said flatly.

"Which is?"

"What I'm about to tell you, must be kept strictly confidential knowledge," Delair started slowly. "You must swear to secrecy, and once told, you're in. One way or the other."

"Before I commit, what do you mean by one way or the other?"

"If you sign on, you'll be in command of the URSHEL KING, which is going to be refitted. And you'll get to hand-pick your crew. However, if after hearing what I have to say you decide that you must decline, you'll spend the rest of the war under security supervision. So you see, either way, you're in."

Beckler could see that there was no way out, if he wanted a ship. He signed on, although somewhat reluctantly. Delair proceeded to explain that by using the old ship as a disguise, he and his crew would transport much needed war supplies, as well as a classified cargo to the front line troops, in preparation for the invasion of Japan.

Delair also carefully explained that the reason Beckler was chosen, first of all, was his experience sailing in and around Japan. Also, because he was single, and he should pick crew members that were as well. Although the Navy wanted the mission to be a success, they realize the risk factor.

"Just how close will we be sailing to Japan?" Beckler questioned.

"We're not yet sure. We need to get as close as possible. But we have to make sure the island to be used for the invasion base is completely secured. But our biggest enemy now, is time. We must act now. Time is our greatest concern, as it is in very short supply. We have less than two weeks to assemble your crew; therefore, you have only twelve hours in which to prepare the list of their names. We will then see to it that they are brought here, and will be reporting to you. Outside, you will find a military sedan, for your transportation needs. If there's anything that I've left out, just ask for it at supply. Use the code name SILVERFISH. They'll be sure you get it. Any questions?"

"How soon do we sail, after the crew gets here?"

"That's why time is the problem. We don't know for sure. As soon as the cargo is readied for shipment, you sail." Delair answered.

"Don't you have any idea? Weeks? Months?" Beckler persisted.

"Not at this time. But as soon as I know something, so will you. Consider this a partnership; I won't leave you in the dark. I'll be in constant communication with you."

"Just what is this cargo?"

"You have no need to know that," Delair sharply replied.

Beckler didn't pursue it; from the lieutenant's expression, he wasn't sure he even wanted to know. Beckler got to his feet and turned for the door, as Delair stepped around him and unlocked it, then held it open for him to go first.

Delair followed Beckler outside and watched as he climbed behind the wheel of the gray sedan and brought the engine to life. Before taking off, Beckler cranked the window down and turned towards the lieutenant.

"One more thing, why the pretense on the phone? Why didn't you just ask me to meet with you? Why the act as if there was somebody else I was to meet?"

"If you had known that it was a lowly Lieutenant that wanted to speak with you, would you have come?"

"Probably not." Beckler smiled, as he popped the clutch and sped off towards the main gate.

CHAPTER THREE
April 25, 1945
10:45
10:45 AM

Milton (Millie) Lambert, the first name on Beckler's list, was enjoying the first leave from the Navy that he had had in over four years. He was sitting on the front porch of his parents home in Cedarville, Illinois. The Lambert home sat squarely on a nice corner lot, facing east. In front of the white, two-story frame structure was Illinois Route 26.

Cedarville was a quiet little town, nestled on a ridge that gently sloped into the bright green fields of clover and summer corn, growing in the fields of the numerous farms surrounding the town. The town's only claim to fame was that Jane Adams had called it home, and now laid buried in the town's neatly-kept cemetery.

Millie loved sitting on the porch, sipping ice tea, and watching the traffic go by. At thirty-five, he'd been all over the world, and for the moment, this was the best of all places to be. He thought back to his youth. He used to love just sitting right where he was now, doing the same thing. Some things never change. He had loved it then and still loved it now.

There were other things about this big old house that Millie held special, like his bedroom being located on the south-east corner of the second story. He had always loved that room, with its tall windows that would allow the early morning sun to awaken him each day, and the way the summer breeze would drift through the screens, laden with all the aromas and sounds native to this midwestern area. The smell of fresh-cut hay and the sweet smell of flowers from his mother's garden. The sounds of the morning birds from the trees right outside the windows, the distant bellow of cattle.

Another advantage to this room's location, was that the kitchen was directly below it. As his mother would make breakfast, the smell of her cooking would drift up through the open grates in the floor, or out the kitchen windows and back into his, allowing him to enjoy breakfast even before getting to the table.

Old Route twenty-six was busier now than then, being the main road between Freeport, just five miles to the south, and Monroe, Wisconsin, to the north. Everyone was going somewhere else; very few ever came to Cedarville, unless they only happened to pass through it.

Millie was about to doze off when he heard the familiar squeak of the front screen door. He looked up to see his mother step out onto the porch.

"Milton, the Navy is on the phone." She said, with a worried expression. "I think the man said he was calling from California."

By three-fifteen that afternoon, Millie was standing on the corner of Stephenson and Adams, a few hundred feet from the banks of the Pecatonica River, at the train depot in Freeport, waiting for the Chicago-bound train. By six, he was boarding a military cargo plane at Meigs Field. After six long hours more of sitting on his duffle bag between crates of military supplies, he stepped out of the plane at Moffet Field in Mountain View, California.

Still not sure about what was going on, he slowly made his way towards the Base Command Center. Stepping up to the first desk he came to, Millie explained why he was there. The young seaman led him over to another desk. Millie went through the explanation a second time. It took about the usual four desks, and four times of explaining who he was and why he was there before he was finally directed to the proper desk for the fifth and final routine.

After receiving the white envelope that he knew contained his orders he quietly left the building and made his way over to a yard light mounted on the exterior corner of the building. He knew the standard form used for this quite well. And for some reason, the first thing he would always look for was the name of the vessel to which he had been assigned. But this time it was different. He didn't recognize the vessel's name, S.S. URSHEL KING. It sounded like a Liberty, or something of that nature. Why was he being called to serve on one of those tubs? Then his eyes shifted to the part about who he was to serve under. He was to report to . . . Captain Andrew T. Beckler, USN. Reserve.

Millie let go with a loud cheer, that echoed off the buildings in the moist night air. He couldn't believe it, he hadn't seen Andy for more than ten years, and now he was going to serve under him? His elation was short-lived, however.

14

There were other things in the orders that didn't make any sense. Millie was now regular Navy; why was he being called to serve under someone who was just in the reserves?

Then there was the part about the address, it was in San Francisco. But it sure as hell wasn't any base he had heard of; he was beginning to smell a rat. If Beckler had called him in all the way from Illinois, ending his leave as a joke, someone was going to pay.

After an hour-long cab ride, Millie found himself standing in front of the address his orders had told him to report to. The anger within him had grown, almost to the point of rage. He was sure that this was some sort of a joke. The address was that of an old run-down apartment building, in a rough section of town. By the sound of it, there was one hell of a party going on inside.

Entering the apartment, Millie couldn't believe his eyes. Most of the entire crew that had served with him under Beckler, the last time he had, was there, including the old ship's Head Cook Delbert (Doc) Lancaster, who was also a first-rate medic. Talking with Del was Charles (Salty) Jackson, who served as Second Cook, and was real handy with a razor and shears.

Then Millie saw Beckler, standing over in the corner talking with the ship's Third Mate Jack Welts. Millie had made it about half way across the room towards Beckler and Jack when someone noticed him, and called out for everyone to look and see what the cat had dragged in.

Upon seeing Millie, Beckler walked over, shook his hand, and told him that he was glad to have him aboard.

"What the hell is this all about?" Millie demanded to know.

"Some big job the Navy has for us to do."

"It had better be a big job!" Millie shot back at all in the room. "I gave up a well-earned leave at home for this!"

The rest of the old crew showed up, one at a time, over the next week. Those that had already gathered didn't waste any time waiting on them. Instead they spent their time painting the town with wine, women, and song. Beckler let them have their fun, for soon he would demand their total concentration. For some it might be their last chance at having fun.

If there was one thing these men knew how to do, it was find trouble. It followed them like a shadow, and the night of April thirtieth was not to be an exception. Before San Francisco's finest could put an end to the brawl, a sleazy waterfront bar had been completely trashed.

Beckler slowly became conscious, but didn't bother to open his eyes. His gut ached. His head pounded. Not sure of what had wakened him, he remained where he was, for he was sure if he made even the slightest movement his body would explode in fits of pain.

As soon as his mental faculties started working again, his mind began to register as many details of the body's whereabouts as was possible without the aid of open eyes. The bed beneath him was solid and cold, the air laden with a strong musky odor, much like that of a crew bunk on an old freighter. He carefully slid his hand out from under his back and ran it along the surface of whatever he was laying on. He now had the capacity to open his eyes, but subconsciously willed himself not to look. If he didn't see it, it wouldn't be there.

The surface beneath his body was cold and hard, with rough spots and small craters. The defects, however, were polished over with a smooth finish that covered the entire area . . . painted concrete!

It was all coming back, the dark and dingy bar that they had visited sometime last night, the cheap booze and even cheaper women. Then someone had insulted one of the hags that one of his men was with; from there, it all happened so fast no one could be sure of what happened.

Then he heard that cold sound again; it had been what had awakened him, the harsh metallic sound of slamming steel. His eyes bolted open. Sight confirmed suspicion; he and his men were behind bars!

"Morning, Skipper. Here's the complimentary breakfast, courtesy of the crowbar hotel." Millie smiled, as he slid the metal tray containing a dried-out roll and cold coffee in an even colder tin cup across the floor to where Beckler was slouched against the steel wall.

"Don't tell me we got thrown in here for protecting the honor of a whore," Beckler sighed.

"Well, actually, Captain," Scotty smirked, "tossin' that joint, 'tis what we're in here fer! The misguided lass had little to do with it."

"Don't tell me," Beckler said with a forced smile. "She was with you."

"Aye, that she was, Captain."

Beckler shook his head and retained that forced smile, as he tried to swallow a mouth full of cold coffee.

"I'm sorry, Andy," Scotty apologized. "But she seemed like such a sweet lass."

"They all seem sweet to you, ya ol' goat!" Fritz taunted. "You only think through your pecker!"

"That's enough!" Beckler yelled before he realized doing it would make his head explode with pain. Lowering his volume, Beckler continued, "Why we are here is not as important, for the time being, as to how we are going to get out."

"Being out won't be all that much fun either," Millie added. "That's when we have to figure something out to pay for the damages to that fire-trap we tore down last night."

"Ah, what could the damages be to that dump?" Doc questioned.

"The biggest problem," Beckler wondered out loud, "is with all of us in here, who do we know out there that could bail us out of here?"

"What about that fat lady? You know, Captain, the one with the diner?" Salty suddenly asked.

"You mean Mama?" Beckler replied.

"Yeah, Mama! Maybe she would spring for us."

"Forget Mama," Fritz said. "She would rather see us rot in here! The Captain is the only one she would spring for."

"Aye, that's for sure," Scotty agreed.

"That may be it," Millie said, with a snap of his fingers. "If she will spring the Captain, then at least we will have someone on the outside who can work at getting us released."

From down the corridor came the sounds of clanking steel doors, followed shortly by the appearance of a guard at the door to the very large holding cell Beckler and his men occupied.

"Beckler. Andrew Beckler!" the guard shouted.

"Yeah, that's me." Beckler answered, raising to his feet awkwardly, realizing for the first time that they had become numb, due to the way he had been sitting on them.

"Are all of these bums with you?" the guard asked.

"Why do you ask?"

"The bail has been made for you, and your friends. Now do you want out or don't you?"

Looking around before replying, he noticed three men he had never seen before, looking back at him with eager intent in their eyes.

"Yes, they are all with me," Beckler replied with a smile directed towards the three strangers.

"Okay, let's go! All of you. Come one, move your butts!" The guard yelled impatiently.

Everyone in the holding cell, including the three strangers, followed Beckler and the guards down the corridors to where they had to sign for their personal belongings. Once everyone had what belonged to them, the group was ushered to a side door and set loose.

Outside the jail, Beckler noticed who it was that had sprung for the bail . . . Lt. Delair was leaning against a light gray sedan, waiting for them. Before Beckler could step over and thank the Lieutenant, the three strangers came up.

"Say, thanks a lot buddy, we were afraid that our Sergeant would have to come get us, and boy, would he have been pissed about that! You just may have saved our necks. Thanks a lot!" One of them said, before they turned and ran off around the corner.

As Beckler stepped up to Delair, the Lieutenant held up one hand and stopped him from saying anything.

"Save it cowboy, let's just say you owe me one. I'll make you a deal," the Lieutenant offered. "I'll give you a lift home, if you promise to keep those idiots out of trouble for two more days."

"I'll try," Beckler replied, trying to sound assuring.

Delair's distorted facial expression showed he had hoped for, but not expected, more. With the wave of his hand, a military truck pulled up and started loading Beckler's men. With the other hand he motioned for Beckler to get into the sedan's front passenger side, as he stepped around to the driver's seat.

To Beckler's surprise, this sedan was equipped with a radio.

"Does it work?" Beckler asked, pointing to the radio.

Without a word, Delair reached out and turned the knob. The light clicked on, and in a few moments the soft strains of music were flowing from the speaker.

"Not standard issue," Beckler mused.

Delair just smiled and drove on. They had gone about a mile when an announcer broke in on the music and said to stand-by for an important message . . .

"Don't tell me Truman is dead!" Delair snapped, remembering back to just a few weeks ago when it had been announced in much the same manner, that F.D.R. had just died.

Then came on an announcer, who lacked all the flair that made newsmen like Walter Winchell great.

" . . . This just in from Berlin . . . Adolf Hitler is DEAD . . . it has been reported over German radio that the Fuehrer died today . . . This information has not been confirmed by any of the Allies . . . I repeat . . . German radio announced that Hitler is dead."

Neither of the two men heard what else was said; they each were buried deep into their own thoughts. After a time the music came back on, as the two men rode along without speaking a word. Each would remember this day, May first, 1945 for the rest of their lives as the day that the worst enemy of free men was gone.

There was still a war going on, but deep down each knew that this marked the beginning of the real end to this nightmare.

The brakes squealed as the sedan slowed to a stop in front of Beckler's apartment. Beckler stepped out with a nod of thanks, closed the door and stepped back as the sedan roared away.

CHAPTER FOUR
May 3, 1945
06:00
6:00 AM

Delair entered the out of the way, cramped office of Admiral Edward R. Danielson, Head of Operation Silverfish. Silverfish was the code name given to the small but vital part of the vastly larger Manhattan Project. The Manhattan Project was itself a code name for the United States' atomic weapon project.

Delair had been assigned to Danielson only four months earlier. Prior to that, he knew nothing about the Manhattan Project. And he was in Naval Intelligence. He remembered being shocked when he was first briefed; that the weapon would be ready in a matter of weeks, two to four months on the outside, was just unbelievable.

Delair waited on a bench outside of the Admiral's office, until the middle-aged WAV with horned rim glasses and plump figure, decided that the wait had been long enough, and told him he could now go in. Delair knew that she really wasn't responsible for the wait, but she seemed to take great pleasure in controlling who went in to see the Admiral and when.

Danielson was intently reading from a file and didn't notice the two standing before him until she announced Delair's name. As the Admiral looked up he returned Delair's salute.

"At ease, Lieutenant," Danielson offered. "Would you care for a cup of coffee?"

"Coffee would be fine, sir."

"Mildred, two cups of coffee please."

Delair received a small amount of satisfaction having that stiff old WAV, Mildred, wait on him. Even if he hated coffee he would have accepted the Admiral's offer just out of spite.

Danielson was a distinguished looking man, somewhere in his mid-fifties. Dark hair, gently graying at the temples, six feet in height, and a trim one hundred and eighty pounds. His speech and mannerisms were that of a man confident in himself.

Delair had, in four months, come to both admire and fear the man. He was methodically intelligent, and as meticulous in his appearance as he was about the small details of his job. In private, he was quietly reserved, and polite. On the job he could be a most ruthless viper.

The admiral offered Delair a seat in front of his desk with a casual hand gesture. No sooner had Delair taken his seat, than Mildred entered with two cups of hot coffee. She delivered the coffee and silently left. Danielson waited to speak until he was sure the door had closed.

"I took a look at that damned old bucket you call a ship yesterday! And when I use the term ship, I use it extremely loosely!"

"It's the best I could come up with, under the pre-set conditions," Delair defended.

"Has Beckler seen it?"

"Not until tomorrow."

"Okay. Beyond the obvious defects, how fit is that old tub? Could she be seaworthy in say . . . sixty days?"

"Sir, that would depend on available resources, both in repair facilities and man-power. Not to mention parts. Those conditions met, why, yes, sir. She could be ready in two months."

"I'll see that she's expected at Mare Island," Danielson said, "but we'll have to work out some security problems first."

"Beckler will want to oversee the refit."

"I was counting on that." Danielson replied, "I'm also counting on him and his men doing a lot of the work themselves. The fewer involved in this the better."

"What should I tell Beckler tomorrow?" Delair asked. "When he sees that ship, he's going to be pissed and ask a lot of tough questions."

"When do you meet with him?"

"Tomorrow, at 06:00 at Alameda."

"Pick me up at home around 05:00; I want to meet this Beckler myself anyway."

The sudden ring of the Admiral's telephone startled Delair. In all the previous meetings the two men had held in this office, the phone had never once rung. Delair heard Danielson tell the voice on the other end to "send him in." This would be the first time Delair had met someone else involved in Silverfish.

As the office door opened, both the Admiral and Delair rose to their feet. Delair was surprised to see an Army Captain walk in. The Captain was thin, and about five feet, ten inches tall, and almost what one would call an albino, except for the fact that the newcomer had the most penetrating blue eyes that Delair had ever seen. Another distinguishing feature was an ugly four-inch scar that ran out and down from the right eye.

The Captain came to an abrupt halt in front of the Admiral's desk and stood at rigid attention.

"At ease. Captain Alan Reynolds, this is Lieutenant Richard Delair," the Admiral announced, as the two men shook hands.

"You two have a lot in common, other than working for me. You're both in the Intelligence sector of your respective branches of service. The Lieutenant here is my man responsible for the ship and the crew being ready on time," Danielson explained, motioning towards Delair, "while the Captain here is doing his level best to see that the proper security levels are kept in regards to our operation."

While the Admiral spoke, the two men were sizing each other up. Both wondered how the other became involved with this operation.

"Captain, Delair here is unaware of your end of this operation. Tell you what, why don't I give the floor to you and let you take it from the top and brief the Lieutenant, while bringing me up to date at the same time."

"Of course, Admiral," Reynolds replied in a soft, almost feminine voice. "As you know, work in New Mexico and Tennessee is going well. I have reports stating that the weapon will be ready by mid-July. The weatherman advises that the more opportune time for its use is early to mid-August, only three short months from now. And, as I'm sure the Lieutenant here already knows, his ship is going to transport the weapon to where it'll be finally assembled and boarded onto a B-29 for a target not yet disclosed.

"The biggest problem we have at this moment is a Japanese general. General Arisue is in charge of the Imperial Army's Intelligence branch. He is a true master of espionage. If he wants to know something, he most generally gets that information."

"He knows about Manhattan?" Delair asked in amazement.

"He knows something," Reynolds continued. "The big question is, what? And how much?"

"Through our sources in Europe, we know where he got what little information he has, his operative in Bonn. We also know that whatever information he has already obtained isn't enough. He has ordered his operative in Brazil to enter this country and learn more."

There was a moment's pause, Delair looked over at the Admiral, who was casually looking at him. Delair was surprised that the Admiral didn't seem affected by what was just said. And even more puzzling, that he wasn't asking the obvious question.

"Do we know who this Brazilian spy is?" Delair finally asked.

"No, we don't," Reynolds quickly replied.

"How long will it take us to find him? And how much jeopardy does this place on this operation?" Delair earnestly asked.

"We have no way of knowing either of those things. All we can do is make it as tough for him as possible to learn anything. That was why we insisted on using a civilian vessel, of as non-descript appearance as possible for our purpose."

"Our little gem fits that bill," Danielson quipped.

"Maybe too much so," Reynolds corrected. "I saw the ship you picked. Will it even make it out of the Bay area?"

"Once it sees the sights of Mare Island," the Admiral smiled. "How are you going to keep it down on the Bay?"

"Won't that look suspicious?" Delair questioned. "A civilian transport being refitted at a crack Naval shipyard?"

"There's a war going on," Reynolds replied rudely. "A lot of things look suspicious. Even the Japanese are doing things a little unorthodox. Besides, the Brazilian could be anywhere . . . Tennessee, New Mexico, or even Washington. All we have to worry about is getting that ship seaworthy, and that cargo on board."

"But how about when it gets to sea? If the Japanese have it pegged, there's nothing to insure that the cargo will ever get to where it is going," Delair persisted.

"We have a plan that will keep them guessing, even if they learn what the cargo is going to be," Reynolds said with a smile. "We'll play a little shell game with them. When we load the cargo on the transport, we will also be loading similar looking cargoes onto combatant vessels. By loading a number of ships at the same time, with cargoes that appear to be normal supplies, which vessel do you think they will go for? Certainly not an old tramp steamer!"

CHAPTER FIVE
May 4, 1945
06:00
6:00 AM

Beckler and his crew were expected at the main gate. After a brief pause there, they were directed to proceed. One of the guards from the gate had joined them, and stood on the running board of the truck and directing the driver where to go. After the truck had come to a stop, Beckler jumped from the passenger side of the cab.

"Okay, let's go! Bail-out! Into the briefing hut."

Briefing an entire crew was a bit unusual, but then this wasn't really going to be a briefing. Delair had told Beckler that the Admiral in charge of the operation wanted to meet him and his crew. Common practice was for this type of meeting to take place on the deck of a ship, but then they didn't have a ship yet.

The briefing hut was a quonset, of about fifty feet in length and fifteen feet in height. Inside there were numerous rows of chairs, all of which faced a slightly elevated platform at the far end of the building. Behind the platform, covering the wall, was a blackboard with a rack of maps mounted just above it. Off to the left was a steel desk.

Overhead, a number of slow-moving ceiling fans kept the air circulating. As the group took their places in the chairs, the guard that had guided them to the hut closed the door and stationed himself in front of it. Beckler and Millie exchanged questioning glances, then took their places at the front of the room.

Beckler and his men were not kept waiting. As if on cue, Delair entered the room, followed closely by Danielson. About half of Beckler's crew came to instant attention upon seeing Danielson's rank. The others simply stood.

"Well, now," Danielson said, as he stood eyeing the roughest potpourri of sailors he had ever seen, "it's easy to see who's regular Navy here."

The majority of Beckler's crew, being rough, and unpolished merchant mariners, certainly didn't fit the "normal" pattern of Navy. The only officer they didn't hold contempt for was Beckler. That was only because he had earned their respect. These men made only the slightest effort to show the appropriate respect for the Admiral's rank.

If that bothered Danielson, he wasn't letting it show. He was far too shrewd for that. He needed this bunch of misfits, and didn't give a damn about protocol. For this operation to work, they would have to trust him. Trust is something that, with this kind of sailor, would have to be painfully earned. It would serve no end to force compliance now.

"I'm Admiral Edward Danielson, head of Operation Silverfish. Glad to have all of you aboard," Danielson started. "I'd like to take a few moments to become acquainted. Over the next few months, we are going to come to depend on each other."

Then turning his attention towards Beckler. "You must be Captain Andrew Beckler."

"That I am," Beckler replied, taking the extended hand Danielson was offering. The gesture of offering his hand won favor in Beckler's eyes.

"And this," Beckler continued, "is my first Officer Milton Lambert, Second . . ."

"Come now, Captain," Danielson interrupted, "I haven't spent all my time in the Navy behind a desk. I spent most of my life aboard a ship, and I know that every sailor has a tag. A nickname of some sorts. It's usually that tag that says more about the man than his given name. So if you don't mind, I'd like to know the tag, as well as the name."

"We call him Millie," Beckler said smiling. "Our Second Mate, Graham (Gramps) Thomas . . . Third Mate Jack (Donk) Welts."

As each man's name was called, he made himself known to the Admiral. And with each one, the Admiral seemed genuinely interested.

"Donk?" the Admiral questioned.

"It's a reference to certain attributes he shares with a donkey," Beckler quietly said, as Danielson expressed a knowing smile.

"Ship's Head Cook," Beckler went on, "Delbert (Doc) Lancaster . . . ship's Second Cook, Charles (Salty) Jackson . . . Bosun, Gordon (Boss) Nashly . . .

Chief Engineer, Patrick (Patty) Briggs . . . Carpenter, Ralph (Scotty) Scott . . . Engineer First Class, Samuel (Fritz) Fitzgerald . . . "

While Beckler was introducing all thirty of the men he had chosen for his crew, Danielson couldn't help but wonder what made each one of these men so special in Beckler's eyes. They certainly were not of the same mold. Their ages varied greatly—some were clean cut, some far from it. If the Admiral had any reservations about this lot, he kept them to himself.

As soon as the introductions were completed, Danielson seated himself on the front edge of the desk.

"Now for the proverbial good news, bad news," he said slowly, as if thinking his words over carefully before saying to them, "Let's start with the bad news. It seems that the Navy, in all its infinite wisdom, has seen fit to award us with less than we had hoped for, where the ship is concerned. However, in view of this, the good news is that I've been able to secure a berth at Mare Island for a complete refit to take place."

Danielson was a real pro, Beckler thought, alienating himself from the bad news, and taking full credit for any good.

"However," Danielson continued, "there are a few points here that should be covered. Although you'll have the finest facilities at your disposal, and all the raw material you'll need . . . "

"We'll do the blamin' sweatin' ourselves," Patty quipped.

"In a manner of speaking, yes," Danielson said, a little irritated by the interruption, "but you'll be aided a great deal by a special Mare Island crew, and the balance of your own crew, when they're assigned to you."

"Rest of our own crew?" Millie questioned. "What rest?"

"The Naval personnel, attached to the URSHEL KING, to man the four-inch guns, and the fifty calibers."

"How many four-inchers?" Beckler asked, "And how many fifties are we getting?"

"Four and six, respectively," Delair answered, speaking for the first time.

"Probably rejects from the tin cans," someone from the back of the room injected.

"Button it!" Beckler ordered.

"That's not true," Danielson calmly defended. "They're top notch."

"That's a lot of fire power," Millie sighed as if not believing his ears.

"Indeed," Danielson smiled.

"Just how bad is this ship?" Scotty questioned.

"Well, I guess the best way to answer that," Danielson replied, "is to show it to you. We've assigned a bus and a driver to be at your disposal so you won't have to depend on cabs. It's parked outside right now, waiting to take you to the URSHEL KING. Lieutenant Delair and myself will join you later. So if there's no more questions at this time, you're dismissed."

The bus left Alameda and crossed back over the bridge into San Francisco, turning south on Third Street for several hundred yards, before turning left into the civilian Bay Docks area. Beckler glanced back at his men to find them looking at him for answers. He shrugged his shoulders and turned back towards the front.

The bus squealed to a halt in front of Pier Seventeen. No one uttered a sound, as if in total disbelief. All eyes were focused toward the pier. It wasn't until after they had exited the bus, that someone broke the silence.

"They must be jokin'!"

"That's a ship?" someone else asked.

"Sure as hell ain't!" Fritz answered. "It's a floatin' scrap heap, that's what the hell it is!"

"Quit your damn bitching!" Beckler ordered. "Let's look her over first. There may be some hidden qualities here."

"If that be true," Boss said flatly, "they're damn well-hidden."

As they neared the ship, it was clear to see, that the URSHEL KING was all the bad things they had said and less—much, much less. The KING was a steel hulled tramp steamer, roughly four hundred and twenty-five feet long, and fifty-three feet abeam. It had a raked bow and a champagne-glass stern. Its steel plates were covered with a thin but complete coat of rust. That made it hard to read the once proud, but now barely visible, white block letters of its name.

Once on deck, the ship looked even more like a derelict. Beckler divided his men up into inspection details, then sent them on their ways, each to explore a different part of the rusting hulk.

Sparks and Shorty were sent up to the bridge deck to check out the radio equipment, if this hulk had any. Millie and the other two officers, as well as the quartermasters and watchmen, made for the wheelhouse, while Boss divided up his deckhands to inspect the holds. Everyone went about inspecting the part of the vessel that would become his domain. Beckler stayed where he was, and slowly paced the open-spar deck. To get a feel, as he called it, for the KING.

Design of the ship was simple, yet functional. The open, upper, or spar deck, as it's called, ran its full length, only to be broken up twice—once by the superstructure of the main deckhouse, amidships, and a small sternhouse aft. Bulwarks lined the deck's sides with the only break abreast of the hatches to number four hold. The KING had five cargo holds, three fore, and two aft. Each hatch had two five-ton cargo booms. Over number four hold, a heavier fifteen-ton boom was affixed to the missenmast, and a heavier yet fifty-ton boom on the foremast, over the number two hold.

One by one, the crew began to reappear from the bowels of the ship. Each time the story was pretty much the same. It painted a bleak picture at best. If the KING was ever to sail again, it would take a miracle.

Holds one, two, and three were dry. But, the forepeak was flooded. Hold five was also dry, but number four had at least a foot of oily water covering its bottom.

"Must be seeping up from the shaft tunnel," Scotty offered, "but the deep tank affixed to the fore bulkhead of the hold appears to be dry."

Sparks and Shorty reported that there had once been a radio, but either it had been stolen, or viciously removed. Millie and the rest of the men that had gone to the wheelhouse reported to everyone's surprise that it was relatively ship-shape.

Patty and Fritz could be heard, cussing up a storm, long before they could be seen. As they stepped out onto the spar deck, with the rest of the engine room personnel in tow, they seemed to be heatedly discussing the virtues of what they had just seen.

"The bloody hold down there is flooded!" Patty announced. "Most likely, it's the flippin' shaft tunnel's outer seal."

"Either that," added Fritz, "or the old gal's got no bottom to her!"

"Scotty confirms the outer seal theory," Beckler said, "because of water in number four hold." He paused for a moment, then continued. "This tub is as bad as she looks. But on the positive side, remember, Danielson did say that we have a date with the boys of Mare Island. And from here, it's not a very long towing job."

"To hell with a refit," Fritz said, "it'd be a damned sight easier to just build a new ship."

"I disagree," Millie stated. "I think that this one can be refitted easily."

"How so?" Beckler inquired.

"Two reasons, really," Millie replied. "First, it's Mare Island, the finest crack shipyard in the world. I've seen them totally rebuild worse wrecks than this, and in a matter of weeks. Secondly, it's the design of this vessel. It's a simple design that's been around for years, and is still in use today. Why hell, if this boat was twenty years newer, it'd be a Liberty ship."

"Big ass deal!" Salty argued. "It's not twenty years newer, and it sure as hell ain't no Liberty ship!"

"Come on Salty," Beckler reasoned. "Millie just may have a point there. Let's hear him out."

"Thanks, Captain," Millie went on, "because of the close similarity between this rusting hulk and a Liberty, spare parts should be plentiful, and easily obtained."

The discussion was cut short by the appearance of a light gray sedan with U.S.N. painted on the doors. The sedan pulled up along side of the gangway. The rear door opened and Delair and Danielson stepped out.

"Permission to come aboard?" Danielson requested.

"Permission granted," Beckler replied, while thinking that the old bastard had class. He could have just come aboard.

Stepping off the gangway and onto the deck, Danielson again offered his hand to Beckler. Again, Andy took it.

"A sight for sore eyes," Danielson said, while looking out over the expanse of the spar deck.

"A broken down scow," Beckler corrected.

"Oh now, it's not that bad," Danielson replied, knowing full well that he was lying through his teeth. But he had to sell them on this old tub. It was all he had, and everything came down to it. "Why, with what we have waiting for her at Mare Island, she'll be the best damn ship you've ever sailed!"

"Is that a fact?" Scotty challenged. "If someone don't get some pumps runnin' soon like, the URSHEL KING'll sink right here! Why the forpeak, number four, and the engine room, have water ass-deep in 'em right now!"

"No need to worry," Danielson answered in a smiling sort of way. "She'll never get the chance."

"How so?" Millie asked.

Danielson didn't bother to answer. Instead he simply motioned towards the two diesel tugs closing in on them.

"Well, I'll be a son-of-. . . " Scotty sighed.

"Let's leave your mother out of this," Fritz laughed.

"They're coming for us?" Donk asked no one in particular.

"Ya bet your sweet ass!" Delair said proudly, causing everyone, including Danielson, to turn back towards him. That kind of talk was common from any of them but him. It seemed so out of character for the Lieutenant. Patty slapped him on the back, and told him that there was hope for him yet.

CHAPTER SIX
May 4, 1945
18:37
6:37 PM

The unmarked, twin-prop plane taxied to a halt at the end of the rough sod landing strip just outside of Sao Bonja, Brazil. As the dust swirled around the fuselage, the side hatch door was swung down, and the plane's lone occupant, Captain Alan Reynolds, emerged.

Waiting for Reynolds was Josè Lomas, Reynolds' Brazilian contact. Lomas was everything Reynolds loathed. He was short and unkempt. When he smiled, Lomas exposed the most unsightly set of teeth. Three of the front ones were missing, the others appeared to be slowly decaying into brownish yellow stubs. His hair lay where it would, matted and oily. Whisker stubbles covered the lower jaw . . . sweat and grime covered the rest of his face.

Lomas' loyalty went to the highest bidder, a fact about which he never pretended. It was his one redeeming quality, his straight forward impudence. Lomas was always up front about his price. And he always did the job his way, usually through ways Reynolds never understood. Lomas always came through with the pertinent information. If the information came from Lomas, it was always on the money.

"Señor Reynolds! How nice it is to see you again."

"And you, Josè," Reynolds lied, while the recipient of the customary embrace that almost turned his stomach.

"You, Señor Reynolds, and I have much to discuss, si?"

"Yes, much," Reynolds said flatly.

"Then come, I feed you a little food, some good wine. Then we talk."

Reynolds knew better than to resist. If you wanted something from Lomas, you did things his way. Lomas placed high value on hospitality. Not to accept was out of the question. But since this was the first time Reynolds had come to Lomas, instead of meeting somewhere in Mexico, he dreaded the thought of eating in this scum's home.

Lomas' modest but surprisingly clean home, a tribute to his plump wife, sat squarely on a knoll just feet from the Argentine border. To smell his flowers, Lomas would say, he had to leave his country.

After a very palatable meal, Lomas led Reynolds into the study. Reynolds couldn't believe he was in the same house. The study was a large room, with rare Carpathian burled walnut, paneled walls. Hundreds of volumes of books lined the neatly organized and dusted shelves. A Persian rug covered the floor.

Lomas parked himself into a high-back, tufted leather swivel desk chair, behind an ornately hand carved mahogany desk. To the right of the desk, affixed to the wall, was a highly detailed relief map of the world. Above the map a series of clocks, one for each time zone could be seen. To the left of the desk, a well-stocked bar. Resting on a bureau, behind the desk, a book rack was filled with leather bound journals. Each journal was coded with numbers and letters. Upon the desk sat four telephones. Arranged in slight angles before the desk sat two tall, straight-back Queen Anne wing chairs, done in a luxurious Belgium tapestry. The study was without windows, although well lit with electric lights.

Reynolds was beginning to understand Lomas' efficiency. His study was pure business. Judging by the decor, Reynolds bet that Lomas not only expected excellence, but demanded it, in the performance of his people, as well as the rewards he gave himself.

"Please be seated, Señor," Lomas offered.

"Thank you," Reynolds replied, settling into one of the Queen Anne chairs.

"At first, I thought this visit to be social, but now I see it is not," Lomas said.

"Why would you think it to be social?" Reynolds questioned.

"Our part of the war is over. Germany is about to sign the declaration of surrender. Hitler is dead. Japan is positioning itself for surrender as well."

"As they say, it's not over 'til it's over. And besides, what makes you think Japan is ready to surrender?"

"Come now, Señor Reynolds. Almost a month ago, on the eighth of April, the Japanese Premier Koiso, stepped down, replaced by Admiral Suzuki," Lomas replied.

"So?" Reynolds questioned, not knowing for sure just how well informed Lomas was.

"The Peace Party!" Lomas testily replied. "The Emperor has thrown his lot their way, as prescribed in the detailed five page report from the Turkish consul to Tokyo. 'SHARK', I believe you call him, delivered it to your late President Roosevelt, on the twenty-fourth of this past December."

"Admiral Suzuki's becoming Premier was so outlined. Japan wants Peace!"

Reynolds sat silent for a time. He had known Lomas since 1939. In all that time, not once did he think Lomas was this well-based. Where did he get his information? Facts like this could come from only one place. Lomas had to have an operative of his own inside Washington.

"I'm impressed," Reynolds finally said.

"Impressed?" Lomas replied. "I think not. Surprised seems more to the point. For years, I have worked with so many men. All different in some ways, but alike in so many others. I have come to study human actions and reactions quite in depth. Judging from your reaction, I sense you find yourself in an awkward position. You have come here under the pretext of needing my services. My guess would be that it has something to do with the Manhattan Project, or more to the point, Operation Silverfish."

"Very good!" Reynolds replied, trying hard not to show his surprise, "but what do you do for an encore? Inform me what the Japanese Emperor is having for dinner this evening?"

"For a price," Lomas laughed.

Reynolds didn't laugh, Lomas was right. He did feel uncomfortable, and not in control of the situation. He had to regain the upper hand. He was there to do the talking, not sit there, like a school kid listening to an upset teacher.

"What I do need, is to find out what General Arisue knows about Manhattan," Reynolds stated.

"He knows a little, but he too, seeks peace," Lomas replied. "If he felt that the war was not already lost, I would consider him a threat. Arisue is a very talented man, possibly the only true peer I have in this world. If he desired such information, he would soon have it. But as I've already said, he seeks peace. Therefore, his energy is spent toward that end, not worrying about your precious project."

"Then someone else in the Imperial Command is concerned. Their Brazilian operative has entered the U.S."

"Just what you wanted, is it not?" Lomas questioned.

"What do you mean by that?"

"Silverfish. Your secret little shell game, that no one knows about, including the United States' Navy, and the heads of the Manhattan Project. Where does this Admiral Danielson get so much clout?"

Reynolds didn't reply.

"Besides, they are only reacting on information gathered by their operative known as 'Tex'."

"Tex?" Reynolds paled noticeably.

"Surely you're aware of Tex?"

Reynolds calm composure returned, as he flatly replied, that he hadn't been aware of any Japanese operative known as 'Tex'.

"Are you certain?" Lomas asked in disbelief.

"Quite certain!"

Lomas thought for a moment, the fact that Reynolds knew nothing of Tex was incredibly odd. He swiveled his chair around and gathered one of the leather journals from the bureau. After quickly checking the index, he turned to the page he had been looking for. Silently reading for a moment, Lomas raised one of his bushy eye brows. Closing the journal and returning it to its proper place.

"And?" Reynolds inquired.

"Nothing," Lomas responded, not at all convincingly. "I was just checking my facts. For future reference, you should be aware that there are two operatives inside your country."

"I'll check it out."

Lomas sat for a moment saying nothing. He hadn't revealed what he had just learned from his journal. He wasn't about to, at least until he had enough time to check out the possibility of his hunch. After a few moments of silence, Lomas went on as if the whole Tex subject had never come up.

"As I see it, you now have the opportunity to test this new weapon, then safely tuck it away, since it's no longer needed."

"Whether or not it's needed is not something for you to decide!" Reynolds said sharply, hoping to intimidate Lomas and failing badly.

"But why use it, when the enemy is already defeated?" Lomas persisted. "Will it bring the war to a close one day sooner?"

"Yes, it will. It will shorten the war as much, if not more, than the introduction of the B-29 bomber has done already."

"Oh Señor, save your propaganda for fools. There is a fundamental difference here. The B-29 was needed. The enemy was not yet beaten. I agree, it has shortened the war. Due to its development, the bomber has been able to take destruction to the heart of the enemy, leaving the enemy broken and beaten, both physically and psychologically. What more is needed? Should this new weapon do the work of two bombs, or ten bombs. How many will you drop? Will it be less than you are dropping now? Or possibly more? Is it your wish to murder Japanese women and children? What difference would there be between what you are about to do, and what the Germans did to the Jews? Is not mass murder the same?"

"No, it's not the same!" Reynolds almost shouted.

"A rose by any other name . . . " Lomas calmly quoted Shakespeare.

"Our only wish is for Japan's unconditional surrender as soon as possible," Reynolds snapped. "What if the Japanese are bluffing?"

"Bluffing?" Lomas asked in astonishment. "Bluffing with what? Most of their planes have been destroyed. Their Navy litters the floor of the ocean. Bluffing? I think not!"

"They sent someone to the U.S., didn't they?"

"What would you do in their place, given the information they have? Failure to react could prove fatal. They are well aware that the end is near, but for every day that the war lingers there is the hope that something will happen to improve their position. When the end finally comes, they would like to be in a position to retain some measure of respect. Some measure of self-will. Even without this new weapon, you bomb Tokyo almost at will. And they do not know this Harry S. Truman. FDR dying changes things. Like the old saying, 'better the devil you know,' so to speak."

The two men argued back and forth, until the night had given way to morning. Lomas was finally able to convince Reynolds that Arisue had not ordered his Brazilian operative into the United States, nor had Arisue's assistant Lieutenant Colonel Kakuzo Oya. But Reynolds was able to persuade Lomas into finding out who in the Japanese military had.

The morning sun reflected off the silver fuselage of the twin prop plane as it lifted off, and roared off to the north and out of sight.

CHAPTER SEVEN
May 4, 1945
14:50
2:50 PM

The URSHEL KING released an agonizing moan as she was gently tugged away from her berth. It was as though her fighting spirit had failed long ago. The desire to be saved had been replaced by a will to decay into such a state as to be admitted into Valhalla. But the metallic grinding that echoed through her empty holds in protest was ignored as the powerful tugs eased her around in the channel, and slowly headed her up the bay.

Beckler and Millie stood on the left bridge wing, watching the screws of the tugs turning the channel water into foam under the burden of their task. The two men stood in silence as they were towed under the San Francisco-Oakland Bay Bridge. Treasure Island Naval Training Station slowly passed off to starboard. While lingering in the light fog that hung over the bay, to port was Alcatraz Prison. In passing it, the two men couldn't help feeling a strange sort of kinship with the inmates there. About two miles beyond the prison, standing as if above the mist, bathed in the warm afternoon sun, was the Golden Gate Bridge.

It seemed to take an eternity before the King was nursed slightly to starboard, to pass between Point San Pablo and San Pablo Point—the gateway, as it were, to San Pablo Bay. Mare Island lay just across the bay.

The Mare Island crews stood on the piers and watched the rusting hulk of the KING being nudged into the waiting dry dock, its home for the metamorphosis that was needed to turn this eye-sore back into a ship.

As soon as the KING was safely inside the dock, the riggings were made fast, gangways were attached, and within minutes, the dock was being pumped out.

Beckler was just stepping off the gangway as a heavy-set sergeant, with crew-cut hair and a half smoked cigar stuck between his teeth, stepped up.

"You Beckler?" the sergeant grunted.

"Yeah, I'm Beckler."

"I'm Sergeant Eugene Germain. Me and my boys gonna rebuild this wreck for ya," the sergeant said, as he stepped past Beckler and Millie as if they weren't there and looked the KING over.

"Wreck?" Millie asked in a fake hurt, sort of tone.

If the sergeant heard it, he ignored it.

"Ya sure you're up to it?" Beckler asked, with a warm smile.

"What in the hell is that supposed to mean?" the sergeant growled.

"Hey, take it easy Sergeant!" Beckler defended. "I was just kidding."

"This old bucket ain't no joke!" the sergeant snapped. "She's beyond being a laughin' matter!"

"Look, Sergeant," Beckler said, "or would you prefer to be called Gene?"

"My friends call me Gene; for you, 'Sergeant' is okay."

"All I meant, SERGEANT," Beckler continued, accentuating the rank, "was that I wouldn't know where to begin."

"Of course you wouldn't! All you wave jockeys know is how to sail 'em. Ya don't know shit about treatin' 'em right!"

Beckler and Millie glanced at each other, but kept silent for the time being. Besides, they had other things to take care of now—things like finding needed supplies for themselves and their crew.

"Say, Sergeant. Do you know where we can find us a jeep?" Beckler asked, hoping that he would loan them his.

"Do ya think that you can treat one of 'em better than ya did this ship?"

"Look Sergeant," Millie protested. "We just acquired this heap. We didn't create it!"

"Oh, yeh?" the sergeant sneered. "Well don't you boys go and buy any used car for me. Okay?"

"Okay, enough about the ship," Beckler interjected, hoping to change the subject to more important matters at hand. "Now what about that jeep?"

"Take that one," the sergeant replied, pointing back towards his.

"Oh, just one more thing . . . " Beckler started to say.

"Now what?" The sergeant snapped back.

"Where's the supply?"

"Damn," the sergeant sighed, while shaking his head, "if I tell ya, you'll only get yourselves lost. Better hop in, and let me do the drivin'."

Beckler and Millie didn't argue. They climbed aboard just as the jeep roared to life. Millie almost tumbled out the back of it, as the sergeant slammed it into gear and popped the clutch. Both men hung on to anything they could grasp, while the sergeant seemed to take great pleasure in racing down the narrow isles of spare parts, ropes, and cables, although he never let it show.

True to form, the sergeant killed the motor and let the speeding jeep coast to a stop, right in front of the main supply depot. By the way the sergeant knew just where to kill the engine, and still reach the depot, Beckler knew he had done it before. He looked over at the mad-hatter seated behind the steering wheel with less than a pleased expression.

"Here ya go, dad!" The sergeant beamed, as if to add salt to injury.

"You know," Beckler growled, "you've got a real attitude problem!"

"Is that a fact?" the sergeant challenged.

"Come on, DAD," Millie laughed, hoping to stop these two before blood was shed.

The supply depot was a large, red brick building, with half a dozen smaller tin buildings, enclosed within a large, fenced in area. Behind the fence stood row upon row of Naval ordinances, miles of ropes, and cables. Stockpiles of iron plates, fittings, and boiler casings were neatly arranged.

Once inside the brick building, the three men stepped up to a long grey metal counter. Beyond the counter were numerous steel desks, occupied by female clerks, busily typing out forms. Over to the right, bent over a filing cabinet drawer, was the firmest, most sensuous looking rump to ever fill a uniform. Lower down, beneath a slightly showing lace slip, were two shapely formed calves that tapered into slender ankles. Beckler felt a pang within himself that had been missing for years.

As if she could feel his eyes upon her, she slowly stood up, and tugged at her skirt, before turning around. Her dark hair was pulled tightly back into a bun, accentuating her high cheek bones, and hazel-blue eyes. As she moved towards the counter, Beckler kept running ideas through his mind, as to what he would say. God, he hated this. He hadn't felt this tongue-tied since he was a teenager.

"May I help you?" she asked in a pleasantly feminine voice.

"Yes. Yes please," Beckler stammered, wishing he could go out and come back in when he had found a way to be impressively clever.

"How can I help you?" she smiled patiently, enjoying the confusion in Beckler she was causing.

Beckler took a deep breath, realizing how stupid he must appear. Then he proceeded, as if nothing had happened.

"I have a list here of supplies needed right away, for my ship and crew."

"Let me have a look," she said, with a tone that had suddenly turned to ice. "The URSHEL KING, is it?"

"That's right."

"First of all, Captain, I don't know how you got that merchant ship into this yard, and I don't care," she started, with a burning glare. "But your vessel is last priority here, we are a Naval installation. Combatant ships come first. And even they must follow procedure. Nobody comes in here and demands supplies right away. Might I suggest that if you want any service at all, you mind your manners, and do things our way."

"Look, I'm sorry," Beckler replied, feeling slightly sheepish, and somewhat pissed by her arrogance, "but I don't like this anymore than you do. I was told to expect great things of Mare Island. I guess I was misinformed."

"Snide remarks won't help you, Captain!"

"Just get me what I need, and send the bill to Silverfish," Beckler said flatly, using the code name for the first time.

A silence fell over the place, as all eyes turned towards him.

"Where did you say to send the bill?" she asked.

"Silverfish," Beckler casually repeated.

"Would within an hour be okay?" She begrudgingly asked.

"Fine."

With that Beckler quickly turned around and walked out. Millie and the Sergeant looked at each other a moment, then over at the attractive female supply lieutenant, who's face was turning red with anger.

"That captain of yours," The sergeant smiled, "has a way with women, don't he?"

Millie didn't answer. He was afraid to. The icy stare of the supply lieutenant told him it was time to follow his captain and depart.

Beckler had paused on the steps of the supply depot to light a cigarette half-heartily out of frustration, and to wait for other two to join him.

"Boy, you sure put it to her," the Sergeant beamed.

"You think so?" Beckler stated, more than questioned. "It was a stupid thing to do! I should have handled it differently."

"Don't worry about it," Millie assured him. "You did the best you could at the moment."

"Maybe, but now every time we need something the process is going to be a tough one."

As the three men were about to climb aboard the jeep for the ride back to the KING, a sailor came running up from the side shouting Millie's name.

"Millie! Is that you?" he said with a beaming smile.

"Jess Tasman?!" Millie replied.

"Yeh, it's me! What are you doing here?"

"Our ship is in for repairs. How about yourself?"

"Mine too! What ship you on?"

Millie hesitated for moment, then answered quietly, "The URSHEL KING."

It took a moment for Jess to comprehend what Millie had just told him. "You mean that tramp they bought in earlier today?"

"I'm afraid so. How about yourself?"

"I'm on the INDIANAPOLIS. Been there for six months now," Jess proudly replied.

Millie turned towards Beckler and the sergeant and made the proper introductions. Then he told them that he and Jess had shared adjoining bunks aboard the NEW MEXICO, when it was commanded by Admiral Zacharias.

"Hear tell, that 'Captain Zach' was shipped back to Washington," Jess said.

"He came from there when he took command of the NEW MEXICO, didn't he?" Millie asked.

"I think Intelligence," Jess offered. "Wasn't the same without him. Had a chance to catch a new ride, so I took it. Almost became a big mistake."

"How so?" Beckler questioned.

"The Indy took a real bad hit off Okinawa. One of those Jap suicide planes. Crashed right into our rear quarter. Almost blew the damn thing right off."

"The Indy is a tough old gal," the sergeant said. "It'd take more than that to sink her."

"I'll say," Jess agreed. "Hey, and guess who is also on the Indy?"

"I don't know. Who?"

"Doc Haynes!" Jess blurted. "Remember him from the NEW MEXICO?"

"You don't say? We'll have to get together sometime while we're here," Millie said as the Sergeant started the jeep.

"Anytime, buddy. Anytime."

The jeep lurched forward as the clutch was released and roared off towards the tired old KING.

CHAPTER EIGHT
May 7, 1945
22:50
10:50 PM

Reynolds stood at the front door of a modest home on the outskirts of San Francisco and knocked. It was a warm, muggy evening. However, a light and steady breeze was blowing in from the coast. It wasn't much, but it beat the stifling closeness of the heat within the city.

The house belonged to Admiral Danielson. It stood at the top of an embankment overlooking the city. On a clear day it also offered a great, although somewhat distant, view of the coast.

Tonight, only the blaze of city lights could be seen. Reynolds loved it here, high above the city, looking down. It gave him a most rewarding sensation of being above it all.

The front porch was the width of the house, with the door into the house being in the center. Off to one side of the door sat two wood rockers with a round table between them. At the opposite end of the porch, suspended by chains from the ceiling, was a courting swing, facing out towards the ocean.

The roof of the porch was supported at its edge by four six inch square posts. Lining the edges of the porch, between the posts, were railings with ornately turned spindles.

Suddenly the porch light came on, and Mrs. Danielson opened the door and asked who it was.

"Captain Alan Reynolds to see the Admiral, ma'am," came the soft, direct reply.

"Just a moment," the frail, but handsome, woman said, as she disappeared back into the house. Reappearing in a moment, she said, "Please follow me."

Reynolds followed her through a foyer, a tastefully decorated living room, and a short hallway before entering a dimly lit study. The Admiral was seated in a fireside wing chair reading Herman Melville's classic nove, *The Whale*.

Danielson's study was of stark contrast to that of Lomas. This one was purely for pleasure, as a large majority of the books lining the shelves were novels. This was where the Admiral went to forget the war and his duties, not conduct them. Even the Admiral's attire was civilian, tan slacks, light blue shirt, argyle socks, and dark brown slippers.

"Edward," Mrs. Danielson said, as if to pull him away from his reading. As soon as the Admiral looked up, she turned on her heels and stepped from the room, closing the door behind herself.

"Excellent writing," the Admiral sighed as he carefully laid the book to rest on the chairside table, next to the only lamp in the room that was lit.

"From the collection on the shelf, I get the distinct impression that you are a true connoisseur of Melville's works. Most of these I've never even heard of," Reynolds stated as he stepped closer to the bookcase containing the Melville works.

"Probably the only collector to own first editions of the eleven best-known Melville titles," Danielson proclaimed proudly, as he watched Reynolds pull his hands back away from the shelf as soon as he heard the words, "first editions."

"Original first editions?" Reynolds asked in disbelief.

"The genuine article."

"They must be as old as hell."

"That would depend on how old you think hell is. As for the books, they age between ninety-nine and twenty-one years old," Danielson replied, "*Typee* was the first, published in 1846. *The Whale*, or *Moby Dick*, as it's better known, was published five years later, but never received much acclaim until after Melville's death. *Foretopman*, the newest of the collection, was finally published in 1924, thirty-three years after his death."

"That's amazing," Reynolds said, not hiding how much he was impressed.

"You didn't come here to discuss my collection of classic novels, so let's get to it."

Reynolds turned towards the admiral, somewhat surprised by his directness, but also savoring the moment of having calmly refrained from stepping into the room and blurting out the information he had just learned minutes before coming here. Reynolds had a flair for the dramatic, a trait that irritated Danielson.

"Germany has surrendered!"

"When?" Danielson flatly asked, masking any sense of excitement, as to spoil Reynolds' moment of glory.

"This afternoon," Reynolds replied in a tone of disappointment. "They will lay down their arms at 23:01 tomorrow night, officially ending the war in Europe."

"That's great, now maybe Japan will follow suit."

"Let's hope they decide to wait a little while longer, or our work will have been for naught."

"What?" Danielson asked in shocked surprise. "Did I hear you right? Are you out of your mind?" We want them to surrender now, or sooner!"

"With all due respect, I disagree with you, Admiral," Reynolds replied, as he fixed an icy stare with those brilliant blue eyes, on the admiral. "Japan may be beaten already, on that point I agree with you. But if the war ends before we have a chance to display the awesome power of this new weapon, we may find ourselves in a different war after the Japanese—a war with the Soviets. I find those prospects a bit unsettling. I'd rather fight the Japanese a few months more, climaxing in the complete destruction of a major Japanese city, showing once and for all, to the entire world, that the United States is indeed the super power of the world! After such a display, the Soviets would think twice about tangling with us."

"Do you realize what this war costs us each and every day, in terms of human life, not to mention weapons, and money?" Danielson countered. "What you are talking about is hypothetical, I'm telling what is real! I would rather have spent my entire life in vain, than for our country to pay the price of fighting the Japanese for even one more day!"

"I understand your position," Reynolds said, "but, mark my words, one day we will have to confront the Soviets. This weapon could mean the difference of whether we fight them directly or indirectly. If we have to fight them directly, the cost may be more than we're able to pay."

"Let's fight one war at a time. Besides, even if we have a chance to drop this bomb, how long before the Soviets build one of their own? We'll find ourselves in a Mexican stand-off. What comes next?" Danielson asked.

Reynolds didn't reply.

"I'll tell you what comes next," Danielson continued, "we'll build a bigger, or stronger bomb, then they will and so on . . . No, I don't care to ponder the future, my hands are full with what lies before us."

Pandemonium was the order of the day, on May 8th, 1945, as President Truman announced to the American people that the German government had accepted complete and unconditional surrender. The cheers within the shipyard were deafening, not to mention the blasts from the horns and whistles of every ship, including tugs within its confines. Even the heavy cruiser, U.S.S. IN-DIANAPOLIS, who was still having the extensive damage to her rear quarter repaired, got into the act.

Beckler was in the supply building, arguing as usual with that same stubborn supply lieutenant, Lt. Hewitt. They had been in the middle of a heated discussion in her office, when the news was announced, having therefore missed it. Both stopped suddenly, however, when all the commotion broke loose, and stared at each other with puzzlement.

Before either could react, someone poked their head into the office, and shouted the joyous news. Lt. Hewitt quickly stepped over to the bureau along the wall and turned the radio on. After the few seconds it took for the tubes to warm up, the solemn voice of President Truman came forth.

As soon as the broadcast was over, no one could be sure of who did what. Nature had taken a hand. Lt. Hewitt was in Beckler's arms, as he twirled her around in the air. The first kiss was innocent enough, a light peck, but the open-mouth kiss that followed caught them both by surprise.

Suddenly Beckler set her down, wiped her lipstick from his lips, and took a nervous step backwards. The moment was just as awkward for her. She first tugged downward on the edges of her skirt, then nudged her hair back into place, before placing a cupped hand to her mouth.

Both started to say something, then stopped, thinking better of it. Beckler decided the situation had become awkward enough, so without a word, he turned and walked out, leaving her standing there wondering. Neither would ever admit it to themselves, let alone to each other, but both had felt something. Maybe it was true, opposites do attract, but these two seemed from the outset to be mortal enemies, fighting and bickering every time they came into contact with one another.

Before he made it to the main entrance to the building, Beckler turned, stealing a glance towards Lt. Hewitt's office door, where she was leaning against the casing, then he stepped outside.

Beckler paused a moment, before climbing into his jeep, and looked back toward the second story window of the depot office that was Lieutenant Hewitt's office. She was standing at the window watching him leave. As soon as he looked up towards her, she quickly turned away from the window.

Upon hearing the jeep roar to life and begin pulling away, she returned to the window and watched him go. She wasn't sure of how she felt. She had enjoyed the kiss, even enjoyed the time they spent arguing over supplies. She had been instructed by Danielson to supply everything Beckler needed, and yet she couldn't bring herself to do so without a struggle.

It had become a game for both of them. Whether or not Beckler would get the supplies was never really in question. She knew it and so did Beckler. Yet the ritual was always the same, he would make the request, she would deny it. He would argue his case, while she gave every reason she could think of to delay the inevitable. Finally, after what seemed to be an appropriate amount of confrontation, the list of supplies would be logged in and begin being processed.

Across the compound the jeep rolled to a stop next to the KING. Work on the vessel had stopped completely. The men were in a party mood, congratulating each other and cheering. Beckler wasn't really in the mood for having work on his ship being halted, but true to his way of doing things, he allowed the men to carry on, as the occasion warranted the festivities.

Millie watched Beckler come aboard, then head straight for his cabin, without so much as a wave to the men. Knowing that something was up, Millie followed his captain.

Millie knocked on the door before entering.

"You okay, Captain?"

"Yeah, I'm fine," Beckler answered. "Remind the men that we are still at war, and that this tub still needs to be finished as soon as possible."

"Yes, Sir," Millie replied. "They're just getting it off their chests! We've been at war with Germany for four years. Some of those men fought in Europe."

"You're right, mister," Beckler sighed. "I'd be doing what they're doing myself, under different circumstances."

"Trouble with supply again?"

"The usual."

"You could get the admiral to set you up so that you could go through someone else," Millie offered.

"I'm aware of that, thank you."

"Then why don't you?" Millie questioned.

"I have my reasons," Beckler stated as if deep in thought.

"I'll give the boys a little more time for their fun," Millie quickly changed the subject, "then it's back to business as usual."

"Thanks."

CHAPTER NINE
May 10, 1945
15:00
3:00 PM

The black sedan slowed and pulled over onto the shoulder of the road, then stopped. The driver's door swung open, and a lone figure emerged. The figure was Latin, medium build, jet black hair, large baggy brown eyes, with a deep tan. The man sported a dark grey, wide-brimmed hat, dark sunglasses, dark slacks, and a dirty white, strap T-shirt. He looked back down the road, and guessed that he was about two miles out of the little town of Rodeo. Then he checked the road for traffic from the other direction. Reassured that there was none, he moved to the back of the car and opened the trunk and removed several large pieces of luggage from it.

Rechecking the road before leaving the car, he then carried the luggage several hundred feet, into a wooded area, overgrown by weeds, on the south bank of the channel across from Mare Island. After making three more trips to the car, he had removed all the luggage. He then opened the back door, and pulled a huge camouflage netting from the seat and onto the ground. Once again, he checked the road for any signs of traffic, and found none. Dragging the netting, he made his way back through the trees and the weeds that hid the view of the channel from the road. He quickly covered the luggage with the net, and returned to the car.

The black sedan pulled a sharp U-turn, and headed north-east towards Crockett. Once on the other side of Crockett, it turned due south for several more miles. Slowing, it turned left, onto a little used dirt road. The dry dust from the road bed swirled around the back of the sedan, as it lazily made its way to a long, winding lane that ran off to the right.

At the end of the lane stood an old, rundown barn. About a hundred and fifty feet from the old barn, covered in a growth of tall weeds, were the crumbling foundation walls of the farm house that once stood there. Thirty feet to the right of the crumbling foundation, stood a steel, skeletal pyramid. The turbine and the wind fan were gone, but the basic structure of the windmill remained.

Surrounding the decaying old farm yard was a rotting old board fence, or what was left of it. Most of the grey weathered boards now hung at odd angles. Some of the posts were missing, leaving the boards that had once been attached to rot on the ground.

The sedan slowed to a stop in front of the barn. The Latin got out and walked over to the barn. Before opening the door, he slowly turned in a sweeping arc and viewed all around himself in all directions. Again he saw nothing. He expected to find nothing. The old barn was all there was for miles, no homes, no ranches, not even the remotest shack for migrant workers. His contact 'Tex' had done well in picking this location.

The huge old wooden door slid open easily on its well-oiled track. Inside, the barn appeared to be deserted. The Latin searched quickly for a well-hidden switch on his right. His fingers found the switch and he flipped it gently with a smile on his dark face. The interior of the barn glowed as the battery operated lights lit the recesses of the large interior. The Latin returned to the sedan and eased it into the barn, and quickly returned to close the door behind himself.

The Japanese had no way of knowing that the code had already been broken. In fact, it had been broken for some time. So when the signal began, Reynolds and his men were ready to listen. The first message was short, merely informing those on the other end, he had made it, was set up, and would transmit on the present schedule.

"That's our man!" Reynolds exclaimed. "Next time he transmits anything, I want to know about it. Also, I want to find out where he's transmitting from."

"Already working on that, sir," an older, gray-haired, man at the control panel replied. "Already we know that the signal is coming from across the bay. My guess would be somewhere in a direct line, south-by-southeast."

The older gentleman and Reynolds stepped over to a huge map that was mounted on the inside wall of the old warehouse Reynolds and his men had converted into a highly advanced listening post. The older man took a red pencil and drew two lines from where their warehouse was on the northwestern edge of San Pablo Bay, across the bay. The first line was drawn over Rodeo, and continued on until stopping at the edge of the city of Concord. The second line was farther south, over Pinole, and stopping at Moraga.

"He's within these boundaries."

"How can you be so sure, Sam?" Reynolds asked.

"Simple. The moment we picked up the signal, we knew which direction it was coming from. Its strength tells us that he's not that far from us. So it's safe to assume that he's on this side of Las Trampas Ridge."

"Great," Reynolds said without emotion. "Let's get two crews set up on the other side of the bay, in mobile units. One in Hercules, and the other in Lafayette. Next time he transmits, we'll be able to narrow the field."

"How often do you think he'll transmit?"

"No way of knowing," Reynolds replied. "Maybe once a day, once an hour, or once a month. Just be sure to listen for him. Once we've picked him up several times, my guess is that we'll be able to detect a pattern, and thereby know in advance when the next transmission will be."

"What should we do if we locate him?" Sam asked.

"Nothing, until I say so. If you find him, stay clear. I don't want to pressure him until I'm ready. Is that clear?"

"Yes, sir," Sam shrugged. "Same holds true for the other one?"

"What other one?"

"The other Japanese informer," Sam said, suddenly aware that this might be the first Reynolds had heard of the second spy.

Reynolds knew, Lomas knew, but how long had Sam known? How many people knew about Tex? Reynolds was irritated every time someone else mentioned Tex, or the other spy. How were so many finding out so soon? The very fact that Tex existed was unknown a week ago.

"Could be the same one using different code names," Reynolds stated.

"Possible," Sam pondered for a moment, before shaking his head. "But not likely. No, I'd sooner say that there are two spies."

"Well, find out what you can by listening," Reynolds said, "then let me know as soon as you're sure about the second. The same orders for him as well. If there are two, I want to be sure of what they know before we put them out of business."

Shortly after the sun had gone down, the barn door was rolled open and the Latin stepped out into the evening air, checking his surroundings for any signs of life, before returning to the barn. A few moments later he emerged, straddling a vintage Indian motorcycle. After securing the barn, he kicked the Indian to life, and roared down the lane.

It was shortly after ten when he neared the place where he had hidden his equipment. Just as he was about to pull over, he saw a pair of headlights down the road in front of him. Cursing to himself, he hit the throttle and sped past the spot. In a few minutes, he rode past the farm truck that belonged to the headlights. He continued on, until he could no longer see the taillights of the truck in his rear view mirror. Ahead he could easily see the lights of Rodeo, but except for that, there were no more headlights from oncoming vehicles. He slowed the Indian down, and pulled a U-turn and headed in the direction the truck had gone.

Easing back on the throttle, and turning off his headlamp the moment he could make out the truck's taillight in the distance. He had no trouble seeing, thanks to a bright moon. And luck stayed with him, as no more headlights appeared before he returned to where he had hidden the equipment.

He slowly rode the Indian into the weeds, before killing the engine, and pushing it the rest of the way. He then returned to the road with a short tree branch, and carefully raked out any trail he had left.

The Latin had planned this mission carefully; he had brought with him only what he felt was vital. The camouflage netting made for perfect cover for his small tent, and the sophisticated telescope. He also had diving gear, photo equipment, and dried rations.

By midnight, he was fully operational. So, he turned in, and got a good night's sleep.

CHAPTER TEN
May 13, 1945
08:00
8:00 AM

Delair's thoughts were on other things as he made his way into Danielson's office. He was hoping that this meeting wouldn't take too long. He had hopes of going to chapel. He hadn't spent much time there since joining the service, but this was one Sunday he wasn't going to miss. He was also thinking about what he had to do after the worship service.

"Good morning, Lieutenant," the Admiral greeted him as Delair stepped through the door.

"Good morning Sir," Delair replied, noticing that Reynolds was there as well. Delair felt slightly uneasy in the Captain's presence. Somehow he seemed to take an unusual amount of pleasure in his job, Delair thought.

"Lieutenant," Reynolds greeted.

"Captain."

"Gentlemen," Danielson began, "a lot has taken place since last we met. Let me bring you up to date. Then in turn, I want each of you to do likewise. First of all, I've been informed that the KING must be ready by no later than the twenty-third of June. She will have her sailing orders on or about the twenty-fifth, and set sail at zero hundred hours, the twenty-ninth. She will sail well to the north of the Hawaiian Islands, making a stop at Midway before proceeding to Wake Island with a final destination of Okinawa. The word is that the INDY will be completed around the same time. It's imperative that the KING get the jump. The INDY will sail on the sixteenth of July, for Pearl Harbor, Tinian, and Guam before reporting for practice maneuvers in Leyte Gulf."

"And finally, no one is sure, but it sounds like the weapon won't be tested until after both vessels have already sailed. Even then it won't be the same bomb, the one to be used against the enemy is a Uranium U-235 while the one to be tested on or about the sixteenth will be Plutonium."

"The KING will be ready," Delair stated. "In the past nine days she has had her hull repaired, for the most part. I believe the hull will be finished in about a week at most. New engines and other vital machinery have been given top priority and should arrive by month's end. That will leave the balance of the time to complete her."

"As for my part," Reynolds started. "I can report that we have attracted an admirer. My people have had this fellow under surveillance since he first arrived in this area. He has sent out two messages. The first, simply saying that he was in place. The second, informing the enemy what vessels were at Mare Island and what their apparent conditions were. He was grasping for straws, nothing more. However, the KING did pique his curiosity. Our efforts on that old tramp steamer really have him baffled."

"How did he get into Mare Island?" Delair demanded.

"Swam in," Reynolds calmly replied. "Simply slipped on a face mask and swam in."

"You knew this and did nothing?"

"There was nothing we could do," Danielson explained. "He was in and out before we knew it."

"That's correct," Reynolds went on. "We're not sure, just yet anyway, just how much the Japanese know. We can't pinpoint his exact location for one thing. And even if we knew exactly where he was, it would serve no end to put him out of business before we are able to uncover the extent of the Japanese knowledge of Manhattan."

"What difference will that make?" Delair questioned.

Reynolds glared towards Delair, then glanced over to the Admiral, who sat there saying and doing nothing. "What difference does it make? Possibly all the difference in the world! The whole idea is to create utter destruction and to do it by complete surprise! Thereby shocking the Japanese into accepting 'unconditional surrender'. If they know what is coming, how far do you think our bombers will get before being nailed?"

"What about the Official Spokesman broadcasts?" Delair questioned. "Shouldn't we at least give them a chance before wholesale slaughter?"

"Look," Danielson replied. "I don't like the idea of sending the weapon or the KING out there any more than you do. That is, however, not our decision to make. Those broadcasts were made five days ago—with no response I might add. For all we know the Japanese didn't even hear them. Or, if they did hear them who's to say what they might or might not do?"

Delair knew that the Admiral was right. The KING and her crew would have to deliver the cargo. He didn't know what bothered him the most, the fact that he himself would do his level best to see that the KING and its cargo carried out their mission—which in turn made him indirectly responsible for the end result. Or that Reynolds seemed to be taking so much pleasure in it.

How could anyone take pleasure in inflicting suffering and death? For that matter why did his own government seem so bent on using this new weapon? It was as if a faction of the U.S. Government, or at least the military was in a race with the process of peace.

Delair had a close friend in the Office of Naval Intelligence in Washington who was keeping him abreast of the diplomatic efforts being made and what the results had been to this point. He knew that the Japanese had made a number of peaceful overtures to no avail. What he was really having a hard time swallowing was the fact that every time a new step was made diplomatically, new pressure was brought to bear on those working on the Manhattan Project.

Delair was convinced that there was someone in the U.S. government or military that was much like Reynolds. The last thing they wanted was for the Japanese to surrender before they could deploy that awesome new toy of theirs. The whole business was beginning to make an old man of him.

CHAPTER ELEVEN
May 19, 1945
16:00
4:00 PM

Beckler descended the companionway on the outside of the main superstructure then headed aft along the main open deck. He was looking for Millie. Someone would have to go to supply and check on the engines that were due in from the Hendy company. Also, there was the much needed, many times promised blankets and sheets for the bunks.

In his mind, Beckler knew that he could go himself, and deep down he really wanted to. But he couldn't bring himself to go. Instead he told himself that he was needed where he was and that Millie could see to the supplies. The real reason was there, buried just below the surface. It was Lt. Hewitt, in her snug fitting uniform that drove his senses wild. Those sensuous eyes, . . . that damn stubborn streak of hers. Why did she always make him feel so out of control?

At least here on the ship he was in control. He was the Captain. Things went the way he wanted them to, for the most part anyway. He didn't need the irritation; from now on he would send someone else down there. He knew there was no hope of anything coming of his seeing her, so what would be the point? So she could get a kick out of playing with him? The more he thought of it, the more irritated it made him.

Beckler had made the entire trip around the main deck without so much as seeing his First Officer when he neared the aft part of the superstructure that had been removed to make room for raising the old engines out and lowering the new ones back down into the engine room flat. Which was located almost amidship, just above the inner bottom.

The removal of the aft half of the superstructure left a gaping hole through which one could peer down into the bowels of the ship from the main deck almost to the keel. Everything aft of the stack and forward of the bulkhead which separated the engine room and hold number four was gone.

Looking down the hole, Beckler heard rather than saw his First Officer.

"Mister?" Beckler called down. "You down there?"

"Yes, Captain," came the reply.

Still Beckler could only hear him, as the bright sunlight outside the hole made the lighting down within the ship seem inadequate.

"Report on the main deck as soon as possible."

"Yes, sir," Millie called out.

Lt. Hewitt was a professional and masked her disappointment well, but Millie had noticed it when he entered her office instead of Beckler. Unlike the episodes with Beckler, the Lieutenant was most cordial in handling Millie's requests.

On his way out, Millie stopped by one of the desks for a quick chat with a female clerk. He had only been there a moment when Lt. Hewitt stepped up.

"Social hour, Ms. Thompson?" Lt. Hewitt inquired in a genuine school-marm fashion.

"I'm sorry," Millie said. "I was just leaving."

"How did it go?" Beckler questioned Millie as he stepped aboard the KING.

"No problems," Millie replied. "Engines should be here in a couple of weeks."

"We need them now!"

"Sorry, Captain. It was the best they could do. We're on the priority list."

"What about the other supplies?"

"Be here yet today," Millie replied, sensing as uneasiness in Beckler.

"Did she give you any problems?"

"None to speak of," Millie sheepishly answered. Knowing that that was what was bothering Beckler more than the engines being delayed.

An hour or so later the supplies were delivered by truck to the ship. As Millie was signing for the supplies, his friend Mary Thompson stepped around the cab of the delivery truck and flashed a sweet smile.

"Hi, Milton," she softly said.

"Hey doll, what brings you down here?" Millie beamed with surprise at seeing her.

"I came to ask you to do me a favor."

"Shoot, anything." Millie smiled.

"Could you bring that Captain of yours along with you tonight?" Mary asked.

"Don't know. The Captain isn't the type to be talked into doing something he doesn't want to do."

"Could you at least try? . . . For me?"

"Well sure, I'll try," Millie knew he was being used, but who cared? "But do you mind telling me why you want Captain Beckler to come along?"

"I've talked Lt. Hewitt into coming with me and I think she needs to see him."

"What? You know how those two get along. It could be a big mistake!"

"Oh Milton," Mary sighed. "You have such beautiful blue eyes and yet you're stone blind. Since you showed up today instead of him she's been a real bitch. I would bet a week's wages that she has a thing for him and just doesn't know how to show it."

"You could have something there," Millie thought aloud. "I think Beckler has a thing for her too."

"Bingo! It's perfect! They'll finally get a chance to get together under the right circumstances," she giggled. "and our lives will be the better for it."

"This little game of yours could blow up in our faces," Millie cautioned. "then our lives would be hell, because they'll blame us for it."

"Trust me," Mary laughed as she walked away.

"Trust me," Millie mimicked her as he returned aboard the KING.

Millie knew better than to try by himself to persuade the Captain to go along. He enlisted the help of the porter, old Pete. Pete had a way with Beckler. He could get the Captain to do more than anyone else. As soon as Millie explained the entire scenario to Pete and explained that a little socializing would be good for the Captain. Old Pete smiled and told Millie to rest easy, the Captain would join him later.

Beckler never knew what transpired. He had returned from supper to find his dress uniform all laid out and ready for him. Upon questioning Pete about it, the porter explained that he wanted him to go with Millie to the Officer's Club.

"But why?" Beckler had protested. "He's a big boy! If he wants to go, let him go! He doesn't need me to babysit."

Pete convincingly argued that Beckler would be doing it to boost morale, both for himself and Millie. Camaraderie and all that. It is a good thing for the two most senior officers of a vessel to socialize together.

To prevent it from appearing staged, Millie pretended not to notice Lt. Hewitt and Mary sitting over in the far corner at a table by themselves. Instead, he and Beckler walked up to the bar, took a couple of stools and ordered beers.

Beckler had just lit a cigarette and was about to take a sip from the bottle in front of him when he noticed the reflection in the mirror behind the bar. He had missed it at first, since they were sitting so far back in the corner. Her eyes met his for an instant before they both turned away. But with each sip of beer Beckler would glance at the reflection in the mirror. More times than not, she was also looking.

Suddenly Millie turned towards Beckler and said he had to go and say hello to someone. Beckler simply nodded and continued nursing his beer. As he watched Millie make his way towards the table Lt. Hewitt was sitting at, a nervous chill went through him. "That's why she didn't give him a hassle!" Beckler thought as he saw Millie grab a chair and sit down at the table. A tingle of jealousy crept in until he noticed that Millie was interested in the companion of Lt. Hewitt's.

Someone started to feed the jukebox and soon the floor was loaded with dancing couples. Millie and Mary were one of the couples. Song after song went deadfully by and yet Beckler could not bring himself to ask the Lieutenant to dance.

As he glanced into the mirror towards her, she seemed to be pleading with her eyes for him to come over. But what if he was just imagining it? What if she turned him down? He would make a fool of himself and she would no doubt enjoy every minute of that. He decided not to take the chance. Yet, other men would step up to her and ask. She would smile, say something to them and remain seated. As each of the suitors stepped away her eyes turned towards Beckler's reflection for an instant to see if he had been watching. He had.

It wasn't that she didn't want to dance; the right man hadn't asked. From the glances in the mirror she felt that he would, sooner or later.

Finally Millie and Mary decided to sit one out. As they returned to the table Mary insisted that he sit with them.

"I'm sorry but I can't," Millie apologized as though it was sincere instead of being a line that he and Mary had just rehearsed when they saw Lt. Hewitt and Beckler might need a little help. "I came with a friend of mine. I can't just leave him sitting alone."

"Well, bring him over here," Mary quickly offered. "You wouldn't mind, would you, Lieutenant?"

"Not at all," Lt. Hewitt politely replied, doing her best at masking any hint of excitement.

"Hey great," Millie winked at Mary. The plan was working so far.

Beckler acted as though it was an inconvenience to move over to the table. As he neared the table his eyes met Lt. Hewitt's. Her hazel-blue eyes were soft and sparkled with warmth. All hint of the fire and ice they held at the office was gone. Still Beckler played it as nonchalant as possible.

"Captain," Millie spoke up. "I'd like you to meet Mary Thompson. Mary, this is my skipper, Captain Andrew Beckler."

"It's a pleasure to meet you, Captain." Mary sweetly nodded.

"I assure you, the pleasure in all mine, Mary," Beckler charmed.

"And I believe you two already know each other," Millie said, worried about blowing it now.

"Good evening Lieutenant, you look lovely."

"Thank you Captain," Lt. Hewitt smiled. God, had he actually paid her a compliment?

"Let's dance, Milton!" Mary urged as she grabbed his hand and led Millie off to the dance floor.

They were adults and yet they were experiencing all the emotional butterflies and awkwardness of adolescence. Beckler kept trying to think of something they might have in common, an ice-breaker of sorts. All he could think of was that when he needed supplies, she was the one he had to fight to get them. It wasn't exactly what he had hoped for, but it was all he had to start with.

"I suppose we could argue over some trivial piece of naval hardware," he smiled.

She laughed a bit and stared blankly into the half empty drink she was stirring. "We don't have any trouble speaking then, do we?"

"We sure don't," Beckler agreed.

"It's not all my fault."

"I didn't say it was anyone's fault," Beckler defended. "I just meant that our voices seem to be in perfect form when we are in our true environment."

"My true environment is a supply depot in a naval yard?" she snapped with eyes that betrayed both hurt and anger.

"That's not what I meant," Beckler shrugged. "I'm sorry, okay?"

As another song on the jukebox went by, they sat quietly and watched the dancers.

"Thanks for getting those blankets and other supplies for Millie today," Beckler finally said.

"I didn't do it just for Millie," she replied. "I would have gotten them for you as well, if you had come to the office and requested them yourself."

"I did, last week."

"I was out then. I really was! There's a war going on, sometimes we run short on things. Even blankets and sheets."

"I believe you."

"I hope that you do. I'm not the wicked witch," she said with moist eyes.

"I didn't say that you were," Beckler couldn't believe where this conversation was heading. "I was just thanking you for the supplies that came today. Hell, I wasn't even thinking anything else. I do have an inkling of the problems of your job."

"Just what do you think of me?" she asked almost in tears.

Before Beckler could answer Mary and Millie stepped up and pleaded with them to dance. Beckler tried to wave them off. Mary ran up and grabbed onto his arm and literally pulled him to the dance floor. Left with little choice, Millie stepped up to the Lieutenant and held his forearm towards her. "May I have this dance?"

She looked up, smiled, and took his arm and was led off towards the dance floor.

The floor near where Beckler and Mary were dancing was too crowded so Millie reluctantly led Lt. Hewitt across the floor to an open area. As they slowly swayed to the music Lt. Hewitt looked Millie in the eyes and asked about that Captain of his.

"What do you want to know?"

"How long have you known him? Where you met him? What kind of a man is he?"

Across the dance floor Mary was taking the lead; not in the dancing, in the small talk. All of which was to plant the seed that the Lieutenant was interested.

Finally, after some careful maneuvering Millie had worked his way over to where he and the Lieutenant were dancing near Beckler and Mary. With that accomplished, Mary looked over towards Millie and beamed, "It's time to change partners!"

"We've been set up," Beckler laughed.

"Looks that way," Lt. Hewitt agreed.

The dance was slow and close. Beckler breathed deeply, tantalized by her perfume. His pulse was rapid and inside he was as excited as a schoolboy. On the exterior he was the calm and collected Captain.

As he led her around the floor, the Lieutenant felt secure and warm in his arms. It was everything she had imagined. She closed her eyes and visioned that he loved her, that this dance was his idea, not a staged event to get them together.

Maybe this would be the beginning of something special. God, she hoped so. But soon the dance was over and Beckler was leading her towards the table. Millie and Mary had already sat down when Beckler turned to Lt. Hewitt and thanked her for the lovely dance. Then he turned to Millie and said that he would see him tomorrow onboard the ship. Without anymore ado, Beckler left, leaving the other three to simply watch in stunned silence.

No sooner had Beckler stepped out of sight, than Lt. Hewitt thanked Mary for bringing her along and left as well. As she walked towards her quarters, Lt. Hewitt angrily cursed Beckler. "Who the hell does he think he is?"

She felt hurt, rejected, and yet intrigued by that rude son-of-a bitch.

Beckler slowly walked towards the KING. He knew that walking out that way was wrong. But he didn't know what to do. He wanted to spend time with her, but at their own choosing, not forced together. If only the ship was done, he could simply sail away like he had done so many times before when things became too awkward. No wonder, he thought, that he was so awful around women. He had spent most of his adult life at sea. The only women he had known were the kind that one bought with a couple of drinks. Not a smart, attractive, thinking woman. Never, he decided, had he ever seen the likes of her.

To make matters worse, he would probably never get another chance, and rightly so. After the way he had behaved, he didn't deserve it. God, if only he could go back and do it all over again!

CHAPTER TWELVE
May 20, 1945
07:00
7:00 AM

Millie made his way towards Beckler's cabin from the wheelhouse. He was troubled with the outcome of last night. He should not have allowed himself to get involved in Mary's little match-maker scheme. If the Captain and Lt. Hewitt wanted to get together, they should do it on their own terms, not be cornered into it. Millie was sure Mary's intentions were good, and she was probably right about the two of them not able to get together on their own. But to trick them into it, then to have such disastrous results. Now he had to set things right with his friend and Captain.

Stopping a moment in front of Beckler's door, Millie took a deep breath before knocking.

"It's open." Beckler called from inside.

Millie reluctantly turned the knob and stepped through the open door. Beckler was sitting at his desk pouring over a stack of paperwork.

"Good morning, Mister," Beckler calmly said, without looking up from his papers. "I'll be with you in a moment, this is part of the job I have always hated. Nobody told me that there would be this much paperwork involved in being a sailor."

"There isn't," Millie grinned nervously. "The paperwork increases with rank. A fresh face sailor doesn't have paperwork."

Beckler stopped what he was doing and pondered that thought for a moment.

"Remember your first voyage, Mister?"

"That and many thereafter," Millie replied. "I also remember the mate that got me the job on my first ship."

"Ever regret it?"

"I have sometimes thought of what I might be doing back in Illinois, if I hadn't gone to sea. But regret it, no, never."

"It's funny," Beckler mused, "that two kids who grew up in the middle of the continent would spend much of their adult lives sailing around the world on ships."

"We've seen it all," Millie agreed, "and much of it together, on one tub or another."

"You're right, we've been through a lot together," Beckler agreed. "I guess I know you better than any other human being. That's why I want you to know that I feel bad about last night."

"Why should you feel bad? I was the one who shouldn't have put you in that awkward position. I'm sorry I let Mary talk me into it."

"Don't be sorry," Beckler said. "I know your heart was in the right place. I was a jerk for walking out like that. I just felt uncomfortable, not knowing what to do or say. I'm a little clumsy around women."

"No you're not," Millie argued. "I remember many ports-of-call that you handled yourself quite well. In fact, thanks to you, the rest of us usually had a good time too."

"That's different."

"In what way?"

"With those gals, I knew that I would never see them again. And the reason for their being there was to spend the night with sailors who had just been paid. It's a whole different ball game with someone like the Lieutenant."

"You like her, don't you?"

"Yes I do," Beckler confessed, "and I don't mind telling you that I feel like a real ass about last night. Thanks to you, I had the perfect opportunity to get to really know her, away from the supply depot. But, like the fool I am, around women anyway, I blew that one chance."

"Hey, I'm sorry I put you into that situation," Millie apologized. "If I had let you in on the game plan, you would have had the time to prepare yourself. I really should have told you."

"Forget it," Beckler forced a smile, "it wasn't your fault, I mean that."

The two sat silent for several seconds before a broad smile came to Millie's face.

"Would you like another go at it?"

Beckler quickly glanced at Millie, thought it over for a minute, then slowly shook his head. "No, I really wouldn't, thanks. Once is enough for me to make a fool of myself. Let's just leave it alone."

"Are you sure?"

"Thanks for the offer, but yes, I'm quite sure. Please don't make the effort again," Beckler replied knowing Millie well enough to know that he wouldn't if he was asked not to.

Reynolds and his men had been narrowing the field of likely places for the broadcasts of this Brazilian spy, whose code name was Felix. Since the last time they had talked about Tex, nothing had been intercepted from him. They knew they were close to establishing where Felix's base was, but were unaware of just how close.

Felix had left his camp area, across the channel from Mare Island, and headed for the barn for some needed rest before moving the radio gear to another location. Felix was a highly paid professional. He knew his job well, and had great respect for the Americans at detecting his location. He knew it wouldn't take long before they knew he was in the area, and not much longer before they began to track down his whereabouts.

His only defense would be to move as often as possible, to broadcast from one location, once or twice, before moving somewhere else. He knew that the time to move was at hand. He had already rented a third story apartment in Fairfax, and another one in Dublin, some distance to the south.

It was getting warm as Felix entered Crockett. The black sedan blended in with all the others. Just as he was about to turn south, Felix noticed a small truck stopped at the intersection. The truck was plain enough, except for a small dish shape affixed to the top of it. Felix felt a cold shiver go down his back as he removed his foot from the brake and accelerated past the truck.

As he drove past his turn-off, he watched through his rear-view mirror, as the truck waited for another car behind to pass, before it pulled out and headed for Crockett.

There was little doubt in Felix's mind that the Yanks had closed in. He thought of waiting for dark to retrieve the equipment, but at night there are fewer vehicles moving, thereby making him stand out even more.

The odds, he thought, were still in favor of getting the radio in broad daylight. Just what the Yanks wouldn't expect.

The only part of the plan that would be changed was which apartment would be used first. By using Dublin first, he might be able to entice those that were seeking him to move their operations farther south. One thing was for sure, he would only be able to use each location once.

Across the Pacific, in Tokyo, Dr. Isamu Inouye sat down before a microphone. After clearing his throat, he turned to another man, who was standing outside the broadcast booth.

With the signal from Inouye, the man outside the booth flipped on the power switch and the good doctor began his 'Official Spokesman' broadcast from Japan to the United States.

In Washington, intelligence officials were buzzing over the broadcast. They had waited patiently for any kind of reply from Japan to Captain Zach's 'Official Spokesman' broadcast. Zacharias and others carefully studied the reply, looking intently at what it did say, and what it didn't say. Zacharaias had spent years in Japan before the war and had a deep understanding of how things worked in that society.

He knew that there were two separate factions within those of authority in the Japanese government. The peace party, and the war party. Each faction was fiercely committed to their cause.

In a secluded office on the second floor of the Imperial Headquarters in Tokyo, four Japanese intelligence officers studied the problem before them. They knew that the enemy had some kind of new and horrible weapon. Exactly what this weapon was, no one knew. Judging from the reports from their operatives within the United States and in Europe, these four men concluded that the new weapon must surely be captured German V-2 rockets.

V-2's made a lot of sense. That's why the enemy was fighting so stubbonrly for Okinawa. The Japanese mainland was within range of V-2's launched from there.

The information had also stated that the weapon would be transported by sea. Their duty, as they saw it, would be to stop that shipment, at all costs.

After pondering all their options, they concluded that the only feasible way to effectively cover all the possible routes from U.S. held bases to Okinawa would be the use of as many Imperial submarines as possible. They would take subs off traditional submarine duty, mainly transport duty, and send them on strictly search-and-destroy missions.

There were still a number of fine points needed for the puzzle, like which ship, where was the weapon's true destination, and if possible, to find out what was the ship's sailing date.

For those answers they could only rely on the two operatives now in the U.S., Felix and Tex. As for which subs they would use for this mission, the four unanimously chose the newer I-Class models. This would allow for extended cruises, and these subs had enough deck space for six kaitens.

'TAMON', one of the gods that protected the Japanese against invaders, was the code name given to this operation. For surely as the deity Tamon had protected the mainland from invasion for centuries, this operation would protect the mainland now.

The Japanese I-Class submarine was one of the largest in the world, with ample stores to remain at sea for lengthy periods of time. Couple the I-Class with the use of the new 'kaiten' torpedoes, or one-man/one way exploding mini subs, and the hunter-killer potential was great. The kaiten was, in itself, a large torpedo attached to the deck of the mother sub. Its lone occupant would climb aboard through a sealed hatchway. When launched, the lone occupant of the kaiten would steer the torpedo towards its target with deadly accuracy. In the nose of the kaiten were three to five hundred pounds of explosives, more than ample to fell a mighty surface ship.

If no exact sailing date could be obtained, these four officers figured that they would have to position a number of these kaiten carrying I-class subs over a large area to destroy any enemy vessels they could, in hopes of stopping the right one.

Due to the diminished reserves at their disposal, they finally decided to dispatch six I-class subs on search and destroy missions from the middle of June on.

In Brazil, Lomas carefully read the cable over for the third time. He smiled, and thought to himself. Maybe peace would come. He had been losing hope. The stubborn Americans had shunned several attempts by the Japanese for a diplomatic settlement. One even came from the Japanese Emperor himself, through the Vatican in Rome. The Americans seemed bent on using this new weapon. Even Russia was preparing to enter the war against the Japanese.

Maybe now the Americans would listen to the Japanese, and settle this blood bath in a peaceful manner.

CHAPTER THIRTEEN
June 6, 1945
13:25
1:25 PM

The sun beat down as the men steadily guided the crane cables. The new triple expansion reciprocating engine for the KING was being lifted off the railroad flat car that had hauled it from the factory in Sunnyvale, California. The engine had been shipped in several huge packing crates that bore the manufacturer's name on their sides. Millie had been right, Beckler thought, the KING was getting the same engine that most of the western-built Liberties were getting, a Joshua Hendy Machine Company engine. The Hendies were damn good engines. Slow, but dependable.

From the railroad car, it was lifted to the ground and unpacked. Then it was hauled up and lowered into the engine room to Patty and his boys, one piece at a time. The going was slow, but between Patty down in the bowels of the ship, and Sergeant Germain on the wall, the progress was steady.

Beckler watched them work for a while and wondered to himself that if ever Patty and Germain got themselves into a cussing match, he wouldn't know who would win. Realizing that there was nothing he could do here, he headed towards the bridge.

Inside the wheelhouse, Millie and Donk had the watchmen and Quartermasters busy painting a new coat of varnish on the woodwork, while they busied themselves with organizing the chart table. Several shipyard workers were installing a new compass, while several more electricians were installing new telephone equipment for intership communications. With the smell of the varnish, and all the bodies already in there, Beckler decided to go elsewhere.

Entering the radio room, Beckler found Sparks and Shorty tidying up a bit. The new radio equipment had already been installed. And her call letters KWHK had been assigned.

"Hey Captain, you slummin'?" Shorty quipped, with a broad smile.

"Naw, just makin' sure you boys are keeping busy."

"We're trying," Sparks smiled, "tryin' to make this job last, 'cause Pete wants us to help him with housekeepin' chores as soon as we're done."

Beckler just smiled, and stepped back out the door. It was just like those two to duck any extra work if they could get out of it. And old Peter Fernburg, the ship's porter, wasn't the easiest person to work with. Pete looked more the part of a rabbi, than a sailor. But, he was one of the most thoughtful persons Beckler had ever met.

At sixty-seven years old, Pete was also the oldest man in the crew. He dearly loved being at sea, and if Beckler hadn't chosen him, he would have been sitting on his front stoop waiting to die in New York City. Besides, everyone in the crew loved the way old Pete treated them, as if they were all his own kids. When they would do something good, old Pete always said a good word. When they acted crazy, Pete would shake his head sadly, and say something like, "Where did I go wrong?" If they did something foolish, another one of Pete's famous sayings was, "I teach you all I know, and you still know nothing. What does that say for me?"

The night air felt good as it passed through the wheelhouse, via the open bridge wing doors, one on either side of the wheelhouse. At last Beckler was alone. The crew was either in their bunks for the night, or down in the engine room helping Patty and the rest of the engineering department. Beckler was unaware of the other person that had just entered the wheelhouse through the starboard wing door. The Lieutenant stood silent, simply watching Beckler as he studied the charts laid before him.

She studied his features, he had the look of a strong-willed man. His rumpled white shirt lay tossed in a ball on the chair at the end of the chart table. His hair was neatly in place, except for a small curl that hung slightly over his forehead. Around his neck, he wore a small medallion, that laid against the few hairs that grew from his chest. If not for the weathered face of a sailor, and the slight graying in his hair, Beckler could have passed for nineteen.

It had been almost a month since that day in her office when they had embraced; it had sparked something within her, intrigue, if nothing else. Even that night, two weeks ago, when they had danced, she knew she wanted him, but he had shunned her. Millie had told her to just pass it off as shyness. But she still wasn't sure.

Against her better judgment, something kept nudging her closer to this moment. He occupied her thoughts, her dreams, and she didn't even know him. The only times they had gotten near each other, there always seemed to be such hostilities between them, except for those two times, and the second time was filled with such coldness.

That day in her office; that was what kept coming back to her, the embrace, the passionate kiss. It was that one fleeting moment, when caution had been thrown to the wind, that drove her desires.

Since that night at the club, Beckler had made himself scarce, sending Millie in for supplies, or Gene. It had even made her feel a tinge of jealousy when one of her clerks asked Millie, where that good-looking Captain of his was?

For whatever reasons, she found herself doing what she never thought she would do, seeking a man out of the dark with passion on her mind. One way or the other, she had to find out for sure if she was the only one to feel the desire that burned between them when they had kissed. Right or wrong, she was here to do just that; it was too late to back out.

She thought she hated him; she thought him arrogant. But suddenly there was this strong attraction. She couldn't describe it. She couldn't even believe that she was here, standing in the wheelhouse of his ship, alone with him!

The perfume she had on, carried by the breeze, drifted over to Beckler. At first he seemed startled, quickly glancing in her direction. Then a look of puzzlement as his eyes narrowed.

"Lieutenant?" he questioned, as if not sure.

"Yes Captain. It's me," she answered nervously.

"Well, come on in."

"Thank you. I will," she replied, feeling clumsy about the situation. "Working late are we?"

"No, not really. Just couldn't sleep, and didn't know what else to do."

"So here you are."

"Here I am," he flatly repeated, wondering where she was headed with this idle chat. He certainly didn't think this visit to be social. She acted like a fish out of water. The Lieutenant was always in command of her thoughts and actions, now she acted giddish. "Are you okay?"

"Oh, I'm fine, really," she replied.

"Then what do you want?" he asked.

She didn't answer at first, instead she walked over to the row of windows at the front of the wheelhouse and peered out over the fore part of the ship. She could feel his eyes upon her back. Thinking of the old saying, that actions speak louder than words, she reached up and removed her uniform cap, pulled the hair pins, and shook her head, and let her long auburn hair fall to her shoulders.

"So this is what it's like to be in the wheelhouse of a ship?" she asked calmly.

"If the KING is a ship, then yes, this is what it's like. You mean, you've never been aboard a ship before?"

"Oh my, yes, I've been aboard many ships, but never in the wheelhouse before. And never at night."

Beckler stood silent. The Lieutenant had the glow of a beautiful woman, with the moonlight through the windows reflecting off her hair—her feminine shape that had been poured into that snug fitting uniform skirt. She seemed so sensual, so delicate, so attractive. He had thought her lovely once before, only to find out he had misread her. He had to push those thoughts aside, she had made a fool of him once. He wasn't going to give her a second go at it. And yet, that day in her office? He felt something, but given how she had always treated him, he had written it off as a one time thing, something that had just happened. The end of the war and all, maybe she just lost her head, as he had done, maybe it had meant nothing. Yet here she was before him, his tormentor, and he couldn't help wanting her!

"You don't like me very much, do you, Captain Andrew Beckler?" she asked, after slowly turning around to face him.

"Haven't given it much thought," he lied.

"I'm just another sailor to you, is that it?"

"Not quite," he corrected.

"How so?" she asked, as she stepped closer to the chart table, with her head tilted slightly, and a sexy expression to her tight smile and a glimmering sparkle in her eyes.

That sheepish part of Beckler's personality was back, and in full force. His face flushed, heart raced, while his brain and tongue seemed to disconnect. He was hating it, as much as she was enjoying his shyness. He turned away from her and stepped over to the ice chest and removed a beer, before moving over to the port side of the wheelhouse, and staring out the side windows.

"You can't run away to your ship now, Captain."

"Look," Beckler started. "I'm sorry about that, really I am."

"Then answer my question," she smiled.

A long pause.

"You're just different," he finally replied.

"In a good sort of way?" she asked, as she stepped up next to him, so closely, that he could feel her hair brush against his bare shoulder, causing a chill to go through him.

"Good," he answered quietly.

"I'm glad," she replied.

"Is this the Jeykll, or Hyde, I'm seeing?" he softly asked.

"Is this what?"

"Is this Jeykll or Hyde? I never seem to know how to read you," Beckler repeated.

"Both. It's the real me. The Rebecca Hewitt, me."

"Who is it that works for supply?"

"Oh that? That's Lieutenant Hewitt. I suppose there's a little of her here too."

"I'd prefer the Rebecca over the Lieutenant."

"How about you? Are you Captain Beckler, or Andrew?"

"Which would you prefer?"

"Depends on what I wanted at the time. At the moment, Andrew would be fine."

"Then Andrew it is." He smiled, as he looked down into her hazel eyes.

For the moment, all around them ceased to be, as they gazed into each other's eyes. All the passion and desire that burned within their souls shown through their eyes. This was a moment to be savored. The ecstasy of being about to enjoy something one has hungrily yearned for, is gone the instant one obtains it, so they lingered, cherishing the sweet taste of desire.

The kiss came slowly, naturally, tenderly. Followed by the embrace, then a second kiss. This time it came with all the fury, and strength, of a lifetime of waiting for this one fleeting second.

With her head pressed against his chest, his strong arms wrapped tightly around her shoulders, they tenderly swayed, in the darkened corner of the wheelhouse, as if dancing to an imaginary band that played in their hearts. The only sound to be heard was the distant hammering of the men down in the engine room four decks below.

"I've been wanting this moment to happen since the first time I saw you," Beckler whispered.

"Me too."

"Really?" Beckler asked in surprise.

"Yes, really," she answered as she looked into his eyes, with the soft glow of the moon lighting her radiant face. "I kept hoping that you would make the first move, then when you left the club, I didn't know what to think."

"I'm sorry. I didn't know what to do, what to say, and above all else, was afraid of making a fool of myself in front of God and everybody."

"That's what Millie told me."

"He did?"

"Yes, he thinks a lot of his captain."

"He's a good friend, and a top notch first mate."

"I think you're pretty special too," she said softly. Beckler didn't verbally answer; instead he lifted her chin with his right hand and tenderly kissed her full and eager lips.

"I'm glad you came tonight," Beckler said.

"I am too," she replied. "although I had second thoughts. I finally said the hell with it, and came anyway."

"What made you decide to come?"

"I thought it was high time that I tour this URSHEL KING myself. And besides, like I said, I've never been in a ship's wheelhouse at night before. I didn't want to miss my chance."

"You couldn't care less about the KING," Beckler smiled.

"You're right about that!" she replied as they tightly embraced.

Each wanted the other, but neither could think of the proper way to convey those thoughts to the other, until finally . . .

"I've never seen the Master's cabin on a ship before either," she finally whispered.

He didn't answer. He didn't have to. He simply cupped her close with one arm and led her away.

CHAPTER FOURTEEN
June 7, 1945
07:00
7:00 AM

Beckler was awakened by a subtle motion along side his bed. He opened his eyes just in time to catch a glimpse of Old Pete carefully laying out the Lieutenant's freshly pressed uniform over the back of a chair. Pete turned, winked, then silently left the cabin.

Beckler turned over and watched the Lieutenant sleep. Her auburn hair covered half of her beautiful face as she slept on her stomach. A suggestion of her perfume still lingered, and Beckler kissed her cheek.

The faint hammer sounds were still coming from below, telling him that the men must have worked down there all night. Easing himself from the bed, he made for the head to shower and shave.

He had just entered the shower when the curtain was pulled back and the Lieutenant dropped the towel she was wrapped in and stepped in.

"I'm great at washing backs," she teased.

"Among other things," Beckler agreed as he turned towards her and kissed her tender lips. With the water spraying around them, they tightly embraced. Body pressed against body.

"Aren't you going to be missed?" he finally asked.

"Seems your crew already wants you back," she said.

"Why do you say that?"

"Someone has gone to the trouble of preparing my clothes for me to go."

Beckler laughed. "That would be old Pete, just doing what he does. He sort of takes care of us. He probably took care of your clothes so you would look great when you left, not that you don't look terrific right now!"

Stepping from the shower they took turns at playingly drying each other off. Then they noticed a delightful aroma coming from the cabin...FOOD. Wrapped in towels, they entered the cabin and found a table set for two complete with a white linen table cloth. A covered dish sat at each place setting. They quickly dressed before setting themselves at the table.

"Who is this Pete?" she wondered out loud.

"Our porter."

"You mean valet, don't you?" she corrected.

"I suppose one could say that, but porter is the job title," Beckler replied.

"Boy would I like to meet him. With this kind of service, I may not want to leave."

Beckler smiled and nodded, while he poured her a cup of coffee from the thermos Pete had left. He was about to say something when a knock came at the door.

"It's open," Beckler said.

The door swung open and old Pete entered. Much to Beckler's and Rebecca's surprise, Pete was dressed in his best dress whites. A towel was hung over one arm and he carried a pitcher of water in one hand. Beckler had never seen Pete in his dress uniform before. Rebecca couldn't believe her eyes. Before her stood a small man with gray hair and a salt and pepper full beard. On his nose sat a round pair of wire-framed, thick glasses. His uniform was freshly pressed with all the brass buttons and black leather shoes spit polished.

"I do hope that the lady finds the meal to her liking," Pete politely questioned.

"Oh my, yes! The food is excellent and so is the service," Rebecca replied in astonishment.

"Pete, I don't know what to say," Beckler added.

"No need, Sir," Pete bowed slightly. "It's not often that the Captain entertains such a lovely creature. It is an honor to have this fine lady join us."

"Why, thank you, Pete," Beckler said. "Pete, I would like to introduce Lieutenant Rebecca Hewitt. Rebecca, this is Mr. Peter Farnburg."

"Just call me Becky. It's an honor to meet you, Peter."

"I assure you, Miss Becky, that the honor is all mine," Pete replied, as he gently bowed and kissed her hand, "and please call me Pete, all my friends do."

"Thank you, Pete," she replied.

Old Pete started to say something else, then seemed to think better of it. Instead he bowed slightly again and turned for the door to leave.

"Was there something else?" Beckler asked.

"Now would not be the time," Pete replied.

"The time for what?" Beckler insisted.

"To make an inquiry."

"Please," Becky intervened, "don't let me get in the way. I have to get ready for work anyway."

"No, wait, please," Pete stopped her. "It was you I wished to speak to. But some other time perhaps."

"Me?" she asked in bewilderment. "Please, now would be fine. What can I do for you?"

"Well," Pete started, not sure just how to put it. "Are you the same Lieutenant Hewitt that works for supply?"

Becky smiled and looked over at Beckler, then back to Pete. "That depends on what the Captain here might have said."

"No one could say anything bad about you, Miss Becky."

"Why Pete, are you patronizing me?"

"Begging your pardon, but the Captain and I have never discussed you before, Miss Becky," Pete shyly replied.

"I believe you," she said sweetly, "and yes, I am from supply."

"What do you need, Pete?" Beckler got right to the point.

"Well, to tell the truth," Pete started uneasily. "I've made up this small list of things I need in housekeeping for this ship. It didn't have a thing when we got it."

"I'll do what I can," Becky assured him.

"Thank you. I really appreciate this," Pete smiled as he handed the list to Becky before slowly backing for the door and exiting.

She turned back to Beckler and teasingly returned his smug smile. "If I didn't know better, I'd say you seduced me for Old Pete's sake."

"Who seduced who?"

"Complaining?"

"Not a chance!"

As Lieutenant Hewitt stepped from the wheelhouse, she became the object of whistles and catcalls. She ignored them and proceeded down the gangway, meeting Sergeant Germain about half the way down. As she passed he paused to watch her go by, then turned his focus towards Beckler who was standing in the wheelhouse doorway, also watching Becky leave. The Sergeant glanced back at Becky, then once again at Beckler. Then with a shrug, he went on about his business.

CHAPTER FIFTEEN
June 8, 1945
15:30
3:30 PM

Reynolds entered the abandoned-looking old warehouse, and made his way past the rows of steel racks that were slowly decaying under a layer of rust. About midway through the building, he came to a grease-stained door with a knob polished by constant use. Once on the other side of the door, he entered into another world, ablaze with flourescent lights and a network of electronic devices.

"Captain," Sam called out to him, "you're just in time."

"What have you got, Sam?" Reynolds questioned. Samuel Cuddy and Reynolds were cut from two different molds. While Reynolds was aloof and distant, Sam was down to earth and friendly. Neither cared for the other very much. For Sam, Reynolds was a young upstart, jackass, sort of boss. But being that he was the boss, Sam treated him with the appropriate respect.

For Reynolds, the association was different. He trusted Sam's ability. Danielson had highly recommended Dr. Cuddy for this project. It had been the Admiral who was able to persuade Sam to take a leave of absence from the university, where he studied ancient languages.

Sam's background made him perfect for the job. His talent was being able to study symbols that didn't have any apparent meaning long enough, with his logical reasoning, to decipher an entire language.

"Felix is about to check in," Sam answered.

"You've got his timing down that pat?"

"No question about it."

"Mind if I have a look?" Reynolds asked, as he picked up a file folder from Sam's desk.

"Help yourself. It contains the notes I've been keeping as to the different transmission times. Thirteen so far, with the next in about three minutes."

"How can you be so sure? It's all Greek to me."

"It's as simple as it is clever," Sam replied, as he leafed through some of the papers until he found the one he was looking for. "The common denominator is sixty-two—forty-seven—thirteen. With a formula of one to four, two to six, three to two, four to five, five to one, and six to three."

"You lost me," Reynolds interrupted.

"Okay, his first transmission was May tenth, at 17:45:02, his second came on May the thirteenth, at 08:32:15. Exactly sixty-two hours, forty-seven minutes, and thirteen seconds after the first. He then made two more transmissions, both of which came at different times of the day, and different lengths of time between them.

But, on the fifth transmission, we got our first break. Up until then, the only thing we could rule out was that he wasn't using certain days, or times of day. It was this fifth transmission, we saw the first pattern. The time between the fourth and fifth transmissions was exactly sixty-two hours, forty-seven minutes, and thirteen seconds. The same as between the first and second.

The sixth transmission was exactly fourteen hours, thirty-six minutes, and seventy-two seconds later. The same as it had been between transmissions two and three."

"Seventy-two seconds?" Reynolds asked.

"Yes, that threw us at first too. But after carefully studying it, we happened upon the formula. Whereby, the first number, the six, becomes the fourth, the second becomes the sixth, and so on. We tested this theory against all the transmission times, and it checks out."

"Just when is the next one?"

"At 15:38:11," Sam quickly replied.

"How long have you been able to predetermine the transmission times?"

"Since the thirtieth. We wanted a few more days to be sure before we notified you of our findings."

Reynolds started to say something, but was cut short by the sound of the receiver coming to life. it was picking up the transmission of the Brazilian Andre Revilla, whose code name was Felix. Reynolds looked up at the large clock, and smilingly shook his head, 15:38:13.

CHAPTER SIXTEEN
June 13, 1945
21:30
9:30 PM

Lieutenant Hewitt pulled up alongside the KING just as Beckler stepped off the gangway.

"Hey Sailor! Ya want a lift?" she called out to him, as he neared the light gray Naval sedan.

"Does your mother know you do this?"

"Of course, who do you think taught me the trade?"

"Miss Becky!" Beckler quipped, in a fake disgusted tone, doing his best imitation of old Pete's voice.

She giggled like a school girl, and slid over, as he sat behind the wheel.

"Where are you taking me, mister?" she teasingly inquired.

"To Mama Freano's place."

"Sounds Italian."

"The best Italian ever. You can't leave this place hungry. Mama won't have it. In fact, if you're able to eat one bit more, she'll feed it to you, herself."

"Oh no, sounds like my grandmother."

"Mine too!" Beckler agreed, remembering back to the days of his childhood, as he drove towards town. Grandma Beckler would seem hurt if you didn't stuff yourself on her cooking. "What's the matter? Don't you like my cooking?" she used to say.

Mama's diner was a tidy little place, just on the edge of town. There were always plenty of cars in her lot. It was the yardstick by which Beckler always judged how good the food was in a strange diner, without going in. He tried never to stop at any place to eat that didn't have a crowd. If there was a wait to get in, there was usually a damn good reason for it. If you went by the red neon sign, you would guess it was a greasy spoon. 'FREANO'S DINER' was all it said, but for the people who did stop, it was a sign that would be long remembered.

After parking the car, Beckler helped Becky out. Her perfume filled his senses, as they slowly walked towards the door. It seemed like the most perfect night in history. The air was warm and fresh, with a light breeze blowing in from the coast. The bright moonlight danced off the enamel paint of rounded car bodies lined up in front of the small diner. You could faintly hear the voices and laughter coming from inside.

"Sure is a quaint little place, isn't it?" Becky said.

"That it is, but once you've been here, and met Mama, coming here will seem like goin' home."

As Andy opened the brightly painted wooden door, they found themselves bathed in a soft light, and tantalized by the sinfully delicious aroma that greeted them.

"Well bless my ever-lovin' soul! If it ain't Andy Beckler! Well, where have you been child?" A huge black woman called out as she made her way towards them.

The surprise was written all over Becky's face. "That doesn't sound Italian," she whispered.

"It's not. She's a true southern belle. But don't tell Papa, it'd kill him to find out now after all these years," Beckler whispered back.

"My, my, my," Mama said, as she encased Beckler in an enormous hug. Becky felt a little nervous that she might be next, as she watched Beckler being held tightly in ebony arms that were bigger around than her own thighs.

Then Mama stepped back, and peeked around Andy's shoulder towards the door.

"You didn't bring those troublesome friends of yours along, did you?" Mama asked.

"No Mama, I left them to fend for themselves tonight."

"That's good! You know you should listen to Mama now, and get yourself some new friends, cause those boys are no good. Are ya a listening to me? I mean it now! Those hooligans are all bad. Can't you find yourself somebody nice to be with . . . " Her voice trailed off as she noticed Becky standing off to the side. "Well, hush my mouth. Why if this isn't the sweetest looking little gal. Boy, you have been listening to Mama after all! Haven't you, Andrew?"

"I've always listened to you, Mama," Beckler smiled.

"If that be true honey, this is the first I've heard of it. And where's your manners? Introduce me to this sweet child."

"Mama Freano, this is Lieutenant Rebecca Hewitt."

"Hi, honey, just call me Mama, everybody does."

"Mama," Becky nodded, not at all sure what would come next.

"Come on babe, come with Mama," Mama said, as she placed her hefty arm gently around Becky's shoulders. "You haf' ta meet Papa. He'll be tickled pink to see Andy finally got himself a gal as pretty as yourself. My, you could sure use a little of Mama's food. How do you keep warm at night with no meat on those bones of yours?"

Beckler just followed. He felt like laughing; he had known this would happen. Mama will talk Becky's leg off. A lot like his own parents would do, if he could possibly have taken her to meet them. That would never be, and things being what they are, coming here was the next best thing.

Meeting Papa didn't take that long. He was a man of few words. He was probably lucky that he could even remember how to talk. Living with Mama would leave little chance for him to keep in practice. Mama then seated them off into a dimly-lit corner table. She always had a knack at being able to tell where folks wanted to sit. After getting their table service set up, she left them to themselves.

"She is unbelievable!" Becky laughed.

"That's Mama all right. At first folks don't know how to take her, but she is genuine. She means well. After you get to know her, you've got to love her. She's the most affectionate person you'll ever meet."

"She's the most of a lot of things."

"You don't like her?" Beckler seemed surprised.

"Oh, I love her. I don't believe her, but I love her! I've never seen anyone like her. How does she do it? Go on talking like that?"

"Papa once told me, if she goes first, he's going to ask the mortician to check and see if that tongue has really stopped. It's the only way he'll know that she's really dead."

"That's awful. True, but awful."

Beckler only smiled his agreement.

"How did you meet Mama?"

"It'a a long story," Beckler replied with eyes that suddenly seemed far away, as if in another time.

"I've got the entire evening," Becky smiled warmly. "I'd really like to know. You two seem so different, yet there is something quite natural between you."

"It was years ago, when I had just started sailin'," Beckler began slowly, as if savoring the cherished memories of that bygone time. Through the tone of his voice, as well as the distant look in his eyes, Becky could sense the deep feelings within Beckler that had laid dormant for many years.

"I was just a kid, working as an OS, Ordinary Seaman, on an old tramp steamer. An independent, as I recall. There weren't many of them then, even less now."

"What do you mean by an independent?"

"The old man owned it. It was his ship. Most ships are owned by a company with the captain being an employee of sorts. On an independent, the captain is the company."

Becky gave an understanding nod, as Beckler went on.

"It was an old ship that always seemed to be on her last legs, so to speak. The machinery was worn out, with a battered hull, but the old man made sure that the old gal was always spotless. If we deckhands weren't scrubbing and washing her down, we were chipping and painting.

In the eleven months I sailed her, I bet we completely painted her from stem to stern, from waterline to the peaks of her masts at least twice. When we were along a pier, he had us scraping barnacles off her bottom with a pair of swimming goggles."

"Sounds like a mean captain."

"Not really," Beckler replied. "He could be, if one crossed him, but for the most part he was fair. He was deeply religious, so we always had Sunday off, with the exception of the watch crew, or if we were needed, like during a hard blow. You could even count on a good hot meal on Sunday, right after a half hour sermon of hell fire and brimstone."

"Delivered by the captain?" Becky laughed.

"You guessed it."

"Why did you leave that ship? Were the sermons that bad?"

Beckler laughed. "No, in fact, if I had listened to them instead of dozing off, I might have turned out better. But then I never would have met Mama, so I guess there's a reason for everything."

"Okay Buster, that's it," Becky warned. "Now I have to know how dozing off during a sermon led to your meeting Mama."

"The Captain took a real dim view of booze, and the 'sin-traps' that peddled the stuff," Beckler started.

"Sin-traps?" Becky interrupted.

"Yeah, that's what the old man called bars," Beckler continued. "We were in port one night, in Mobile, Alabama."

"In Mobile, Alabama!?"

"Do you want to hear this story or not?" Beckler quipped.

"Yes I do," Becky giggled. "I won't interrupt again, but how did she and Papa get here?"

"They moved, people do that nowadays," Beckler sarcastically replied.

"I know they move, but why?"

"Work for Papa was slow; he was an iron worker, one of the best I'm told."

"Not by him, of course."

Beckler's only reply to that was a fake stern glance.

"I'm sorry," Becky grinned. "I just couldn't resist."

"So they packed up and moved west. Not an easy thing for anyone to do, even harder if you're colored. He finally found a job; he got the chance to prove his talents, and never lacked for a job in the bay area after that. He even helped build the Golden Gate."

"Great, now what happened in Mobile?"

"Well, we had just been paid and several of us decided to spend the night on the town. Since we were to be in port for three days, the old man had given us each the time off for a well deserved shore leave. We figured that we would have plenty of time to sober up before we had to report back to the ship. One thing led to another, and the next thing I knew—I woke up in jail."

"Really?" Becky laughed with an amazed look on her face.

"Really," Beckler smiled as he slowly stared at the last swallow of beer in the bottom of his glass as he slowly swirled it around. "While Papa was between jobs, Mama worked at the jail as cook and cleaning lady. When the Captain heard that we had landed in jail, he decided to let us rot there. He hired replacements from the local docks and sailed off without us.

I spent 32 days in that jail, and would have spent six months, but Mama took pity on me and paid my fine out of her meager earnings."

"How could they afford that? Didn't Papa get upset?"

"No, he really didn't, and no, they couldn't afford it; that's just the kind of people they are."

"How much was the fine?"

"I don't remember the exact amount, but I took a job painting houses for rich folks to earn enough money to pay them back, not that they expected it. You see they never had any kids of their own, and as it turned out, I was like a son to them for the time I was there. After that, we always kept in touch."

"What a touching story. No wonder you think so much of them, and they of you," Becky smiled.

"Did you ever see that Captain or his ship again?"

"No. I did, however, hear that the ship broke up in a bad storm somewhere near Bishop's Rock. All hands were lost."

"Really? How long after you had left it?"

"Three or four years," Beckler replied just as the food arrived.

As always, the lasagna was excellent. Beckler and Rebecca talked about a variety of subjects. The topic finally came around to where they grew up.

"I was born and raised in Marshall, Michigan," Becky began. "If you ever had visions of what the ideal American hometown would be like, Marshall would be it."

"Why do you say that?"

"Well, it's the perfect place to grow up. It has everything a larger town would have, like stores, movie theatres, library. They hold the county fair there, on Capitol Hill."

"Capitol Hill?"

"Yes, they call it Capitol Hill, because when the new state was looking for a place to build the state house, Marshall lost to Lansing, by only one vote. The people of Marshall were so sure that they were going to become the state capitol, that they set aside this land as the ground for the new state capitol. They even built a governor's mansion."

"Really? What happened when Lansing became the capitol?" Beckler asked.

"Nothing really, other than all the new lawmakers still had to ride the train to Marshall, then rent a horse and carriage to drive the final forty miles to Lansing. You see, Marshall was also a rail center, whereas Lansing was little more than a fork in a muddy road."

"Politics and politicians, two things I never could understand."

"Tell me about your hometown," Becky insisted.

"Well, I didn't grow up in town. Instead I grew up on a farm, five miles south of Freeport, Illinois. As a matter of fact, our farm was on Illinois Route 26. Millie Lambert, my first officer, and I lived on the same road, only about twelve miles apart. Millie lived in Cedarville, which is five miles north of Freeport. As a kid, my family didn't get into town that often. Actually, the town I spent the most time in was Forreston, fourteen miles to the south. That's where I went to school. It's funny, but you know what I remember most about growing up?"

"What's that?" Becky questioned, as she leaned slightly closer, with the light of the candle reflecting in her soft eyes.

"I remember doing the field work with my dad and grandfather. Most of that time was spent with Granddad. He was the one who taught me how to drive the team. And if I had to come up with the most memorable moment of all it would probably be a time when I was about thirteen years old. It was June twenty-first, the longest day of the year. Granddad and I had been working the ten acres down by the creek. Just before the sun set, we stopped for the night. Instead of heading for home, we just sat there, outside the gate, and watched the sun set. I can still hear him saying, 'Whenever you watch a sunset, remember this night, it'll be our moment. It may not be anything spectacular, but so long as you remember it, it'll be special.' He was right, it is special. Even after more than thirty years."

"That was wonderful. I'm glad you shared that story with me. I would have liked to have met your grandfather; he sounds like a special man."

"After leaving Mama's, they drove along the coast, stopping at a scenic, sandy beach area. They removed their shoes, and stepped out along the water's edge. The night breeze coming off the ocean was warm and heavily laden with pungent odors of the sea. Looking out to sea, the water grew continually darker until it melted into the total void where sky met sea. The slow breakers tumbled softly, lightly slapping at their toes.

They strolled along silently, holding each other closely, and feeling the warm waters of the Pacific washing over their feet; each enjoying the magic of the moment, the tenderness of an enchanted evening.

"What's it like out there?" Becky finally asked.

"You mean the sea?"

"Yes, what is it like? Why did you leave Freeport to spend your life out there?"

"That's a tough question to answer. Right now, it isn't that great to be out there. But there was a time, before the war, when being out at sea was the greatest thing in my life. I'm not sure really just how to explain it. But when I'm out there, I'm truly at peace with myself. I feel contentment, fulfillment, satisfaction. As to how a farm kid from Illinois ever fell in love with the sea? I haven't a notion."

"It's so hard to believe that on the other side of this peaceful water, there is a war going on. People are fighting and dying," she said softly.

"The sea can be misleading. Even when there isn't a war going on. One moment she can be calm and peaceful, then in a matter of hours, she can be trying to swallow you and your ship up. In fact, she's a lot like a woman I know."

"Is that right? Is this woman anyone I know?"

Beckler had backed himself into a corner. A tender kiss was his only escape.

CHAPTER SEVENTEEN
June 14, 1945
08:00
8:00 AM

Beckler was finishing the writing in his daily journal; old Pete stood beaming in the doorway.

"What's got you so happy this morning?"

"She did it!" Pete blurted out. "Miss Becky got me all the supplies I had asked for. Every one!"

"Hey, that's great Pete," Beckler said while he thought, if only he had started to date her sooner, maybe the KING would be at sea already. Boy, wouldn't she be pissed if she knew he even thought that!

"Yes sir, it sure is!" Pete answered as he started to leave.

"Oh, Pete," Beckler called after him.

"Yes Captain," Pete replied returning to the doorway.

"Would you send Patty up here?"

"Sorry sir, but I don't think that Patty can come just right now."

"And why is that?"

"There's smoke coming from the funnel. I believe that they have fired the boiler."

Beckler jumped from his chair and rushed past Pete without a reply. His heart raced as he made his way through the chart room and the wheelhouse. Could the men possibly have the machinery working already? It had to be too good to be true. If the machinery was indeed ready, then the final completions could not be far off.

Stepping out onto the port bridgewing, Beckler could hardly control his jubilation. There was indeed smoke coming from the stack. Stepping back inside the wheelhouse he turned the dial of the intraship telephone to the engine room position and lifted the receiver. After several rings, Engineer Second Class Lucky Martz answered it.

"Engine Room."

"Lucky?" Beckler questioned.

"Yes, Captain, what can I do for you?"

"Is the boiler fired?"

"Yes, Captain, it is. So are the generators."

"That's great! Any major problems?"

"None that we can see yet, sir."

"Good. Also, would you have Patty come to my office as soon as he's free?"

"Yes sir."

"Thank you," Beckler said as he returned the receiver to its cradle. He turned and stepped back unto the bridgewing. Far below some yard workers were putting the finishing touches on the repair job to the hull.

Beckler climbed down the assortment of ladders into the basin of the dry dock. Sure enough, there was Sergeant Germain, inspecting the job his men had done on the installation of the new propeller shaft bushings.

"What ya got on your mind, Beckler?" the Sergeant grunted through teeth clenched on the butt end of a cigar, without even looking at the Captain.

"Good morning to you too, Sergeant." Beckler smiled, while underneath he loathed this fat-headed jerk.

"Morning, hell, the day is half over. If you weren't up all night on *navel* explorations with that tight-assed Lieutenant, you might be able to get up with the rest of us."

Without so much as a clue of intentions, Beckler decked him. Then he hovered over the Sergeant, ready with more. As blood trickled from the corner of his mouth, the Sergeant roared with laughter.

"I'm impressed, Captain! A damn nice right cross!"

"You thick head, pompous swine. The only thing you can appreciate is a belt in the mouth. All I came down here for is to find out when this tub will be ready for her sea trials. Where do you get off insulting Lieutenant Hewitt for no damn reason?" Beckler threatened with clenched fist, and tight lips.

"She means something to ya, huh?" the Sergeant asked matter of factly, while not bothering to get back to his feet.

"Yes, she does!" Beckler snapped. "And so does this ship and its crew. Now when will she be ready for trials?"

"Take it easy, Captain. I didn't mean anything by it. As for when the KING will be ready for trials, I doubt that she'll have a chance to get them. I've got orders to have her ready by the twenty-third. Those orders came from Hunter's Point; seems they have most of your cargo already waiting."

"The twenty-third?" Beckler questioned.

"That's what the man said," the Sergeant replied, picking himself up at last.

"What man? Who gave you that order?" Beckler demanded to know.

"Some sawed-off Lieutenant. Don't remember his name."

"Delair. Was his name Delair?"

"Yeah, come to think of it. Yeah, it was Delair."

Beckler thought a minute, then turned back to the Sergeant. "If the ship is almost ready now, why can't she have a sea trial? The twenty-third is over a week away."

"Because I have about four days worth of work here before she's ready to leave this dry dock. At least five more days here in the fitting-out basin. That is, of course, if I don't get interrupted by some hot-headed Captain!"

"You had that coming," Beckler replied as he turned and started to leave.

"One more thing, Captain, before you leave."

Beckler turned around to see what it was. Before he could maneuver, his face met with a solid wall of knuckles that sent him sprawling to the concrete floor of the dry dock basin.

"You can call me Gene," the Sergeant said smiling, as he lit a fresh cigar and started to walk away. "Oh, and by the way, thanks for bailing those three bums of mine out of the county jail a number of weeks back."

Beckler simply watched him step around the corner of the stern without saying a word.

After wiping the trace of blood from his split lip, Beckler picked himself back up and made for the basin stairwell. As he hurried up the stairs, Beckler cussed beneath his breath, not at Germain, at Delair.

He kept remembering Delair's words, "We're in this together, partners. When I know something, so will you!"

"Some partnership!" Beckler said through clenched teeth, as he made the top side of the basin and quickly stepped towards the ship.

"How's that skipper?" Millie asked as Beckler walked right past without acknowledging him.

"Get Delair on the phone," Beckler ordered without repeating what he had said, "and tell him I want to see him now or sooner!"

"Right away," Millie answered as he spun on his heels and made off.

CHAPTER EIGHTEEN
June 18, 1945
11:00
11:00 AM

At last the moment had arrived. The filling valve to the dry dock basin was opened and water rushed in. It took a while, but ever so slowly, the KING would groan and creak as she started to lift off the shoring blocks that had held her during the refit.

Workers were already crawling all over the ship, looking for any signs of trouble. The hatch covers were off, and teams of men checked each cargo hold. Patty and his men were down in the engine room checking seals and bulkheads for any signs of excessive seepage. Scotty was in the aft peak tank, checking the outer shaft seal. Fritz was crawling through the shaft tunnel.

After more than an hour of checking and rechecking, Fritz and Sergeant Germain seemed confident in the KING's water-tight integrity. The yard tugs were summoned, and the huge gates to the dry dock were opened.

After forty-three days of resting in this basin, while being transformed from a rusting hulk of scrap iron into a working, 'fit', vessel, the URSHEL KING was at last towed from the dry dock, and moved to the fitting-out pier.

As Beckler watched the yard crews fasten the cables to the bollards, he noticed Lieutenant Delair making his way up the gangway. He was beginning to hate to see this s.o.b. show his face. Every time Delair came around meant one thing, trouble. What would the jerk want now?

"Hello, Captain," Delair said with a smile as he entered the bridge door. "The old girl never looked better, gray must be her color."

"Can the small talk and get to the point, Lieutenant."

"Is there somewhere we can talk in private?" Delair questioned, trying not to offend Millie, who was also standing in the wheelhouse.

"We can talk right here; Millie knows all about the sea trials. Unless there is more bad news? Then I think you will want Millie to be here so he can try to stop me from doing something you'll regret."

"Look, Captain, I'm not the enemy," Delair defended.

"It's getting hard to tell."

"What I am here for," Delair went on, ignoring that last shot, "is to offer you something in lieu of the trials. Personally, I wish there was time for the trials too. But there isn't, and that's that."

"What would take the place of a proper sea trial?" Millie inquired.

"The whole purpose of a trial, is to shake her down. Find out what doesn't work right. Then bring her back, and get the new parts. If bringing her back is out of the question, take the parts with you. Use spare parts as part of your cargo. That way if something breaks, just fix it on the run, unless of course, it can't be done without a shipyard. In that case, I made other arrangements."

Neither Beckler, or Millie said anything. They just watched, and listened. The Lieutenant seemed to be making sense.

"Here are your sailing orders. Remember, these are confidential. You're leaving Hunter's Point at midnight of the twenty-eighth. From there, you will sail north of the Hawaiian group, to Midway. However, should there be any problem too large for you to handle at sea, you will turn south and make for Pearl."

"Not bad, but we will have to have damn good mechanics on board," Millie said flatly.

"True," Beckler added, "I'm not at all sure if we would have enough, should anything major come up."

"What's the point?" Delair interrupted.

"Throw that ugly Marine Sergeant Germain in on the deal," Beckler replied.

"Like you said, he's a Marine. He's not mine to throw in."

"Then what is he doing here in the first place?" Millie asked.

"I'm not sure, but it was some deal Danielson worked out, before the KING came here. The Sergeant grew up in Portland, his uncle owned a shipyard that worked on this type of vessel. The Admiral borrowed him just long enough to get the KING into shipshape."

"Well, get the Admiral to borrow him a little while longer."

"If I am able to do it, we got a deal?"

"Just one more thing."

"Now what? I suppose you want radar, or something?" Delair snapped.
"Bingo!" Beckler replied.
"Are you crazy?!"
"Should I be?"
"I can't get you a radar system, there's no way in hell I could that!" Delair shouted.
"Thought I'd ask."
Delair shook his head and stormed out the bridge door, slamming it behind him. Beckler then turned to Millie, "Get Gene up here!"
"Right away, Captain," Millie said with a smile on his face.

"You wanted to see me, Beckler?" the Sergeant grunted.
"Yes, Gene, I did. What do you know about radar?"
"Radar, huh? Where you going to steal one of them?"
"Who said anything about stealing one. The question was, what do you know about radar?" Beckler persisted.
"Well, I know what one is. I'm sure I could hook it up. But them babies have to be calibrated if you want it to work," Gene replied.
"Think you could find me one?"
"I knew you were going to have to steal it. Now you want me to steal it for you? What's in it for me?"
"How about a nice long vacation from the Marine Corps?"
Gene thought it over for a moment, and nodded his head. "Where do you suppose is the best place to look for an extra radar system, complete, just laying around?"
Beckler shrugged. "I don't know, but right here would be my guess for the best place to start looking."
"I'll see what I can do," Gene said. "I'll let you know if I find anything."

Delair kept thinking about the radar system all the way back to his office. If the KING could be equipped with such a system, it would shorten the long odds against them. The more he thought about it, the more he liked it.
He had almost made it back to his office, when he spun his car around and headed back towards Mare Island. There had to be some vessel at Mare having radar installed. Typographical errors were as common as rain drops, especially in over worked supply offices. Another slight typo was about to happen.

Delair spent less than twenty minutes pouring over order forms until he found the one he was looking for. Two complete radar systems had been ordered and delivered within the last three days. He carefully edited both sets of forms to read as if only one set had been ordered and received.
Next, he went into the secured storeroom and hunted through the massive

building until he located all the pieces for one complete system. Removing all trace of what they actually contained, Delair neatly printed S.S. URSHEL KING, Mare Island, across the outside of the crates.

Then, he returned to the supply office, and made out the necessary paperwork to have those crates delivered to Captain Andrew Beckler personally. On the line for contents, Delair printed . . . 'Captain's Personal property.' Then, he signed the inspection release.

At three that afternoon, a delivery truck rolled to a stop along side of the KING. The driver was none too happy about having to look the Captain up.

"You Captain Andrew Beckler?" he asked.

"Yeah, I'm Beckler."

"Good," the driver sighed. "I've spent the last ten minutes looking all over this tub for you."

"What do you have?" Beckler questioned. "Why didn't you just have the First Mate sign for it?"

"Couldn't. I have your personal stuff," the driver explained. "Got to have your autograph, then set it in your personal cabin. Them are my orders."

"Personal belongings?" Beckler started to question. Then realized that Gene might have come through. He signed the form, then quickly read it. Delair had released it!

Beckler didn't say anything to the truck driver, instead he called Millie and Gene up to the bridge while the driver placed the crates into Beckler's cabin.

After the delivery truck had left, the three men carefully opened each crate before inspecting what they contained.

"I'll be damned!" Gene smiled.

"That shrewd little bastard did it" Beckler exclaimed. "Keep it here until you're sure that everything is here. Then once the number of bodies floating around has dropped, we'll get to installing it."

"We still have to find a way of concealing it from the inspectors," Millie stated.

"I'll come up with some way to hide it," Gene replied. "But, we still have to find someone we can trust to calibrate the thing."

"Millie, you handle finding the proper technician," Beckler instructed. "Gene work on concealment. I want this thing operational before we leave here."

CHAPTER NINETEEN
June 20, 1945
22:47
10:47 PM

    Becky made her way up the gangway to the spar deck of the KING. Night had finally settled in and had started to cool things off a bit. A light mist was beginning to roll over the bulwarks. The ship lay quiet; the yard crews that had been busily installing the new Naval ordinances were gone. That dockside, fishy odor was strong, mixed in with the smell of bunker fuel. The combination was almost enough to turn Becky's stomach. The vessel had a most eerie sensation about it.
    She had made it as far as the companionway leading from the spar deck up to the bridge when the sudden sound of something metallic reverberated off the steel deck right behind her. She clutched her chest as her blood ran cold, and took refuge on the stairs that led up to the wheelhouse. She quickly turned and peered into the darkness towards the direction of the sound.
    The ship was not in total darkness, as a minimal number of decklights were lit. But, with the machinery and the packing crates from the guns that were being mounted, the deck was awash in shadows.
    "Who's there?" she called out in a choked whisper.

"Take it easy, Lieutenant, it was just a wrench," Sergeant Germain laughed as he made his way down the companionway to retrieve the lost tool.

"What are you doing here, Sergeant?" she demanded to know.

"Just doing a few odds and ends for the old man. How about yourself?"

"That's none of your business."

"Didn't think so," Gene smiled smugly as he walked past her.

Becky felt a bit embarrassed about being so easily frightened and a bit angered by the Sergeant's arrogance. She felt like telling him what she thought of his attitude, but decided against it. Instead she continued her climb up the companionway towards the wheelhouse.

Beckler was studying the charts of the North Pacific when she entered the wheelhouse. Off to one side someone was installing a new counter, the top of which lay off to one side. A trouble light was draped over the edge. Inside the counter, Becky could see what looked like a radar console.

"Been shopping the midnight parts supply I see," she said calmly.

Beckler looked up from his charts for the first time, then his eyes followed hers to the new counter. He wished that she hadn't seen that. But there was nothing he could do now.

"Your competition was having a sale."

"Must have been a good price."

"Couldn't say no," Beckler answered wondering where this was headed.

"Germain's pretty talented. But how will you hide it from the inspectors?" she asked.

"Shucks mam, that's the easy part," the Sergeant replied as he stepped into the wheelhouse from behind her.

"How's that?" She smiled at the surprisingly different manner in which Gene had answered her. She was used to only the gruff side of him. To see that he had a sense of humor was refreshing.

"Just like this," Gene said as he lifted the top of the counter into place. The counter top was complete with sink and faucet.

"But what if they try the water?"

"Water is what they'll get," Gene replied.

"How? That counter is a fake."

"Oh, contraire! With the use of some flexible hosing, this lavatory will really function," Gene beamed.

"How about the tower and the dish up topside? How do you propose to hide that?" she persisted.

"No need to hide that. We won't install it until we're at sea," Beckler answered.

"But don't these things have to be tuned or something in order to work?"

"Already done. We had it on long enough for the men to calibrate it earlier. All we have to do now is keep everything out of sight until we're out of sight," Beckler answered.

"Well, you both get an 'A' for creativity," she laughed. "I just hope that that unit isn't from my inventory."

After the Sergeant had left, Becky walked over to the edge of the chart table and silently watched as Beckler carefully drew out his route. From San Francisco to Midway, then on to Wake. He stood several moments as if in deep thought. Slowly he marked off an area on the map and wrote a small caption next to it, (31' north, 157' west, decision must be made.)

"What does that mean?" she quietly asked.

"I will have to decide by then whether or not to turn back towards Pearl, or continue on towards Midway. If the ship is doing fine, we'll continue. If not, we will turn south and make for Pearl Harbor, seven hundred miles due south of this point."

"Is Wake Island your final destination?"

"No, I'm not sure what our final destination will be. They haven't said as yet. So far all I do know is that we will make calls at Midway and Wake. From there, only they know," Beckler lied.

Becky turned away from the chart table and stepped toward the forward bulkhead windows. Beckler watched in silence. She stared out across the shipyard, now shrouded in evening mist, through teary eyes. How could she convey to him the fear she felt? Something was tearing at her insides. Somehow she felt an urgent sense of foreboding about this whole voyage.

Beckler stepped out from behind the chart table and walked over to her, gently grabbing her by the arms and turning her around to face him. He was puzzled by her tear streaked cheeks, and the tenseness of her trembling body.

Instead of having him see her crying, she embraced him and buried her face into his chest. She never wanted this moment to end. He felt warm and strong. He gently held her in his arms and kissed the top of her head. But whatever had brought this on, he hadn't a clue.

He cupped her chin and lifted her face until their eyes met.

"What's the matter?" he asked in a tender whisper.

"I'm frightened, so frightened for you. I don't want to lose you."

"Frightened? Lose me? What on earth are you talking about?"

"Look Andy, don't play me for a fool. I think this whole operation Silverfish is dangerous," she said, stepping back from him, but taking the handkerchief he offered. "I can't say why, but my woman's intuition tells me something is dreadfully wrong."

Beckler didn't answer, only watched as if pained by her hurt, and flattered by her concern. Nobody had ever given a damn about him before; he wasn't sure if that was good or bad.

"It's just doesn't make any sense! Why is the Navy spending so much time and energy on an old tramp steamer like the URSHEL KING? Why, of all people, did they pick you to command it?" she cried.

Again Beckler remained silent. What could he say? And if he could tell her what he knew, would it make a difference for the better? He thought not, so he kept silent.

"And most of all," she went on, "why, after all these years of looking for someone to love does it have to be you, now? Here, under these circumstances? In a couple of days you're going to sail out of here, most likely never to return. What am I supposed to do then? Simply turn my feelings for you off and forget we ever met?"

Before he could find the words to say, she started to pound on his chest with her fists. "Answer me, damn you! Answer me!" she screamed through tear-streaked, trembling lips.

Beckler was able to wrap his strong arms around her and stop her fists. As he held her tight, she sobbed violently against his chest.

"I don't have all the answers," he soothingly whispered, "but I do know that I love you so very much. I don't know why it had to happen now either. But I'm glad it did. I've waited all my life for someone like you to come along; it never happened until now. Why? I can't say. But one thing is for certain, I will come back. This war isn't going to last forever. If you feel as strongly about me as I do about you, a day, a week, a month, a year won't matter. All I know is that I will have something to look forward to at the end of this voyage. You! It's the first time in my life that I couldn't wait to get back before I ever set sail." With that he gently kissed her moist lips. The salty taste of tears melted into the warm tenderness of her eager mouth.

"Do you really mean that?" she softly sobbed.

"Of course I do! I really love you."

"I've wanted to hear you say that for so long."

"If you ever doubted it, why didn't you just ask?"

"It's not the same," she softly replied. "I dearly love you and didn't want to force you into saying something that you didn't mean."

"I do mean it, I really do. I should have told you sooner, but please remember that I'm rather new at this. I've never felt this way before. I simply had to be sure that true love is what I've been feeling."

The morning sky was growing brighter as Beckler sat with his back against the forward bulkhead of the wheelhouse with Becky's head on his lap; yes, he did indeed truly love her. As he lightly stroked her soft auburn hair, he wondered about the future, the voyage, Becky, and beyond.

CHAPTER TWENTY
June 5, 1945
05:30
5:30 AM

Beckler was awake before the alarm went off. This was the morning he had been waiting for. The KING would leave Mare Island under her own power. There were times during her refit he doubted whether she would ever sail again. His desire to be at sea again was something he could never reveal to Becky; she would not have understood.

Upon reading the letter she had left, he got a lump in his throat. He did love her with all his being and her short letter confirmed her love for him. It explained how she hated long goodbyes and that she wanted to have a tender memory of him until he returned.

He tucked the letter into the top drawer of the desk, and went about getting ready for the big day.

Around six, old Pete entered with his breakfast and informed him that Patty had the boilers fired already. Beckler told Pete to inform Patty that he wanted to see him, Boss, and Millie at 06:30 in the bridge.

* * * * * * * * * * * * * * * * * * * *

Felix had wasted no time in gathering up his gear. He already had rented an apartment close to Hunter's Point. From the smoke coming from the KING's stack, it was clear that she would be underway very soon. His job here would soon be over; he would be glad to get back home.

* * * * * * * * * * * * * * * * * * * *

06:30: Beckler entered the bridge as Millie hung up the intraship telephone.

"That was the engine room. Patty is on his way up. The boilers have gotten up to full steam," Millie said.

"Good," Beckler replied. "The tugs will be here in about fifteen minutes to turn us away from the pier. How about the deck hands? Your men ready, Boss?"

"That they are, Captain," Boss answered.

Suddenly, Sergeant Germain burst through the door with a sheet of white paper in his hand.

"Is this your idea of an extended vacation?" he demanded to know.

"What are you talking about?" Beckler played dumb.

"I've been assigned to this tub!"

"I think you deserve a cruise," Beckler smiled.

"WHAT?" Gene asked in disbelief.

"Who would you rather spend the rest of the war with? The Marine Corps, or us, your friends?" Beckler replied.

"Some choice; I'd rather stay right where I am, thank you."

"That wasn't one of the options. Besides, Patty could use your expertise in keeping this ship afloat."

"What about my gear?"

"Already on board," Millie answered. "We had it loaded an hour ago."

Gene didn't answer; he just shook his head and stomped out of the bridge.

After Patty arrived, Beckler gave each of them last minute instructions. Each went over what could happen in the way of problems within their respective departments, and what they thought could be done to remedy it. Patty's engineering department was the biggest concern. Without the sea trial anything could go wrong, an engine, the propeller, anything.

"We'll see that we take on an extra prop, and I want you and Gene to make out a list of the most likely parts to give you a problem," Beckler instructed.

"The chances of a prop going bad are slim. Even if it did, how would we be able to replace it at sea?" Patty asked.

"Like you said, the odds of that happening are remote at best," Beckler replied. "If it does happen, there's damn little we can do except call the Navy tugs to come and tow us back to Pearl."

The discussion was cut short by the arrival of the tugs. Within minutes everyone was at his station. The cables were laid out and the tugs took the KING into tow. This time there was no groaning or hollow, metallic grinding noises coming from the ship. She seemed eager to be turned around, anxiously awaiting the chance to bite into the bay with her blade.

The crew including Beckler, was filled with the same anticipation. He was standing in the front center of the wheelhouse, next to the ship's telegraph, itching for the moment he would move it from the 'STAND-BY' position into the 'AHEAD SLOW'.

With everything that was going on, no one noticed the tall, slender redhead standing next to the jeep parked at the edge of the pier. She stood with dignity, no tears, not the slightest trace of emotion showing externally. But within her, her very being was threatened by a swelling tide of emptiness and sorrow.

At last the tugs were released and a wave of thanks paid the due. Beckler reached down and pushed the telegraph forward then pulled it back to 'AHEAD SLOW'. The KING bit into the water, and slowly leaned into it. She was moving away from Mare Island under her own steam.

Arriving off Hunter's Point Naval Shipyard, the KING dropped anchor several hundred yards out. It would be here that she would take on her load. Barges of cargo would be brought out to her side. The crew remained on board. Only Beckler could leave the ship. He was to report to the harbor master's office for his manifest, and Delair would provide him with the final destination.

* * * * * * * * * * * * * * * * * * * *

Felix had chosen his apartment well. With the aid of a telescope he could watch all that took place on or around the URSHEL KING. Keeping careful notes of all that he witnessed, he was surprised to note that the Americans took no precautions in disguising what it was that they were loading. Every crate, every barrel, and every box had what he believed was really inside it written in bold print on the outside.

His notes included what the cargo was, and where on the ship it was stowed. For the last week he had been carefully studying the silhouette of the KING, looking for any distinguishing features it might possess that would make it different from a hundred other tramp steamers. Since there was no way he could get actual pictures of the ship to the Japanese, he had to find a way for them to be able to recognize it from a distance. Also, since he had no way of knowing what the Japanese planned on using to destroy the KING. He had to be able to describe how it looked from the air as well as from the sea.

Try as he might, there was really nothing that made the KING stand out. She was like any other tramp steamer he had ever seen. Then he noticed something that he couldn't quite make out. There was a small bracket affixed to the forward part of the stack, with a steel shelf extending out from it. Maybe it was nothing, but it was the first thing he had seen that was different from any other ship of this type.

He zoomed the scope in tighter for a closer look. No wonder the shelf had passed unseen before, it was painted to match the funnel. There was however, nothing on it. What was its purpose? He very slowly moved the scope around, then he saw it! A cable! That shelf was installed to hold a radar dish! Now he had something the Japanese would definitely find interesting. He followed the cable down the side of the stack to where it disappeared into the bridge. There could no longer be any doubt, this ship was not an ordinary tramp steamer!

There were also a number of other oddities, in the form of canvass-covered crates fore and aft. They could be crates containing cargo, or they could be concealing deck guns! The only guns Felix could see were of the anti-aircraft variety mounted aft of the wheelhouse.

Since it would be some time before he was due to radio his information, he decided to take a stroll down by the waterfront in hopes of getting closer and possibly picking up some needed information. He still had to find out the departure time, and destination, if at all possible.

As Felix stepped from the front door of his apartment building he didn't notice anything unusual about the mechanic laying underneath the car at the service station across the street. Or the older gray haired gentleman sitting on the corner bench reading a newspaper. Or the window washer on the building two doors down, or the four other seemingly innocent, trained security people. All of whom were trailing his every move.

CHAPTER TWENTY-ONE
June 28, 1945
23:30
11:30 PM

The cargo boom slowly lifted the fifteen-foot wooden crate from the barge. While two marines carried an eighteen-inch diameter lead bucket up the gangway, supported by a bar over their shoulders. The wooden crate was lowered down into hold number three, just forward of the superstructure amidship. The lead bucket was taken up to Millie's cabin and fastened into metal straps that had been welded to the floor.

Accompanying the precious cargo was a dozen heavily armed Marine guards. Millie would be bunking with Gramps and Donk for this trip. The regular Navy guys came on board as well. They would be responsible for manning the guns that had been added to the KING at Mare.

Around midnight the pilot came on board, and the barge pulled away. Beckler picked up the telephone and ordered the anchors raised. He then turned the dial to the engine room and asked Patty if he was all set.

At five minutes after midnight, the KING eased ahead towards the channel. Beckler stood back and let the pilot handle the bridge.

High up in his apartment overlooking the harbor, Felix had just put his headset on and didn't hear the door to his apartment open. He felt the cold steel of the silencer next to his left temple. The icy fingers of total fear filled him; he turned around to face his captor, but before he could recognize the face there was a sudden flash. The bullet impacted in the right eye, and exited just above the left ear, sending skull fragments, blood, and brain tissue splattering against the walls.

Reynolds packed the inert form into a black canvas bag, and hoisted it onto his shoulder. After dumping the body into the trunk of his car, he returned to the apartment to clean the place up.

Becky had made it as close to the base of the Golden Gate Bridge as she could. She knew that it would probably be futile, but she couldn't help herself. At forty minutes past midnight the lights of the KING could be faintly seen through the mist. She could no longer fight back the tears for the man she so dearly loved. He was so near, but yet so far away. She felt like demanding from God that the ship stop and let Andy off. Something kept telling her that if he left now, she would never see him again. That was something she couldn't let happen, and yet, couldn't stop.

The KING was gliding under the bridge. She knew Andy was in the wheelhouse. In her mind's eye, she could see him standing there. Was he even thinking of her? Was this as painful for him as her?

The mast light could barely be seen from the bridge now as the fog seemed to close in behind the ship.

"Bye, my love," She whispered in a painfully choked voice, "Please come back to me."

She turned away, and stepped off into the darkness.

At five miles out into the Pacific, the lights of a small craft came into view. The KING slowed to a stop and allowed the launch to come along side. Beckler thanked the pilot, and sent him on his way.

As soon as the small motor launch was a safe distance, the KING's screw started churning up the ocean as she steamed away from San Francisco.

CHAPTER TWENTY-TWO
June 29, 1945
01:00
1:00 AM

Reynolds carefully picked up Felix's apartment and cleaned the walls of blood and removed the bullet from the wall into which it had imbedded itself after exiting Felix's skull. Then, he filled the hole with toothpaste, taking time to smooth it out as to render it invisible from any distance. Next, he packed all of Felix's radio gear and clothes, and carried them down to his car. Once he felt confident that no one would be the wiser, he locked the door and left.

He drove to Hamilton field, where his plane was already fueled and waiting for him. He stopped the car on the far side of the craft, so as not to draw attention to himself. The lights on this end of the airstrip were spaced far apart, leaving the area rather darkened, which suited Reynolds' needs quite well.

After wrestling the body from the car's trunk to the floor of the cargo hold, Reynolds took a few moments to catch his breath, then moved his car into one of the hangers, parked it there, and returned to the plane.

Prior to seating himself at the controls of the plane, Reynolds opened the canvas body bag, and fastened several concrete blocks to the body, to insure that it would stay where it was to be put.

The engines sputtered to life and Reynolds went through a last minute checklist. He released the brake and taxied out towards the runway. Requesting and receiving clearance from the tower, he nosed the craft into the wind, roared down the pavement, and lifted off.

Arching to the west, he flew over the sleeping city and out over the coast. He lowered his altitude to five hundred feet once he had cleared the coast, and switched off his navigational lights. From this vantage point he should be able to see the lights of a ship without them being able to detect his darkened plane.

He didn't have far to go. The lights of a ship appeared faintly below through the fog. He raised his field glasses to his eyes and studied the vessel below him, it was indeed the KING. A feeling of satisfaction came over him as he turned the plane towards the southeast, doubting if he would ever have to look at that ship again.

As he crossed over the limits of United States national waters, he fixed the controls, and eased out of the pilot's seat. He stood and watched the plane fly itself for a time, to be sure everything would be all right, then he made his way aft to the cargo hold. He opened the cargo door and heaved the body out.

Darkness prevented him from seeing the body hit the water, but he watched it fall as far as he could before closing the door and making his way back to the cockpit and taking back the controls.

Onboard the KING, the crew had settled in for their first night at sea. Beckler had retired to his cabin just beyond the chartroom. Due purely to preference, Beckler granted Millie's request to change which watch the first mate stood. Millie had the twelve to four watch on the bridge, unlike the traditional watches where the First Officer stands watch from four to eight. His wheelsman was Eric (Mad Dog) Sanders, and the watchman was William (Willy) Collins.

Millie and Mad Dog had served together before, but Willy was a newcomer to this crew, so Beckler put him with Millie, knowing that Millie was a little bit easier to work for than Gramps, or Donk.

Shortly after three, a light rain started to fall. It was a welcome friend to Millie. He opened up the wing doors and let the light breeze blow in, carrying with it the familiar scent of the rain at sea. The rain also broke up the monotony of the watch. The night was ink black, and the sea was calm; only the slight vibration of the engines turning the prop and the splatter of rain against the windows and roof gave a sense of being alive.

Shortly before four, Gramps entered the wheelhouse to relieve Millie. Then Ephraim (Newf) Young, replaced Mad Dog at the wheel, as James (Sandy) Sanford relieved Willy. Millie went over the instructions Beckler had left and showed Gramps where they were on the chart. Millie commented that he'd be glad when the radar was functional.

At seven, Beckler entered the wheelhouse, checked the chart, and chatted with Gramps for several minutes before going to the dining room for breakfast.

At eight, the third watch relieved the second. The third watch consisted of the Third Mate Donk, James (Jimmy) Castle as Wheelsman, and John (Oscar) White as watchman. By the time the first watch was to relieve the third at noon, Gene had the radar in working order, enabling the crew to see what lay fifty miles ahead.

CHAPTER TWENTY-THREE
June 30, 1945
07:00
7:00 AM

Lieutenant Hewitt silently stood waiting to board the transport plane that would take her to Great Lakes Naval Training Center in Chicago. The transfer had come as a surprise. At first she didn't want to take it, as it would put more distance between her and Beckler. But, Chicago was only a few hours drive from her parents home in Michigan and if she wasn't able to see Andy, then at least she would be able to go home and see her parents and friends on her time off.

As she stepped aboard the plane, she took one last look around; she would miss California, but looked forward to getting home. She hoped that Andy would get the letter she had sent. Maybe he would take a leave when he returned and come to Chicago, since he had grown up only a hundred miles from there.

Now that Danielson had been able to get Hewitt out of the way, he proceeded in having all the records of the KING ever having been at Mare Island removed from the yard. Operation Silverfish was proceeding as planned. His only concern at the moment was how to improve his swing for the base golf outing.

Shortly before sundown, Reynolds landed his plane on Lomas's sod runway. As usual, Lomas was there to greet him.

"Señor Reynolds, glad to have you back."

"Señor Lomas, got any of that old brandy left?"

"Always have some for friends," Lomas replied, as he embraced Reynolds in the customary way.

As before, Lomas entertained Reynolds with a fine meal then they retired to the study. This time however, Reynolds brought along a metal briefcase. As Lomas took his seat behind his desk, Reynolds laid the case upon the desk then spun it around so the latch would be facing Lomas.

"Your reward for a job well done." Reynolds said.

"I thank you, Señor Reynolds," Lomas replied, while trying to hide the disgust he held for the American. Lomas had the distinct feeling that Reynolds thought of him as a cheap whore. Even the manner in which he paid his bill bothered Lomas, not to mention sliding that metal case on his fine desk. Without saying what he felt, Lomas simply picked the case up and set it on the floor next to the desk.

"Not going to count it?" Reynolds questioned.

"Should I?" Lomas replied, "Would you be so foolish as to cheat me?"

"It's all there," Reynolds assured.

Lomas had tact. He entertained Reynolds for the evening, even offered a place for the Captain to spend the night. Reynolds kept the talk light and spoke of everything except the war. Lomas was as patient as a poker player casually playing the small games straight, while holding the ace up his sleeve for the big game of winner take all.

At the first light of day, Reynolds was awakened by the sweet smell of breakfast cooking. After a hearty meal, Lomas drove the Captain to his plane. Reynolds thanked Lomas for his service and the hospitality, then turned and boarded the plane. The two men who had stood guard over the plane at night, walked over and stood by their employer.

"There goes a dangerous man," Lomas said. "He thinks little of human life. Of all the people I have worked for, he is the lowest."

"He is gone, do not worry over him," one of the men said.

"Did you service his plane properly?" Lomas questioned.

"As you wished," came the reply.

The twin engine plane roared down the runway and lifted up into the face of the bright orange morning sun before banking to the north, then to the west and out of sight. Lomas was glad to be rid of Reynolds, and Reynolds of Lomas.

Reynolds pulled back on the controls and took the plane to ten thousand feet.

He followed his westerly course until he cleared the coast of Chile then banked toward the northwest and home.

With the roar of the engines sounding in his ears, Reynolds began to think of how clever he had been, everything had worked like clockwork. The Japanese had fallen for his well-laid trap and soon their stupidity would cost them an entire city. He felt proud. Because of his genius, tens of thousands of those bastards would burn.

He could almost see the horror in their eyes, a slight smile crossed his lips. Then in an instant, there was a blinding flash, a crushing pressure, and Reynolds and his aircraft was no more. The wreckage rained into the ocean, while a huge white cloud, fringed in black, that had been the creation of the blast, drifted on the breeze.

Lomas's trump card had been played. He had hated Reynolds from the beginning, had hated the idea of working towards the goal of Reynolds choosing, all of which he could bear, but when Reynolds had no qualms about murdering thousands of innocent people, Lomas had drawn the line. His honor made him finish his job, his moral conscience forced him to see to Reynolds' demise.

'Tex' was dead.

CHAPTER TWENTY-FOUR
July 14, 1945
07:00
7:00 AM

The New Mexican desert at Los Alamos was already getting hot. It was a harsh environment, cold at night, and unbearably hot during the day. By the way the temperature was rising already, this day would prove to be a scorcher.

Since just before daybreak, a convoy of eight vehicles gathered inside the compound of the Manhattan Project's Trinity Camp. The convoy consisted of seven black sedans, and one enclosed black truck.

As the convoy pulled out of the camp, four of the sedans took up the lead, with three to the rear, all with four heavily armed security forces inside. The truck, with its lone occupant, was in the middle. Destination for this convoy was the Air Force base at Albequerque.

Riding in the back of the truck were two objects. The first, a fifteen foot wooden crate, containing most of the conponents of a Uranium 235 bomb, known as "little boy". The second object was a lead cylinder of about eighteen inches in diameter by about twenty-four inches tall. This lead bucket, as it were, contained the highly volatile uranium projectile.

The convoy arrived at the airbase and proceeded towards the three waiting Air Force DC-3s. The precious cargo was loaded into the middle aircraft and fastened securely to the cargo hold floor. Two of the armed guards joined the cargo, and would be with it at all times until it reached it's final destination, Tinian. The balance of the security forces divided up into the other two planes.

As with the truck, the plane carrying the cargo was kept between the other two. It took off second, and landed second at Hamilton Field in San Francisco. Even in the air, it was always protected by the other two planes.

They arrived on schedule, and were greeted by a waiting armed detachment that would escort them to Hunter's Point Naval Shipyard. Once again the components were loaded into the back of a black, covered truck. This escort included eight sedans; four were to the front, and four followed.

The convoy exited the base and turned south on route 101, Redwood Highway, and started the thirty mile drive to Hunter's Point. Local police had all the major intersections along the route blocked for them. This was war time, and there were always plenty of military convoys. Motorists paid little attention to this one. Even on the eight-year-old, six-lane, 'man-made wonder', Golden Gate Bridge, the motorist would whiz by, only occasionally glancing over at the nondescript faces in the sedans. Finally the convoy turned off onto Third Street, continuing in a southerly direction before turning left into Hunter's Point Naval Shipyard.

Seeing them coming, the guards at the main gate stepped back and allowed them to pass unchecked. Since the U.S.S. Indianapolis was not due until the next morning, the lead bucket would be placed in the office of the Port Commander, accompanied by the same two guards. The fifteen-foot wooden crate was left in the truck, while the truck was parked in a heavily guarded garage.

The following morning the Battleship Indianapolis, CA-35, arrived just off Hunter's Point and anchored almost in the precise spot the KING had occupied. The Indy had also just left Mare Island. The heavy cruiser had a new coat of gray paint covering the major repairs that were rushed to completion for his mission.

Around noon, the ship's crane hoisted the large wooden crate aboard, while two marines carried the two hundred pound lead bucket up the gangway, supported by a shoulder bar. The wooden crate was secured to the hanger area of the Indy. The lead bucket was taken to the Fleet Commander's cabin and welded to the the floor.

This weapon had been the dream of the late, great President Roosevelt. It seemed ironic that the major components of the bomb would rest here, in this cabin. In late 1936, FDR himself had occupied this very room, on his South American goodwill visit.

As before, the same two guards took up their stations keeping watch over the lead bucket. But, this time the accomodations were far more to their liking. But, the pressure was wearing on them; this assignment couldn't be over too soon.

No one was sure what it would take to set the uranium off; as of yet the U-235 components had not been tested, there hadn't been time. Both men thought of home, their friends, and loved ones. Would they ever see them again?

CHAPTER TWENTY-FIVE
July 16, 1945
05:10
5:10 AM

The authoritative voice that was carried over an array of speakers, intercoms, and radios, announced the beginning of the twenty minute countdown. Listening intently to his every word, were the numerous scientists that had labored for the past three years getting to this point. It all came down to this, an untried bomb affixed to the top of a hundred foot tower in the middle of the New Mexican desert. The tension was great; zero hour had been intended for 04:00. Due to constant rain, the test had to be postponed twice. The first postponement lasted an hour, the second, a half hour. If the weather hadn't broken when it did, the test would have been scrubbed.

At last, zero hour was rapidly approaching. It was this very moment that all the work here at Trinity Camp, Los Alamos, New Mexico, had been all about.

Only one newspaper reporter was allowed to witness what was about to change the course of life forever. From this moment forward, all of humankind would live under the shadow of threat. Never again would simply protecting American shores be sufficient.

At first, the voice counted in five minute intervals, then in minutes, and at last in seconds. At T-minus forty-five seconds, the main switch that controlled the automatic timer was thrown. At T-minus twenty seconds, breaths became short, hearts seemed to beat so hard, as to be felt in the throat.

"TEN . . . NINE . . . EIGHT . . . SEVEN . . . SIX . . . FIVE . . . FOUR . . . THREE . . . TWO . . . ONE . . . NOW!"

Suddenly, a boiling eruption of light of extreme intensity, instantly turned the darkened desert to day, brighter by twenty times than it had ever been at midday. Its brilliant orange, gold, gray, blue, and violet colors being seen as far away as one hundred and ninety miles, the flash was blinding, even with one's eyes closed.

After the flash came a sudden rush of air racing to fill the void of oxygen the explosion had caused. Finally, after more than a minute came the shattering concussion that seemed to last an eternity.

No one knew what to expect; some thought that it might ignite the atmosphere and destroy New Mexico, maybe the world. All were in awe of the fury they had just released.

The huge eruption boiled skyward, slowly cooling until it reached its zenith, almost six miles straight up, and gently as if in slowed motion, curled back downward into a mammoth mushroom shaped cloud.

The "Fat Man", a plutonium bomb, had exploded, marking the first detonation of a nuclear device by man in history.

08:00: At Hunter's Point in San Francisco, the USS Indianapolis weighed anchor again, and headed for the open expanse of the Pacific Ocean. Half an hour later the heavy cruiser sailed beneath the Golden Gate Bridge.

As the Indy made for Pearl Harbor at full speed, twenty-five percent of her crew were green recruits, and relatively unfamiliar to the workings of a battleship. To compound Captain McVay's problems, the military passengers always seemed underfoot. An even greater concern for the Capatain was that secret cargo.

He had been told that he had no need to know what it was—only that it was of extreme importance. So important, he was told, that should anything happen to the ship before reaching Tinian, the cargo was to get top priority. If only one lifeboat could be lowered, it was to contain the lead bucket. Even if that meant the loss of all the lives on board.

While the Indy was making for Pearl with all haste another killing war machine was also heading out to sea. The 2,600 ton I-58 was setting out on its fourth patrol of the war. The I-58 was part of the six Japanese submarines that made up the Tamon Group. The Tamon Group was unique amongst Japanese submariners due to its mission, "attack and destroy the enemy."

The Tamon Group was the first and only Japanese submarine squadron to have search and destroy be the foremost priority of their mission. All other

Japanese sub's priority was supply and transport; attack was secondary, if such an occasion would arise. Often these transports had had the opportunity to attack American surface ships and had not done so.

Even the name 'Tamon', had historical and religious implications. In the Japanese Buddhist faith, the deity Tamon was one of four deities that protected the Empire from its enemies. The I-58 made its way south to Hirao, where it stopped to have six Kaiten torpedoes strapped to the upper deck of the sub. Each Kaiten torpedo was in fact a one man submarine nearly fifty feet in length and weighing eight tons. Much like the standard Japanaese torpedoes, the Kaiten was oxygen powered and could race toward its destiny, a glorious death for the Emperor, at thirty knots.

Lieutenant Commander Mochitsura Hashimoto stood silently as he watched the large Kaitens being strapped to his boat's back. He reflected back to the previous September, when he had first taken command of the then-new I-58. The boat had been commissioned on September 13, 1944. Days later he took her out into Hiroshima Bay for its first test dive. From the moment he stepped aboard her, he loved her. The I-58 was the envy of the world. She was larger, faster, and heavier-armed than any other class of submarine in the world.

Hashimoto loved the smell of the freshly painted interior, loved the feeling of power the new boat gave him, and rightly so. The I-Class subs carried 19 wakeless torpedoes, all forward. It had two diesel engines that pushed it through the swell at fourteen knots and electric motors that gave her a submerged speed of half that.

Considering the storage allotment for food and fuel, the 'I' boats could cruise for three months with a range of 15,000 miles. Each carried a crew of around 105.

The test dive had not gone well; at a depth of two hundred feet, a seal in the forward torpedo room had failed to hold and the new boat damned near sank.

After the necessary repairs were made, the boat was tested again and this time achieved the three hundred foot depth and then returned to base for preparations for its first war patrol.

It had been in March of 1945 that the I-58 was chosen as one of the subs that would carry the new Kaiten torpedoes. The "I-58" legend was removed from the sides of the conning tower and replaced with a neatly painted Kikusui banner just above the rising sun emblem. The Kikusui flag was a tribute to an ancient Japanese warrior who had courageously fought knowing he could not possibly survive. A fitting symbol for the Kaitens.

Hashimoto shuddered for an instant as he recalled the first war patrol as a Kaiten carrier. The I-58 had been sent to Okinawa along with a number of other Japanese subs. While enroute, the I-58 picked up a reconnaissance report that stated that a large American battleship was limping away from Okinawa, badly damaged. Hashimoto longed to go after the target and finish it off, but due to the distance between his boat and the target, he passed on the opportunity and allowed the U.S.S. INDIANAPOLIS to limp home for repairs.

Okinawa was a nightmare for the I-58. From the time the sub arrived to the time it was ordered to return to base, it was attacked no less than fifty times. It had been bombed, depth-charged, and strafed, spending most of the time playing dead, submerged, while the Americans on the surface hammered away, anxious for the kill.

Although he had taken a beating, Hashimoto was resentful for being ordered back. He was a professional, he felt that his job had not yet been done and returning home without a kill was a disgrace. He was sobered a bit by the fact that his boat was the only Japanese submarine sent to Okinawa that returned.

At last, the Kaitens were securely fastened to the deck, the six very young pilots cheerfully stepped aboard. Hashimoto was deeply saddened by their smiling innocent looking faces. His was inwardly sickened by the fact that his country's war effort had gone from cool, calculated planning that smacked of genius, to last ditch heroics orchestrated by a few fanatic zealots. The Japanese leaders spoke of the sea running red with American blood. The sea was running red with blood, but it wasn't American.

The Japanese Navy was no longer a serious threat to the enemy. Hashimoto likened it to the bee that would sting the hand that went to pick a flower; the sting would exact a small price but not save the flower.

As the I-58 headed for sea and its fourth war patrol, the thirty-five year-old Hashimoto speculated about what lay in store for him this time. He was confident in his boat and his hand-picked crew. He had always stressed competence over senseless heroics. The only thing that troubled him about the mission was those Kaitens. It would be up to him when they would be used. He would decide when another young Japanese boy would die.

Most troubling of all was the fact that they pleaded to go, they wanted to die. But, he had decided on his first trip out with the Kaitens that he would only use them when the success of the standard torpedoes was in doubt. Because, above all else, he would have to live with whatever decisions he made.

CHAPTER TWENTY-SIX
July 17, 1945
03:00
3:00 AM

The Imperial Japanese submarine I-72 was the third chosen for 'TAMON.' The mission was simple enough, seek out and destroy a certain American freighter, namely the URSHEL KING. The I-72 had been at sea sixteen days, sixteen long and trying days. She had spent the last thirty-six hours simply trying to stay alive. Capatain Yuko Shoji's only immediate concern was to be able to stay on the surface long enough to recharge the batteries.

Three days ago contact had been made with a small enemy convoy. The convoy included six merchant vessels heavily laden and riding low in the water, and two fast American Destroyer-Escorts, or DEs as they are called. The speed of the convoy was held to that of the slowest merchant—just a little over six and a half knots.

The DEs were constantly racing around their charges and generally keeping a smart lookout for trouble.

Luckily the I-72 had just completed recharging the batteries and had just submerged at the first light of dawn, a scant fifteen minutes before sonar contact was made.

The convoy had steamed over the curve of the earth on a course directly for the sub's position before altering course and turning away again. Yuko would like to have brought his boat to the surface and beat it around the convoy at fourteen knots. But the American DEs forced him to be more cautious. Submerged, he still could travel slightly faster than they could. It would take far longer to stalk his prey submerged, but with four kaitens still strapped to his back, the last thing he wanted was a confrontation with those DEs.

Fourteen hours later, the I-72 came to periscope depth five thousand yards ahead and slightly to port of the slow-moving convoy. Luckily, one of the DEs was off on the starboard side while the other brought up the rear, giving the I-72 an ideal set-up. A fat tanker was leading the convoy with two loaded freighters off either beam.

Carefully studying the outline of each oncoming vessel, Yuko was disappointed none matched the description of the vessel he was sent to find and destroy. Nevertheless, he wasn't about to let this opportunity pass him by. He could launch two kaitens toward the outer two freighters and shoot a salvo of four torpedoes with the standard three degree spread towards the tanker in the center.

That would hopefully create enough confusion as to allow himself to drop down to three hundred feet and let the remaining convoy pass over him before returning to periscope depth for a shot up their sterns.

At three thousand yards he ordered the two kaiten pilots into their death traps, allowing himself only the slightest moment to remember his long lost friend Hideyo. He kept his eye firmly pressed to the rubber eye piece, watching and waiting. The sonar operator kept calling off the distance separating the convoy and sub, while in the background, noises of slamming hatch doors and muffled farewells could be heard.

"Open torpedo doors and stand by to fire one through four."

"Doors opening now," the Executive Officer responded. "Doors now open."

At last the kaitens were ready, and none too soon. A few seconds more . . . "all torpedo tubes forward ready and standing by." A few seconds more . . .

"Fire one!" Yuko bellowed.

"One away." An officer called out as the swoosh of water rushed against the conning tower as the oxygen drive of the first kaiten drove it from the sub's back.

"Fire Two!" Yuko ordered after a ten second interval from the first.

"Two away," came the direct reply.

"Standby torpedoes."

"Torpedo room standing by."

Twenty seconds after the first kaiten had left the sub, the first conventional torpedo raced from the forward tube. In the conning tower a young Japanese sailor wrestled with the large controls. In a matter of thirty seconds, more than sixteen tons had been removed from the sub's displacement; keeping it from bobbing to the surface took total concentration.

Suddenly the two destroyer-escorts appeared from the rear and far side of the convoy and headed directly towards the I-72. Maybe the kaiten pilots had seen them as well! The other four fish had been fired in order; Yuko felt confident that the small destroyers could do little to stop six incoming torpedoes.

Whisps of smoke followed by splashes in the water along the flanks of the DEs told Yuko that the destroyers had fired their own torpedoes!

"Crash dive!" he called with his eye glued to the periscope. "All head full! Dive! Dive! Dive!"

If there is one thing a submariner has complete respect of, it's a torpedo. His only safe haven was the darkness of the deep. It seemed to take forever for the depth gauges to start moving. The boat had reached a depth of about eighty-five feet when the first concussion rocked the steel hull with such force as to knock cork insulation loose and shatter light bulbs. This was followed in quick succession by another shattering explosion. This second one was closer than the first, rattling the copper tubing and bouncing anything that wasn't secure onto the grated deck.

Yuko hoped that the kaitens had seen the destroyers and had altered course and attacked them. That would leave the convoy sitting ducks for him to eliminate. Then two more explosions were heard, these sounds very much like conventional torpedoes hitting home, probably those he had fired at the tanker. He hated being blind, but didn't dare go up for a look; instead he turned to the sound man.

"Report," he ordered with eyes that demanded instantaneous response. "How many contacts? How fast are they? What are they doing?"

The sound man turned the volume control back up, and listened intently for a moment before responding.

"Multiple contacts, Sir!" he snapped, while trying to get a fix on how many. "Two are moving very fast, possibly thirty knots, coming this way! And pinging!"

"Damn!" Yuko thought, somehow the two destroyers had survived and were now coming after him. He glanced over at the depth gauge which showed that the boat was at two hundred and seventy feet and still diving.

"Going to short scale!" the sound man called out, meaning that the destroyer felt he had a good contact and was switching to the much faster short range sonar. Now those in the boat could plainly hear the nerve racking pinging pulsating throughout the steel hull of the I-72.

It was easy for the Japanese sailors in the sub to know when the Americans were starting a depth-charge run, the beat of their propeller rapidly increased its tempo. Thum-thum-thum-thum . . .

"Depth charges!" the sound man called out, as everyone held their breath for the inevitable.

The first thing you hear from a depth charge blast is a clicking noise, this click is really the explosion, but it takes a moment for the WHAM to hit you, then the rush of water through the external superstructure of the sub. The length of time between the click and the WHAM tells you just how close to the bullseye the depth charge was.

Just as the sound of the enemies' propeller starts to fade, click . . . WHAM-click, click . . . WHAM-WHAM-WHAM-WHAM-WHAM-WHAM-click . . . WHAM-click . . . WHAM. The Americans definitely had a fix on them.

As soon as it was clear that the last depth charge dropped by the DE on the first run had exploded, the sound man quickly put the earphones to his head and listened intently for what was happening on the surface. For the moment he was the Captain's eyes.

"The second destroyer has gone back to the stationary target," he called out in little more than a whisper. "The first is turning around for another depth charging run!"

"Range?"

"2500 yards and still turning."

"Right full rudder," Yuko barked. "All ahead full!"

"Right full rudder. All ahead full."

"Range?"

"1800 yards bearing two-eight-zero."

"Rudder amidship, all stop."

"Rudder amidship, all stopped, Captain."

As the sub grew dead quiet the sound of the DE could be heard once again. THUM-THUM-THUM-THUM-THUM . . . suddenly the tempo quickened and the soundman once again heard the sounds of the depth charges striking the water above.

The Japanese crew took a severe beating; many were jolted right off their feet. The air in the sub was filled with fine particles of cork and paint dust, the steel hull creaked and groaned under the stress of the onslaught.

CLICK-WHAM-WHAM-WHAM-WHAM-WHAM-WHAM-CLICK-WHAM-CLICK-WHAM-CLICK-WHAM . . .

"What's the depth?" Yuko calmly questioned, masking any sense of the terror that he truly felt.

"Three hundred!" was the crisp reply from the white knuckled helmsman, as he fought to keep the tortured boat on even keel.

Three hundred feet was the maximum design depth for this boat to go, Yuko thought. But how long could it stand up to the beating it was taking?

"Take it deeper," Yuko ordered, knowing that the pressure at the greater depth might crush his boat. Then again it might not. The Americans were sure to blow him apart if he didn't do something. He also remembered a time when the I-18 reached nearly 400 ft. and survived.

"Going deeper."

"Hold it at three-thirty, and let me know the moment you reach that depth."

"Three-thirty, Captain."

"All-stop. Dead silent."

"All-stopped, dead silent."

Now the Japanese waited; there was nothing more they could do for the time being. The sound of the American propellers would pass overhead then the depth charges would slam against them, but not as severely as before. From time to time the Americans stopped and just listened, trying to confirm contact.

While the Americans were trying to listen, so were the Japanese. The Japanese sound man picked up six distinct propeller noises and the sounds of the seventh vessel breaking up. Yuko correctly assumed that the kaitens had failed. The four torpedo salvo had indeed struck the tanker. It was the tanker they heard breaking up. While one destroyer hunted the I-72, the other was standing off the tanker to effect the rescue of its crew. The other five merchant ships were hightailing it out of there.

Secretly, Yuko admired the determination of his American foe. It was clear that they were not likely to be easily fooled. Evidently their sonar was better than he had been led to believe. They had retained contact no matter which way he turned. The only thing that had saved him so far was the extra depth. At this point he was confident that the I-72 could take the pressure at 350 feet, but what about those two kaitens still strapped to its back, could they?

After several hours of playing dead, Yuko grew tired of passively waiting while the determined Americans kept passing over and trying to blow him apart.

Yuko decided that it was time to act. He waited for the next depth-charge run, then during the terrific pounding he made his run for it.

"Left full rudder!" he quietly called out. "All ahead full!"

"Left full rudder, all ahead full," came the reply.

He had caught the Americans off guard, but only for a moment. By some stroke of luck they made sonar contact again and the pounding continued.

By the time they were finally able to creep away from the American destroyer-escort, the air inside the sub had already been through someone's lungs at least once. The heat had built up to an unbelievable height and the batteries were almost totally drained.

The sub rose to periscope depth. There Yuko carefully searched the surface through the night scope. Finding nothing, he turned to the sound man and asked if he could detect any contacts. Finding none, the boat was finally ordered to the surface. Once on the surface the valves were switched, the ducts and exhaust manifolds opened, then the diesel engines started and charging began.

While the much-needed charging was taking place, the boat was pumped full of fresh air and the debris from the attack picked up off the decks. The I-72 had survived the ordeal with one possible kill on the tanker, and the loss of two kaitens, probably destroyed by torpedoes from the American DEs. For the sub, it was a perfect night. Pitch dark. No moon to give them away to passing enemy aircraft that seemed to be everywhere nowadays. By the way the sea was kicking up, they were probably riding on the tail edge of a good-sized storm.

Yuko was glad to be standing in the open breathing fresh air. The angry sea was sending spray high into the air, soaking the men in the open tower, yet he felt safe, in control again. This was his element and he loved it.

As soon as the proper lookouts had reached their posts and their eyes had grown accustomed to the darkness, he went below to study the charts and plan his search pattern for the target he was sent to intercept.

Before retiring to his cabin, Yuko turned the bridge over to the executive and stopped by the Radar Operator.

"Any contacts?"

"None, Captain," the soundman replied. "But that last beating we took didn't do the radar any good; it's not working as well as it did."

"How so?"

"It seems to fade out in one direction."

"Can you fix it?"

"I don't think so; it'll have to wait until we reach our base, but I'll try."

"Very well."

Yuko didn't like not being able to see in one direction, so he informed the Executive Officer to alter course every half hour to bring that blind spot around to avoid having an enemy vessel get the drop on them. The lookouts kept a constant watch in that direction.

Yuko stripped out of his sweat soaked uniform and threw himself onto his bunk naked. It was the only way he could rest in this heat. As he closed his eyes he listened to all the racket the rats were making in the galley. Try as they might, they could never get all the rats out of the boat; every boat and every patrol had been the same, infested with a large colony of rats.

As he lay in the darkness he thought back to Hideyo and the letter that he had been given just before Hideyo left the I-18. Hideyo had known that the trip would be one-way, and he had gone willingly to die for the Emperor. A glorious death for a noble cause would ensure Hideyo a righteous place in the world beyond.

But what about Yuko? His war record had left much to be desired. He had left the I-18 just weeks before it was lost southwest of Rendova Island to a U.S. submarine on January 2, 1943. In fact the tanker was the first kill Yuko had any part of. With the war nearing an end, unless someone pulled off a miracle, the homeland would soon be over-run by the enemy. Yuko vowed to himself to be the one to do that something! He would find the URSHEL KING! He would drive his boat hard, attack the enemy hard, or die a glorious death trying!

Eight hundred miles to the north-east the URSHEL KING was fighting another battle of her own. This was however, a battle for which she was well suited. It was a battle against the sea. The KING had fought many such battles over the course of her life time and the proud old ship seemed to relish the challenge.

Beckler had altered course slightly and was running into the sea bow-on. It was like being on a eternal roller-coaster. The bow would run down the back side of a wave before plowing into the bottom of the trough before rebounding and climbing up the next. On the biggest waves, as the KING would start down the back side of a wave the stern would rise and bring the prop right out of the water which in turn would cause the engine to race for a moment, until the prop bit into the sea again.

It was hardest on those below decks, most of which were suffering from varying stages of sea sickness. Along with the up and down motion the ship was pitching back and forth on its beam ends.

The engine room personnel hung tightly to anything they could get a hold of to keep from being tossed around like rag dolls. Even the old seamen would cast a worried eye towards the incline meter. At times the meter showed that the ship had rolled to forty, forty-five, even fifty degrees one way or the other. Each time the proud old KING fought back and came back to even keel before taking the next roll.

If there had been any doubts among the crew about how good this old ship was built, this storm quickly dispelled them.

At 0400, the Captain of the United States submarine LIONFISH Carl Samson was called from his bunk to the conning tower by the young radar operator Charles 'Chuck' Smith.

"What do you have?" Samson asked.

"Not sure, Sir," Chuck puzzled. "I keep getting a funny signal, like I'm getting interference or something."

"Let me see," Samson studied the scope for a moment before quickly realizing what is causing the problem. "Secure the radar!"

The lad instantly turned the radar off. "What do you think it is Captain?"

"Another radar set, probably a Japanese sub!" Samson sighed with an air of conviction. "Sound general quarters."

Samson rushed to the plotting table and, along with the Exec, started calculating how best to handle the situation. Luckily they had picked up the Japanese sub first, instead of the other way around. By securing their own radar they hoped to keep the enemy from discovering them.

to literally spring to life as the throttles to the big diesels were pressed against their stops. It was known that the Japanese had radar, although not as good as the American radar. Samson planned to conduct the entire operation on the surface. His plan was to do what was called an end around. In effect it meant to race up ahead of the target and then lay in wait for the enemy vessel to simply cross your path before you let him have it.

As is the problem with most plans, it sounds easier than it really is. Samson would have his work cut out for him. First he would have to get ahead of the Japanese sub and do so without being detected himself. But he also had to keep contact with the Japanese as long as he could to be sure that he himself hadn't suddenly become the hunted.

This was done by turning the radar back on periodically, just long enough for contact to be made, hopefully, with the better equipment, not long enough for the enemy to be the wiser. The next problem was, once he got himself and the LIONFISH into position, he would have to turn his boat around and shoot from the tail since all he had left were stern torpedoes, and only two of them at that!

Samson was very careful to keep the distance between himself and the enemy to the maximum range of his own radar, the idea being that he could watch them without being seen himself.

The I-72 was plowing the heavy swell at fourteen knots, holding a steady course of one-eight-three. This pleased Samson. It would afford him the time he would need to get far enough ahead as to be able to swing around and back in towards the enemy before he came back into radar range.

The biggest concern that worried Samson was the chance that the Jap sub might alter its course between the time last contact was made and renewed contact. This meant that the LIONFISH could be laying in wait for the Jap to pass a thousand yards astern, when in fact the enemy would come up with the LIONFISH laying broadside across its bow. Hunting another submarine is always a very deadly game. The slightest miscalculation could mean disaster and few survivors are ever recovered from a sunken sub.

When Samson felt confident that they had travelled the proper distance ahead of the enemy to give LIONFISH enough time to turn around and close the range toward the track, he didn't hesitate. He could still avoid this fight, he could wait for a target less threatening. But then that was never Samson's style.

"Distance to track?" He called out.

From plotting came the quick reply. "3000 yards."

"Right full rudder. All ahead two thirds!"

"Right full rudder. All ahead two thirds." The exec repeated as soon as it had been carried out.

"Keep feeding me distance to track."

"2700 yards . . . 2600 yards . . . 2500 yards . . . 2400 yards . . ."

"Commence radar. Let me know the moment you have something."

"Commencing radar sweep."

"I need to be sure that he is still on this track, as soon as you have that confirmed secure radar."

"Aye Captain," the radar operator replied.

"2000 yards," the exec announced.

"Left full rudder. All ahead full."

"Left rudder, ahead full."

"Amidship rudder, all astern two thirds," Samson called as soon as the LIONFISH had spun around and lined her stern up with the Jap sub's track.

"Rudder's amidship, two third astern."

"Any contact with target?"

"No contact Sir."

"Distance to track?"

"1500 yards to track and closing."

"All astern one third."

"One third astern Sir."

Samson searched the night sea for any glimpse of the enemy to no avail. Deep within the pit of his stomach he was beginning to have self-doubts. They should have re-established radar contact by now.

"Range to track?"

"1100 yards to track."

"All stop."

"All stopped."

The suspense within the LIONFISH was intense. Where was that damn Japanese sub? Was it at this moment bearing down on the LIONFISH? Was the hunted now the hunter?

"Contact!" the radar operator shouted. Plot quickly had a fix on him; he was still plodding along as if he was asleep, still on course of one-eight-three.

"Range?"

"3000 yards."

Samson wanted to do this right; if he missed he would have no recourse but to run and hide. With no more ammunition, the first try would have to do.

"Open stern tubes," Samson called down the voice tube. "Commence radar and keep feeding information to myself and plot. Also watch him for any signs that he sees us."

"Aye, Captain, commencing radar."

The I-72 continued on his course, totally unaware of the LIONFISH, at least so far. The Japanese radar operator has been working tirelessly on his set trying to get the clarity back. Once after adjusting the cable feed from the mast, the clarity had been restored. From that time on it had worked pretty well, the quivering happening only intermittently. Each time it happened he reached under the scope and jiggled the cable and the scope returned to normal. He was convinced that there must be a loose fitting somewhere.

"2000 yards and closing," Chuck calls out.
"All ready aft?"
"All ready aft, sir."
"1500 yards."

At last Samson could make out a dark shape low in the water. He had the drop on the Jap sub! Samson steadied the TBT binoculars on the target and shouted down to the exec to stand by for a bearing. As he heard plot call off 1200 yards he squeezed the handle of the TBT and called 'MARK.'

The exec took less than a second before responding. "Mark."

On the I-72 the irritating quiver was back on the scope, now stronger than ever. A solid blip suddenly materialized; the operator was stunned. How could that be? He finally realized what he was looking at was very real!

"CONTACT! CONTACT! 1000 YARDS!" he screamed.

Yuko heard the scream of a contact and rushed to the control tower without bothering to grab any clothes. As he reached the control room he saw the radar operator's face white with fear. Too late Yuko realized what had caused the fluctuation in the scope.

"Dive! Dive! Dive!" Yuko bellowed.

It took a moment for Yuko's eyes to adjust to the darkness. He quickly ordered the periscope up and pressed his eye to the rubber eye piece and spun it around to the direction of the contact. "Enemy Sub! Enemy Sub!" he shouted as he saw the low dark shape of the LIONFISH. "Crash Dive! Get this boat down!" he screamed, as it seemed to take forever for the I-72 to start down.

The unsteady wavering of the scopes in both submarines suddenly became constant as the Japanese operator steadied his beam on the American sub.

"He has us!" Chuck shouted. "The Jap has seen us!"

"Fire One!" Samson bellowed, as he felt the pitch of the boat as a thousand pounds of death raced from the stern tube. "New bearing, mark!"

"One away. New bearing, mark!" the exec repeated.

"Fire two!"

"Two away!"

Samson watched as the white streak from the steam torpedoes shot straight for the low fat body of the enemy. Too late he had seen the LIONFISH. Samson couldn't help but feel a little remorseful. Sure, that target out there is the enemy, but they are submariners just as he is. He could only imagine what they must be thinking at this very moment.

The Japanese sub had started a dive, but it was too little, too late. Much of the Japanese sub was still above the surface as the LIONFISH's first torpedo found its mark.

Suddenly the dark night was lit up like a hundred suns. Samson had no way of knowing that his first shot had hit the enemy in the forward torpedo room where fifteen of its own torpedoes exploded in a searing white flash, which in turn ignited the 1000 lbs. of explosives in the two kaitens still strapped to the I-72's back. The shock and the blast to those on the LIONFISH was spectacular, the likes of which they had never seen. Those below in LIONFISH felt a tremendous hammerblow against their hull as the Jap disintegrated.

The I-72 blew with such tremendous force and so suddenly that fragments were thrown high into the air, leaving nothing for the second torpedo to hit when it reached the spot just occupied by the Japanese I-boat. In seconds there was nothing left, except the hollow feeling in Samson's gut.

CHAPTER TWENTY-SEVEN
July 29, 1945
06:25
6:25 AM

Since the second day out, Gene had been teaching Beckler and the officers how to read the radar. Other than Gene, only two other crew members were familiar with radar. They had gained their experience while serving on Naval ships. One was able seaman, James (Ace) Kemp, and the other was ordinary seaman, William (Gilly) Gilberry.

After leaving Wake, Beckler considered his vessel to be in hostile waters, and ordered that the radar be monitored constantly. Gene took the first watch, Ace the second, and Gilly the third.

As it was nearing midnight, the first watch was coming on to relieve the third. Beckler was having an uneasy night of it. Within a few hours, the KING would pass between the Mariana Island group, a hundred miles to the south, and the Bonin Islands, one hundred and twenty miles to the north. The Marianas were in American hands; the Bonins, Japanese. Slightly off to the northwest, at only about eightly miles, lay the Volcano Islands, three small, rocky, volcanic islands that rose up from the sea, with the middle island being known as Iwo Jima. The Volcano group was now in American hands, after being bought with much blood.

"What's the compass heading?" Beckler questioned.

"2-8-9," Mad Dog replied.

"Riding the Tropic of Cancer," Millie said, looking up from the chart.

"Should the moon decide to make an appearance tonight, resume the zigzag," Beckler ordered, as he stared out into a night void of light.

"Aye, aye, Captain," Millie replied, as Beckler retired to his cabin.

For an hour Beckler laid on his bunk, looking at the ceiling. Sleep just would not come. Finally, he stepped over to his desk and retrieved a letter from its top drawer. The letter was starting to show signs of wear. He had read it a dozen times by now, but it still offered an escape. It made him long for this voyage to end. Never before had he wanted to return to port as he did then.

The letter had been waiting for him when he arrived at Wake. Simply reading the letter made him feel close to Becky. If only he could hold her in his arms, say the things he wished he had when he last held her.

She told of her sudden transfer to Great Lakes, in Chicago. How she planned on going to Freeport, to see where he had grown up. It also told of her love for him, and her longing for him to return to her. Beckler smiled as he saw Becky in his mind's eye. He held the letter close to his face and smelled of the fine perfume she had misted it with. It had been his favorite. Then, he slowly slipped it back into the envelope and placed it back into the drawer.

Beckler was awakened by a loud and rapid knock on his door. It took a moment for his mind to clear and recall where he was; he had been dreaming of Freeport, meeting Becky there and gazing into her hazel eyes. He felt a pang of sadness when realization set in. Before he could answer, the door was being pounded again.

"What is it?" he demanded to know.

"Bogey on radar, sir!" came the quick reply.

Still dressed in the uniform he had had on the night before, Beckler jumped to his feet and bolted for the bridge.

"What have you got?" Beckler demanded, as he raced up to the console where Ace was intently watching the sweep of the light bar.

"Not sure, Captain. But it appears to be a single aircraft about thirty-five miles out, and heading in this general direction," Ace replied.

"Sound the alarm! Every man to his battle station!" Beckler shouted, as he glanced up at the clock that read 6:28.

In moments, men were scrambling all over the ship to get to their appointed stations. The gunners prepared their weapons; bulkhead doors were closed and battened down—even the fire control party got their hoses in order. Beckler stepped out onto the starboard bridge wing and studied the sky with the field glasses, as Ace called out the distance between the bogey and the KING.

"Ten miles out, and about two degrees off our starboard bow," Ace called out. "Nine miles, eight . . ."

"There it is!" Beckler shouted, masking the fear of uncertainty that welled within him. He could easily recall a morning much like this one, on the North Atlantic, when the war came to visit his ship. What was once a small dark speck grew larger and darker with each passing second. "At one o'clock!"

Millie passed the information on to the gun crews, who could now see it, and were following it in their sights.

"It's a Jap spotter plane!" Beckler warned. "Tell those men in the gun tubs to bring it down as soon as possible before it tells the entire Jap Navy we're here!"

It was already too late, Sparks had picked up the plane's signal. It was already relaying the KING's position back to its base. Then, for some reason, it turned and came in lower for a closer look. The gunners did not let this opportunity pass them by. As soon as it came into range, the stern gun opened up, and literally blew it out of the sky. There would be no need to check for survivors.

"Well, Dad, so much for the welcoming committee," Gene smiled.

"Maybe, but now they probably know we're here," Beckler replied.

"Sparks confirms it," Millie said, as he returned the telephone to its cradle. "He picked up a transmission from that plane. He doesn't understand Japanese, but he's sure of what they were probably saying."

"Yeah, I'm sure too!" Beckler seemed resigned, "bring her to course 2-7-5, QM."

"Coming to course 2-7-5," the quartermaster replied.

"What's next, Dad?" Gene asked.

"Depends on how important they think we are, and what they have in this area to throw at us. Maybe nothing, then again, maybe all hell will break loose very soon," Beckler answered.

"On course 2-7-5," the quartermaster announced.

"Hold steady on this course for an hour or so before returning to our previous course," Beckler instructed Millie.

"Aye, aye, Captain," Millie responded.

"Wonder where it came from?" Gene asked, to no one in particular.

"I can't say where it came from for sure, but my guess would either be the Bonins, or from some Japanese battlewagon, possibly even an I-class sub," Beckler answered.

"I thought the Bonins were ours."

"No, the Japas still have the deed. We've attacked them, but haven't taken them. No need to, really. Japan itself is only seven hundred miles from there. Why go for the small fry, when you can have the whale?"

"If it's that close, wouldn't it be perfect for an airfield for strikes against the mainland?"

"Too small. The Bonin Island group is made up of ninety-seven small islands, with only a total land mass of about thirty square miles. None of them could accommodate a strip long enough for our bombers."

"But they are big enough to play home plate for a flying fish?"

"Right. All they need is a pier for loading fuel, but my guess is that that plane belonged to some Japanese destroyer. By this time tomorrow, we'll know for sure, maybe sooner," Beckler replied.

Beckler had been absolutely correct. Shortly after four P.M., a ship appeared on the radar scope. Beckler ordered the alarm to be sounded. From here on in, anything showing on that screen would be sufficient to have battle stations called.

"What's the plan, Captain?" Millie questioned.

"We'll hold a steady course," Beckler quickly replied.

"Why not turn south and keep as much distance between us and them?"

"Wouldn't do much good. Their speed is much greater than ours; sooner or later, they would catch up. And the moment we turn off this course, we send them a signal that we have radar. So long as they don't know that, we still have a slim chance. Also, I'm counting on them thinking that we are a Liberty," Beckler answered.

"I fail to see the point," Gene spoke up, trying to figure Beckler's scheme. "Why would it matter if they think we are a Liberty or not?"

"Fire-power," Beckler shot back. "We have four times the fire-power of a Liberty. Danielson may be a first class jerk, but he sure knows how to arm a transport."

"I've heard tell that our radar is far better than anything the Japs have," Millie stated. "Maybe they haven't pinpointed us yet. They wouldn't even know that we've turned away."

"Our radar is better," Gene agreed.

"So is our fire control," Beckler added. "We not only pack a damn good punch for a freighter, but we had the latest in range finding equipment installed at the same time. In short, we can see farther, shoot straighter, but not outgun them inasmuch as their range is longer, and they pack more guns. Our safest bet is to let them think that we're sitting ducks."

"But they might not even know we're here; we're miles from where we should be," Millie countered.

"Then again they may," Beckler coolly replied. "Get canvass pulled over both aft guns and one of the forward guns."

Ace kept up a steady report of distances between the target on the radar screen and the KING. Beckler had several members of the bridge crew keep a close watch for this 'target,' through field glasses, while he himself tried to do some thinking. Once again he recalled that morning on the Atlantic. He remembered the utter destruction, the screams of the dying, the wounded, the stench of burned flesh, the mangled and misshapen inert forms of former crew members. Above all, he remembered death. Those who died in the attack, those who died before he could give the order to abandon ship, those who died jumping from the dying ship, and those who choked to death in the oil-coated water.

He looked out the rear of the bridge, across this ship the URSHEL KING. It was a different ship, a different ocean, a different crew, a different enemy. But for the moment he couldn't recognize the differences. He could only wonder, how many of this crew would die? How would the old KING hold up under the impending onslaught of an enemy warship?

At five miles out, they could see the brilliant red sun against the field of white, flying from the mast.

"It's a Japanese tincan!" Millie shouted, waking Beckler from his torrid memories.

There was little doubt where the plane had come from, and what the intentions of this Japanese destroyer were. At three miles distant, the destroyer altered course and swung its bow towards the KING.

Beckler's deception was working. The enemy was moving in for an easy kill.

"Hard to starboard!" Beckler ordered. "Keep your bow towards him, it'll make a smaller target."

"Hard to starboard," the Q.M. repeated, "keeping bow on."

"Have guns stand by, ready, but do not fire until we can be sure of a hit."

"Guns standing by," Millie replied.

At a distance of two miles the flash of the destroyer's forward guns could be seen. Then, a shrill scream, and somebody shouted 'DOWN.' Suddenly the scream of the raining shell stopped and a muffled explosion off the starboard side sent water rocketing up in a huge geyser which then collapsed across the roof of the bridge and the KING's boat deck, pulverizing boat number one as it did so.

Beckler jumped back to his feet.

"Bring her five degrees to starboard," Beckler ordered. "Have the guns fire at will!"

Another flash from the destroyer, and this time the shell hit the water off the port side, just as the canvass covering was pulled away from the KING's three hidden guns. The range had been constantly monitored by the KING's fire control, and number one forward gun already had a steady line on the Jap destroyer and commenced firing; the second four incher was quickly brought to the proper elevation and opened up with its first salvo seconds later.

Now, less than a mile separated the two vessels. Another flash from the destroyer, but this one seemed different somehow. It took a moment to realize it, but this flash had been caused by the Jap being hit by a shell from the KING.

The forward gun crews of the KING started shouting joyously, "We hit the Jap bastards! We did!"

The hit had been taken right in the forward gun battery. Heavy black smoke and bright orange flames boiled around turret number one, but the fight was far from over. The destroyer again altered course and brought its stern guns to bear. The KING's forward guns kept up the pace, load . . . fire . . . load . . . fire . . . , as the KING swung its bow away from the destroyer. On the stern, the rear gun crews were bringing their guns around towards the enemy.

The Japanese had taken several direct hits and were having difficulty in maneuvering. Suddenly the KING was rocked by several huge explosions almost at the same time. The concussions sent the old freighter reeling over to an almost five degree list, throwing Beckler and the others on the bridge to the floor. The KING's gun crews were the first to recover, as they went back to work, loading and firing their guns.

For Beckler the nightmare had just started all over again. Rancid smoke was rising up from several different places on the KING. Screams of injured men could be heard, but nothing could be done for them right now. If any of them were to survive, he would have to ignore their pleas, and fight with all the courage he had to save the others and the ship.

The gun crews were an odd sort of lot. They seemed to be enjoying their task. They were totally oblivious of the carnage happening around them, as if controlled by a total single-mindedness, (load that blasted gun, aim it, fire it, and reload it). It was that concentration on doing their job that might just save the KING.

Delair had provided Beckler with an exceptional group of gunners. They knew their job, and did it very well, much to the horror of the destroyer.

The Japanese took several more hits; this time they totally lost all but the stern gun turret, but that was bombarding the KING with deadly accuracy. A shell hit the KING's reinforced breastwork at the base of the superstructure, sending white hot shrapnel bouncing and ricocheting off anything that wouldn't absorb it. The blast shattered the windows of the wheelhouse, sending fragments showering around those inside. Luckily, most of them heard the shell coming and covered their faces. Ace wasn't so fortunate. He had covered his face, but the concussion jolted him from his seat at the radar console, and sent him reeling into the cascading shower of glass.

As the rest of them slowly started to pick themselves back up, Millie rushed over to Ace and helped him over to the port side of the wheelhouse with blood rushing from every part of his head and shoulders. But there was no time to offer any more help than that. The KING was taking hits almost every second. Unknown to those in the bridge, she was also dishing out as many hits to the enemy.

Then, number two stern gun took a direct hit, followed by another hit somewhere astern of the superstructure.

With flames and shrapnel all about them, the remaining three four-inch guns on the KING kept up their unrelenting work. Between the heat of the gun, the tropic sun, and flames and smoke of their own ship burning, the gun crews worked on. Choking and gasping for breath, stripped to the waist, sweat dripping from every pore, they fought on.

Finally, after twenty minutes of fierce fighting, the destroyer's guns went silent. Its bow was dipping low into the calm water of the Philippine Sea. Beckler ordered the KING in closer, and had his own gun crews hold their fire, but cautioned them to keep the destroyer in their sights.

The fight was over; the Japanese were taking to the lifeboats while their ship slowly rolled over and sank, taking many of them with it. The KING slowed to a stop, and Beckler ordered boats to be lowered in an effort to assist survivors. Only twenty Japanese sailors could be picked up, the rest swam wildly away from their rescuers, rather than surrender. Beckler called the boats back. If those still in the water didn't want help, there was nothing he could do about that.

The KING then swung her bow back around and resumed her course at greatly reduced speeds.

Beckler ordered all hands to help with the fire-fighting details, and sent for the carpenter, Scotty. He tried to phone the engine room, but the lines had been damaged, and communications were out. He then ordered Gramps to hold the prior zig-zag course and keep speed to four knots.

As soon as Scotty appeared, Beckler ordered him to sound the ship. They would have to decide whether to continue on to Okinawa, or turn back to the Marianas for repairs. To turn back would be in direct violation of orders; Danielson had made it clear that the KING was to proceed at all cost to its destination.

But all costs could possibly mean the loss of that precious cargo. Beckler would keep his options open, but, for the time being the KING would sail on until Scotty was done with the sounding of the ship.

CHAPTER TWENTY-EIGHT
July 27, 1945
15:45
7:45 PM

The URSHEL KING had left San Francisco with seventy-seven souls aboard. Thirty-one regular crew, Gene, and five of his mechanics, sixteen Naval gunners to man the four-inchers and twelve gunners to man the six fifties, and finally, twelve marine armed guards to protect that damn precious cargo. Less then five hours before, all seventy-seven were still alive. Now fourteen were dead, nine wounded. Five of the wounded would most likely die as a result of their wounds.

The dead included two of Gene's men, all four of the Naval gunners from number two stern gun, two of the 50mm gunners, one of the marine guards, and five of Beckler's men, Fireman Donald (DD) Donaldson, Machinist Mate Issac (Zek) Waters, both Communications Officers, Sparks, and Shorty, and Able Seaman Gerald (Jerry) Gault.

The KING had taken ten direct hits; it was a wonder that she rode the swells, let alone be able to produce steam in her boilers. The breastwork at the base of the superstructure was scarred and dented, but intact. It had been the fragments of that shell that had cut Zeke and Jerry to pieces. They must have been running past that point at the exact time the shell hit.

129

Zeke had always worn a pair of cowboy boots that he was real proud of, and Jerry had the name MARY tatooed on his left bicep. Finding these trademarks was the only way they could be identified; not much else remained.

The four gunners who had caught it in their bucket had fared no better. The hit had set off the live ammo they had been preparing to fire in their gun. The detonation produced such immense heat as to buckle even the barrel of the gun. Two of the gunners in the next bucket were hit by flying debris.

Another shell had hit the boat deck aft of the main superstructure, obliterating that section of deck, leaving only half of one davit, and that was in near perfect condition. It looked as though a cutter's torch had snipped off the upper section of it, leaving the lower unscathed. But then exploding shells can do that, mangle everything but some insignificant piece, and leave that as if nothing had happened.

Beckler was staring dumbfoundedly at the wrecked boat deck when he noticed a drip of dark red fluid drop down from the upper bridge deck and sizzle on the hot steel deck plates. Looking up he saw the two limp forms of the two 50mm gunners who were manning their gun just two decks directly above. The shell had exploded beneath them, tearing away the corner of the lower bridge deck, one deck below and slamming through the steel plates they stood on, killing them instantly. One body was held by a section of the railing almost as if the railing had opened up and allowed him to pass half the way through before closing and skewering him through the chest. The other laid entangled in a molted mess of steel; only one arm protruded out beyond the drooping deck. The fingers of this hand were curled back with only the index finger pointing outward. It was from this finger that the blood had slowly dripped, running down the arm from an unseen hole that had once been his chest and dripping onto the hot deck below.

His attention was drawn to the crumpled form of one of the marine guards, or at least what was left to be found. The flesh had been burned away leaving a rancid pile of smoldering tissue.

There had been two other hits forward; one eliminated the foremost cargo boom and deformed the hatch covering to hold number one. The second had pierced the starboard side of the hull just below the bulwark and exploded in the 'tween deck' just above hold number one. This area of the ship had been filled with, of all things, army boots. Case upon case of leather boots were smoldering away and covering the view from the now almost open bridge with gagging thick smoke.

D.D. met his fate when a shell hit the spar deck in the area of hold number five. D.D. looked all the world like nothing had happened. He just sat there staring off towards the sea. He had caught a piece of white hot shrapnel in the heart; as it had entered, it seared the wound, preventing even the slightest amount of bleeding.

Number four hold had taken the brunt of the damage. It had taken two direct hits, and one more hit just aft in the 'tween deck' between it and number five. It was in this 'tween deck' that two of Gene's men were killed. An exploding shell in a steel cave leaves little of a man to bury. But then again it can leave some things alone, or just do a little damage if it wishes. Such was the case with O.S. Thomas (Sammy) Sampson, and three of the marine guards. They were in the same area as the other two, but Sammy only received slight wounds as did one of the marines. The other two marines were injured far more seriously. Neither was given much of a chance to live.

Little remained of the cargo held in number four and the raging inferno down there kept the fire crew busy fighting to contain it to that hold. Just five feet above the waterline to number four, a shell had blown clean through, opening a six foot hole to the sea. Luckily it was above the waterline. Smoke and steam from the water that was being sprayed into the hold, billowed as well as an occasional tongue of flame escaped through the hole and wrapped around the hull, trying to strike at those who were fighting it.

As Beckler saw it, he had really only two choices. Neither of which he liked very much. One, he could stop the ship until the fires were brought under control. But what if there was another Jap warship out there? Staying where he was would make it all too easy for them to find his ship. The second choice was to continue on at reduced speed, and hopefully not create too much draft, as to hamper the work of those fighting the fires in number one 'tween deck' and number four hold. But at these slow speeds, they wouldn't be able to run very far, and if the flames were still with them come nightfall, the KING would be very easy to spot indeed.

By the way the flames were licking out of that crater left in the hull's side by the Jap shell, they would have to slow down even more than the four knots they were steaming at now. Judging from the persistence of the fire, each knot of speed might mean an extra hour of fighting flames. There may not be anything left of the KING for the Japanese to search for unless the forward momentum of the ship was checked, at least until the fire was manageable.

Beckler ordered the electrician Wilbur (Irish) O'Connell, to get to work on the intraship telephone. Doc, Salty, and Hank had already set the dining salon up as a temporary hospital. The tables served as operating tables; auxiliary cargo lights were brought in and rigged up. Boss had only two men left in his deck crew now, with Jerry being dead and Ace and Gilly being reassigned to the radar duty, but the bosun wasn't the type of man to let something stand in the way of doing his duty. Now, he and able seaman Joe Simms worked at blacking out the remaining salon windows, and covering those that had been blown out. As soon as Sammy was able to return to duty, he would join them.

Beckler sent Millie forward to bring the vessel to 'ALL STOP', and Gene with him to keep a close eye on the scope of the radar. That's all they would need, another damn Jap to sail over the earth's curve towards them.

Finally, with no other choice, Beckler looked toward the radio shack door blown inwards by the blast. The framework around where the door had been was jagged and burnt. The heat must have been intense, as the fire had been put out some time ago and yet steam from the water standing on the shack's floor still billowed from the gaping hatch.

Nearing the shack, Beckler could see that the water on the floor was nearly boiling from the hot deck plates. Nothing inside was recognizable; a few bare strands of copper wire, that had once been coated with rubber, stuck out at odd angles. Bulkhead panels that had once been the solid steel walls of the radio shack now buckled in several directions to allow Beckler to see through them. Off to one corner was all that remained of the two men that lived and worked within these walls. The blast had cooked them, and the water of the fire hoses had rinsed their bones clean before washing them into that corner to where it could push them no farther. Which bones belonged to which man? No one would ever know, for they laid in one unsightly pile, together in death as they had been in life.

Beckler fought to keep the bile out of his throat, and turned away from the charred tomb.

"Poor lads," old Pete offered, as Beckler almost bumped into him just outside the door. "I'll take care of sewing what's left up, for a proper burial and all."

"Thanks," Beckler said, still trying to hold his stomach's contents. "I'll see that Boss, and Scotty, and whoever else I can find help you out."

"If they just help get 'em out here on the deck, the bag sewing I can do myself," Pete replied.

"There's fourteen men to be buried. You sure you don't want some help with the canvas?"

"No, but thanks just the same."

"For God's sake why?" Beckler questioned.

"I started my life at sea on the schooners; I've buried many a shipmate. Ya see, it's somewhat an honor to sew the canvas for a mate. Kinda like payin' one's final respects and all," Pete solemnly stated.

Beckler nodded that he understood, and started to step past the old porter before stopping alongside him and patting him on the shoulder.

"You're a damn good man Peter Fernburg, and a damn good friend. There's regal honor inside that meek being of yours," Beckler quietly said. "As you wish, old friend, as you wish."

By the time Beckler entered the bridge, the KING had lost almost all of her headway. Soon, she would be dead in the water; a sense of foreboding told Beckler that he had better keep the boilers to full steam in case he would have to make a run for it. Since they had traveled only about eight thousand miles since leaving San Francisco, and their cruising range was around eighteen thousand miles, they had more than enough fuel. Now was no time to be thrifty.

"Keep those boilers fired to their fullest," Beckler ordered, as screams of agony from the wounded carried up from the salon. "Get all the booze on board rounded up, and deliver it to the salon," he ordered the watchman Sandy. "Let's hope that it gives those poor souls some peace."

"Which course do we take as soon as the fires are out?" Millie asked. "South by east, toward Guam?"

"West by nor'west," Beckler replied without addressing his first officer's puzzled stare. "We continue on toward our final destination, Mr. Lambert! We sail for Okinawa!"

"But Captain," Millie pleaded, "my God Man! What of the wounded? They need more than we are able to offer, they won't live to see Okinawa."

"And you think they'll live long enough for us to reach Guam?" Beckler snapped. "We have a job to do! Whatever that damn cargo is below, it is imperative that it arrives as soon as possible. Thousands of lives could hang in the balance, not just nine!"

"The hell with you and that damn cargo," Millie glared. "You rotten bastard, Beckler. You just turned aour little make shift sickbay into death row. Those men, YOUR men, will die, simply because you won't go out of your way to help 'em!"

"Listen to me, Mister!" Beckler growled, as he grabbed Millie by the shirt and slammed him against the bulkhead. "I've already been down there and appraised the situation. Four of the wounded will survive with what we can do for them right here. The other five won't live to see the sun set tomorrow, no matter what direction we're heading. So you better get your tail in line and follow orders without question or I'll boot your smart ass out of here, and have you down there swabbin' the flippin' decks! Understand me, Mister Lambert?"

The fight seemed to have gone out of Millie, as he simply nodded. Beckler released him and turned away to face the unbelieving stares of the other watch members.

By midnight the fires were coming under control, the coolness of the night air felt refreshing to those men who now laid exhausted on the open decks. Old Pete had ten of his fallen shipmates already sewn into their canvas burial bags that had only a few hours ago been their mattress covers. Each was carefully weighted so as to make their final voyage a swift one, right to the bottom of the ocean.

By o-three-hundred, two of the wounded had died, just as Pete was completing the final canvas of the first fourteen. Now they too had been sewn in and laid next to the others. As the living gathered around them to pay their last respects and give them a fittin' funeral for a sailor, all thoughts were grim.

Beckler said a few kind words over each, then nodded, as the bodies were tilted up on the slide board, and slid into the waiting arms of their eternal grave, the sea.

Shortly after the last of the sixteen bodies had splashed into the sea, Beckler turned towards the sullen group of sweat and grime blackened men before him.

"We came this far to do a job, to do what we do best; deliver precious cargo from one distant shore to another. There are no assurances that before we reach port, many of us won't join them. There's a war going on. And since the beginning of time men have died fighting these wars. The reason they fight is because they believe in something. They stand for something. Their death stands tribute to those beliefs. But before those deaths can ever be justified, the task for which they died must be seen through. If not, they died for nothing. Turning back now would mean that we came all this way just to have them get killed, nothing more, for that's all we would have accomplished. I think that would be a sin that we would never live down."

After slowly looking over the filthy faces that stared back at him, and finding no resentment, he continued . . .

"Prepare to get underway. That is all."

CHAPTER TWENTY-NINE
July 28, 1945
05:00
5:00 AM

Sleep had been evasive for Beckler, and he tired of the struggle. The ship smelled of death—the bridge, the stern, even his cabin. Stepping out onto the bridge wing, he realized that he wasn't alone. Normally the spar deck would be deserted; this morning it appeared as though half of the crew was having the same trouble as himself. The sky was still dark, while the eastern horizon astern of the KING was growing brighter with each passing minute, casting images of those who wandered the decks aimlessly below, not as men, but as darkened shadows.

Not sure if he was up to it, he descended the ladder to the main deck and made for the salon, without giving it much thought. Beckler entered the darkened foyer that Boss had set up, then closed the door behind himself before opening the curtain and entering the salon proper. The foyer bit had proven to be a great invention of the bosun's. It allowed access to the salon without emitting bright light to show. It would certainly catch a Jap lookout's attention, to be scanning the dark horizon, then to see a sudden flash of white light.

Doc was just pulling the cover over the face of one of the wounded when Beckler stepped in. Two of the less seriously wounded had already gone back on duty, of which Sammy was one. That left four wounded men remaining, two of which appeared to be doing as well as could be expected. The other two lay in suspended limbo, somewhere between the dead and the living, belonging to neither.

One of the two had taken a hit to the head. The shell fragment had buried itself deep within the skull. All Doc could do for him was make him as comfortable as possible, which included inserting a long metal rod in the hole and clearing away any blockage that would cause pressure. After each cleaning, the patient rested calmly. When the pressure started to rebuild, breathing would become labored and rapid.

Nothing could be done for the second. Half of his right side had been blown away, and yet he continued to breathe.

"I jus' pray that one dies soon," Doc whispered. "If he ever regained consciousness the pain would be unbearable. He's going to die anyway, I just don't want to see him suffer."

Beckler didn't reply, just nodded his head and walked out. Old Doc was made of strong material, but how long could even he hold up under the strain?

Walking back to the bridge, Beckler felt very much alone. Sure, there were sixty men still aboard his ship, but the radio was out, eliminating any contact with the outside world. And the only ones that seemed to know they were there were the Japanese.

The stillness of the morning was suddenly shattered when the battle stations alarm went off. It had caught Beckler off guard, and it took a moment for the shock to wear off before he started running the final distance to the bridge ladder.

"What have you got?" he questioned as he entered the bridge.

"Ten fast moving bogeys, coming out of the northwest!"

"Vampire bats, straight from the gates of hell," Beckler corrected, meaning aircraft, direct from the Japanese mainland some six hundred miles to the northwest.

"Who on board knows the most about enemy aircraft?" Beckler questioned.

"Issac did," Gramps replied, "but next to him, I think Machinist Mate Henney."

"Get Stub up here at once!" Beckler ordered. "How far out are those bogeys?"

"Thirty-seven miles and closing," Gilly shouted.

The bogeys were only twenty miles out when Stub came rushing into the bridge, all out of breath.

"You sent for me, Captain?" he asked between his gasps for air.

"Yes," Beckler replied, taking him by the arm, leading him to the front of the bridge and handing him a pair of binoculars. "Look at those planes and tell me how much time they have before they will have to return home for fuel. They've already come about six hundred miles."

Stub looked at the Captain for a moment, before putting the glasses to his eyes and studying the incoming aircraft.

"Six hundred miles you say?"

"There abouts, yes."

"Those planes happen to be . . . "

"I don't give a damn about what kind of plane it is, just how much fuel do they have?"

"Should have turned back already."

"What do you mean, should have turned back already?"

"Those planes are Mitsubishi Zeros. They can fly three hundred and forty-five miles an hour, but their range is limited to only about six hundred miles, unless they employ a drop-belly tank," Stub explained.

"A drop-belly tank?"

"Yes, an extra fuel tank carried under their belly. They use that first, then drop it off, and start using from their regular fuel cell."

"What if they use those tanks, how much extra time does that give them?" Beckler demanded.

"Doesn't matter, cause those planes didn't use one," Stub shouted, as to be heard over the thunderous noise around them, as the first wave of planes came in.

"How can you tell that?" Beckler shouted in Stub's ear, as they both ducked below the steel forward plating of the bridge for cover as bullets from the planes ricocheted all about them.

"Cause they have bombs where the tanks would have been! They couldn't have carried the tanks!"

The cold fear of knowing the truth slowly sank in. They had no intentions of making it back home. Their mission had been a one-way trip. To sink the UR-SHEL KING!

"Bring her hard to starboard!" Beckler barked, as he strained to be heard over the roar of the KING's guns and the scream of the deadly attacking aircraft.

The first pass by the planes had been a simple strafing run; they were checking the ship out. Or possibly the pilots weren't the gung-ho type. Beckler knew that they would waste no more passes; their fuel was almost gone. The only place for them to land was into the steel plates of the KING.

"Hard to port!" Beckler shouted. He knew that his only hope was to make it as difficult as possible for the planes to hit him, maybe it would give the gun crews the precious time they needed to knock out the kamikazes.

On the first pass of the planes, gun number one forward got lucky and made a direct hit. The Zero exploded instantly in a brilliant flash, then fell into the sea in a rain of parts ringed in dark smoke. The last remaining aft gun also made a hit, but not as direct as number one's. Its target took the blast in the canopy, killing the pilot instantly, but not destroying the plane. The crippled craft flew directly over the KING, streaking the sky with a tail of smoke, gradually losing altitude before impacting into the sea a thousand yards off the port side.

"Hard to starboard!" Beckler shouted as he watched and prayed for space. The planes were sticking to a plan of some kind, as only two or three would actually try to crash into the ship each time they passed. But the others did let go with bullets and bombs. So far the KING's luck was holding. The Japanese had made two passes, and no direct hits on the KING as yet.

The eight remaining planes broke off in two formations. Four circled wide and lined up with the port side of the KING, while the others banked the other way and flew off to the west before turning back around and making for the bow.

By now even the Marine guards were kneeling on the deck of the ship with their rifles trained on the incoming planes. As soon as the range of the four planes coming in from the starboard side were in firing range, the number one forward gun, the aft gun, and the remaining two-fifty calibers opened fire.

The zeroes appeared to be lined up wing tip to wing tip. It looked as though all four were going to attempt to crash into the KING together. Again the armament and the talent Danielson had provided for them proved to be up to the challenge.

First, one of the middle planes was hit and started going down, slowly. It looked as though it could still reach the side of the ship, but impacted with the sea one hundred yards away. Then, the plane on the right outside was hit squarely in the wing, tearing that wing away and driving the careening Zero into the side of the one flying next to it.

The lone attacker bore in with the blind determination to die a glorious death for the empire. As the plane dropped too low for the four-inch guns to depress far enough to be able to hit it, the job was entirely left to the fifty-calibers hammering away from the upper bridgework of the superstructure.

Luck held with the KING again; a split second before the plane could hit the side of the ship, it exploded into an orange fireball raining scathing parts and fire onto the deck, but little structural damage was done to the KING.

Two of the Marine guards that had been kneeling with their rifles were hit by the holocaust and died instantly.

The forward guns were at the ready when the four remaining Zeros came swooping out of the sky in single file. The whine of the planes' engines as they gathered speed during their steep descent caused the blood, even in the bravest of the gunners, to run cold. Then, planes leveled off at a height just high enough to clear the KING's masts and raced in from directly ahead of the bow.

The first plane caught the wrath of both forward guns, disintegrating instantly. But before the two guns could be reloaded, the second plane was upon them and strafing the entire open deck. Two of the gunners in tub number one were hit. The first caught a bullet in the teeth, exploding his mouth and nearly ripping his head off. His body flew backwards and now hung draped over the side of the tub. The second caught it in the side, just below the armpit, dropping like a stone to the bottom of the tub for the others to stumble over in their fight to stay alive.

Passing over the KING, the second plane released a bomb that dropped into the remaining forward boom and exploded, tearing a gaping hole where the boom had once been affixed to the deck.

Luckily, the boom came crashing down between the forward two gun tubs. However, these men didn't have time to consider how lucky they were. They were desperately fighting for their lives.

The third plane made it through the first two guns as well and released a bomb that crashed through the upper hatch cover to number three hold before exploding and obliterating everything in that hold, including Danielson's precious fifteen-foot wooden crate.

The second plane continued over the ship, strafing as it went, and releasing its second bomb towards the stern. But it had held the bomb too long; the bomb dropped safely astern before exploding and sending a geyser of saltwater laced with cordite skyward.

Once again two planes raced towards the ship, this time much closer together than before. The forwards guns could do nothing to stop them, but the 50mm kept hammering away from the upper bridge deck, just above the wheelhouse. The first plane cleared the forepeak of the KING and released its payload right into number three hold, just fore of the superstructure.

Beckler had ordered, "Hard to port!" But the KING couldn't turn away fast enough. Millie had arrived on the bridge just as the fighting had begun. Seeing the trouble they were having in number one gun getting it reloaded, he didn't wait for Beckler's permission, he just dropped down the bridge ladder and started running for the gun.

Now the planes no longer flew in formation, instead, they attacked like angry bees just knocked from the hive. The KING would take a hit and roll from the concussion, clawing at the sea to right herself in time to take another hit from the other side.

Then, one of the planes pancaked into a flaming ball of destruction into the forepeak of the ship, sending flaming fuel and flying debris across the foreward decks and spilling into the sea. Beckler had seen it coming, but was helpless in stopping it. Now, he too was running toward what had been the forward gun tubs. He had left Gramps in charge of the bridge, to do whatever he could to keep the ship alive.

Beckler was half way towards where he had last seen Millie when a deafening explosion happened directly behind him. He didn't have a chance to see what happened before being slammed down on the steel deck and sliding to the bulwark through strands of licking flames. To his surprise he'd been only bruised; the force had thrown him across the deck so quickly that he didn't have time to get burnt.

Stumbling to his feet, he swiveled around to see that a kamikaze had crashed into what had been the bridge, totally obliterating it in a flaming holocaust of melted steel and incinerated flesh.

Before he could move, he detected a strange sensation. He couldn't fathom it at first, then it hit him, silence. No more screaming planes, no more gun-fire, no more explosions.

Then, the silence was broken again, this time by pleas for help, screams of anguish, and the voices of the uninjured shouting for someone to help them remove a friend from the wreckage. Looking aft, it appeared as if the entire length of the KING was aflame.

Turning around to face forward once again, Beckler could still only see flames and thick black smoke climbing in the intense heat. Uninjured members of the crew were already manning the fire hoses as Beckler walked past them in a daze, with his eyes fixed on what had once been the forward gun number one. Nothing seemed to sink in. There was so much going on around him, and yet nothing.

Stepping through the carnage of wrecked plane and ship, and finally emerging from a wall of black smoke, Beckler stood facing the gun tub. He hadn't given any thought to what he might find. At the moment he lacked the capacity for competent thought.

What he did find stopped him in his tracks. Millie was still alive, propped up against the mangled steel side of the gun tub. His hair was all burnt off, and his skin was blackened and blistered. A patch of his forehead had been peeled down and now covered his left eye. The flesh of his upper torso had baked in the extreme heat, removing the natural fluids in it, leaving it dry and splitting. The legs laid still at odd angles. One missing below the knee, the other missing the foot. Somehow parts of the uniform, only parts, had survived. The bronze rank markings on his collar had melted into the fabric that had held them.

"Andy?" Millie asked through burnt lips, breaking Beckler out of his trance.

"Oh, Millie," Beckler sighed, as he reached down for his First Mate, only to have Millie's flesh peel off in his hands.

"Please, please, don't touch me," Millie pleaded. "Just stay with me for a while."

Beckler could say nothing as tears welled up in his eyes, and his throat swelled shut from the pity he was feeling for his life-long friend.

"Tell," Millie started, trying to raise enough strength to talk. "Tell my folks . . . tell 'em . . . you know . . . jus' tell 'em, Andy."

"I will, Millie, I will," Beckler promised, as he looked into the fading sparkle of his friend's eye.

Then Millie gasped his final breath, and tumbled back into the riddled bucket.

Drowning in sorrow and anger, Beckler stepped onto the burning deck and shook his fist towards the heavens, and screamed . . .

"YOU BASTARDS!"

CHAPTER THIRTY
July 28, 1945
0800
8:00 AM

Beckler was running again, this time towards amidship. Through the heavy black smoke and the rancid odor of death, he made his way past where the forward cargo booms had been. The superstructure, or what was left of it, was hidden from view by the flames and smoke belching from hold number three.

It seemed so senseless. He knew that precious cargo of Danielson's, and the men who guarded it, were no more. The fifteen-foot wooden crate had been affixed to number three's floor.

Upon reaching the booms between two and three, Beckler stopped for a moment; something was wrong. He didn't know what, but something wasn't as it should be. At the moment he was standing out of the smoke, and breathing fresh sea air. In his dazed mind, he tried to figure out what was out of place; what was happening that shouldn't be? He stepped over to the port side of the spar deck, just as Gene ran through the smoke and into Beckler, sending them both crashing to the steel deck.

Gene was the first to get back on his feet, and race over to Beckler, who had made it to a sitting position, but no farther.

"You all right, Captain?" Gene asked as he grabbed Beckler by the arm to help lift him up.

"Yeah, I'm fine," Beckler replied, with a blank expression on his face.

"Ya got to snap out of it, Captain," Gene shouted as he shook Beckler, trying to get through to him. "There's a lot of lives dependin' on you! This ship is dying unless we can control these fires, and real soon!"

"The engines!" Beckler suddenly shouted, as he leaped to his feet.

"What about the damn engines?"

"Gotta stop those engines, they're feedin' the flames!" Beckler shouted as he pulled free of Gene's grip and started running again. Gene didn't know what else to do, so he ran after Beckler.

Beckler fought his way along the port side, the rudder must have been jammed to port, as the ship seemed to be endlessly turning in circle. For the moment he was thankful for that, since the flames and smoke were being fanned over the starboard side. He finally reached what was left of the superstructure and deckhouse amidship, where he ran into the remnants of his crew.

Of the original seventy-seven man crew, over two-thirds were now dead. Only twenty-two men were still alive, four of which were so badly injured they could only lay in anguished torment. The deckhouse had once towered four decks above the spar deck; now the steel skeletal outer bulkheads of two decks were all that remained.

All living quarters, the galley, the salon, the food stores, everything that had been housed there was gone, including the men that were in it at the time. The dead included all the ship's officers, Quartermasters, cooks, everybody except those whose battle stations were elsewhere on deck, even the twenty Japanese prisoners from the destroyer.

Beckler was surprised to see that the engineering staff had survived and now had joined their shipmates in battling the fire on deck.

The crew paid little attention to what was happening around them; each concentrated on the task before them. Most hadn't even seen Beckler run up, so when he grabbed Patty and pulled him away from the fire, the Chief Engineer acted as though he had seen a ghost.

"Thought you got it when the bridge was hit," Patty shouted to be heard over the roar of the fire and those fighting it.

"Must stop the engines!" Beckler shouted into Patty's ear, ignoring the Engineer's comment.

"Can't get to 'em! Fire is blockin' the blessed entrance! We'd been damn lucky jus' to get out!"

"Have everyone direct their hoses into the passageway! We must get to the engines and shut them down!"

"Aye, aye, Captain," Patty shrugged in reply, as he turned back to direct those closest, where to point the stream of water from the hoses.

"Get everyone to bring their hose to bear on the engine room hatch!" Beckler shouted at Gene.

Gene didn't reply, instead, went right to work gathering men and all fire fighting equipment to the engine room hatch.

After an eternity of breathing heavy black smoke, battling intense heat from the fire under an unforgiving tropical sun, Patty, Fritz, Lucky, and Bobby were able to enter the hatch and make for the stairs that led down into the bowels of the dying ship to the engine room.

Descending the stairs was a trick in itself, as the hand rails were far too hot to touch. Boiler number two had blown its high pressure fitting and was filling the room with super heated steam; luckily the steam was directed towards the steel ceiling, allowing the men to enter the room beneath it. After much difficulty, they had wrestled a fire hose down the companionway into the engine room and across it to the control panel. Working in a steady cool mist from the hose Patty was able to disengage the engine. Then, they went to work to shut number two down. Number one would have to be kept going in order to run the pumps.

As soon as the four men had entered the engine room, Beckler ordered three men with hoses to stay at the hatch and keep the fire under control. Another three were sent to hold number three to battle that blaze; three more were sent forward to number one and the forepeak. The final three were sent to the rear of the superstructure to battle the blaze from that side. Then, turning towards Gene . . .

"You, Sergeant, are now my First Mate! Get aft and see what can be done about navigating the ship from there."

Gene simply gave a nod of his head and was gone. Beckler suddenly felt the vibration of the screws die away, as the draft created by it lessened. As soon as the draft had faded sufficiently the smoke no longer drifted off the starboard side, instead, much to his dismay, there was a slight breeze from starboard which brought the smoke right in on top of them.

Around midday, the fires within the deckhouse were finally extinguished, enabling the six men that were battling those blazes to assist the others forward. Gene reported the auxiliary helm on the poop deck was functional, but with all the navigational devices and charts being destroyed, making any port would be purely guesswork.

Sometime after two, the sea started to pick up, and clouds rolled in overhead.

"The Gods must be with us yet," Gene stated, looking skyward. "Hope that rain comes soon."

"So do I," Beckler agreed, "but why won't the fire in three go out? What was in that crate that could burn so long?"

"Maybe nothing," Gene thoughtfully answered, "maybe that hit blew the bottom out of the hold and opened her up to the fuel oil in the double bottom tanks."

"If that's the case, how much heat will the outer hull plates take before they buckle open to the sea?"

"No way of knowing; if the sea can dissipate the heat fast enough . . . " Gene was cut short by old Pete running up.

"Captain, come quickly, we've got ourselves some real problems!" Pete quickly pleaded.

Beckler didn't have the time to respond before Pete was running forward again, with Beckler and Gene in close pursuit. Reaching the open hatch cover to number two, Pete stopped and pointed into it.

"This cargo is getting real hot!" Pete warned.

Bending over the coaming, Beckler and Gene stared into the darkened hold. The forward half of it was occupied by drum after drum of aviation fuel, while the second half was filled with neatly stacked cases of armour piercing, anti-tank missiles. Beckler felt sick; he didn't know if he was lucky or damned. Lucky because this hold hadn't been hit directly, damned because it could go up at any moment from the heat being generated from the fires on either side of it in holds one and three.

"Wonder how hot they are?" Gene asked.

"Not sure," Pete quickly replied, "but how hot can they get before blowing us all to kingdom come?"

Beckler silently stared into the hold and weighed his options. Seeing no other choice, he finally rose to his feet and sent old Pete down to the engine room to retrieve everyone except Patty. Patty would have to keep the boiler going by himself. Of the men fighting the fires, he cut their number in half.

"What's the plan, Captain?" Gene finally asked. "Gonna have a go at removing that stuff and dumping it over the side?"

"Bingo!" Beckler replied. "Get something to use as a sling . . . Scotty, get this boom swung out over this hatch, extend it far enough so it'll reach out over the port railing here . . . Boss, get a rope over here so we can get some bodies down in there."

Beckler was the first to lower himself down into the hold. He carefully landed on top of one of the drums of aviation fuel. Slowly, he bent down and put his palm on the top of it. Warm, but not hot, that was good! But this drum was in the middle of the hold, what about the ones near the forward bulkhead? That bulkhead was all that separated this deadly cargo from the inferno in number one. Carefully, making his way over to the bulkhead, he felt each and every row of drums. The nearer he got to the bulkhead, the warmer the drums became.

Two rows from the bulkhead, the drums became hot to the touch. It would only be a matter of minutes, maybe seconds, before the contents of these drums would send this ship and her crew to hell in pieces.

One by one, others slowly joined him in the hold, as the sling attached to the boom was lowered down.

"Feed a hose down here," Beckler ordered.

In moments the hose was being lowered, and as soon as it was firmly in their hands the water was turned on.

"Keep misting those drums nearest the bulkhead," Beckler instructed. "While we remove the first row, then we will slowly move those away from the heat."

"Think we'll make it?" Joe inquired, "before they blow?"

"There's only one way to find out," Beckler replied. "They're damn sure going to blow if we don't try!"

Every head in there turned towards Beckler. That wasn't the answer they were looking for. And if there was a damn good chance that this lethal cargo was going to blow, in the same steel hole with it, was not the place they wanted to be!

It was back-breaking work, moving those fifty-five gallon steel drums of highly flammable fuel into the cargo netting. The net could accommodate ten drums. To entirely remove one full row it would take four trips, as the drums were twenty across and two high. There were twelve rows of drums, making a total of twenty-six thousand, four hundred gallons of this deadly cargo!

Six o'clock came and went. It was usually dinner time, but no one even mentioned food. Just as well; there wasn't any to be had. The problem for some was that it had been more than a full day since they had eaten. The planes had hit before breakfast, and with fighting fires, and burying their friends last night, few had been able to eat then. Everything was beginning to work against them; the heat, the hunger, the exhaustion. Possibly the only thing that drove them on was the very fact that their lives could well depend on it!

By seven, they had been able to burrow down the middle of the rows and remove the first two rows that were against the bulkhead. The spray from the fire hose had kept them cool enough, long enough. However, the work was far from over. The bulkhead was starting to allow smoke from the fire in number one through its seams into number two. Beckler didn't have to point out the danger, everyone saw the threat.

"Hey, it's raining!" someone hollered down to them.

"Better late than never!" Gene quipped.

"Probably won't help much," Beckler stated flatly, "at least not in number one. That fire is being fed by the fuel oil stored in number one and two deep tanks in its bottom!"

"Not only may it not help, but it could kill us," Irish corrected. "Feel the ship!"

Nobody spoke. They all stood dead still. It was there, slight, but there! The ship was starting to roll in the swells. To unload the drums, they had to unlash them. If the ship rolled too much, there was nothing to stop the drums from tumbling down and rolling right up against the hot bulkhead!

Now, more than ever, it was a race against time. Beckler ordered the men to lash as many of the drums as they could, which would do little good with the center of the rows now missing. But they would have to do all they could to buy time. The boom seemed to take forever to return from dumping its last load. While it was gone, the men would move drums from the nearest row to the bulkhead towards the center of the hold. The boom returned and lowered the sling down to them, they would load the drums they had collected.

The fire in three was finally dying down, as the last case of missiles was hauled over the coaming and dropped over the rail. Hold number two was empty, and it was as though their bodies knew it. They couldn't muster the strength to climb out. The boom was called back to the hold one more time, to lift them over the coaming.

The rain was a gift from heaven as it beat down against their bodies. Beckler had had no idea how hard it was raining until he was lifted from the hold. Number one was still ablaze, but the superstructure and number three were finally out.

The ship, like the night and sea around it, was void of any light, with the exception of number one. It was doing its damnedest to light up this part of the world! A cold shiver went down Beckler's back; the thought of that fire burning so brightly scared the hell out of him. It would serve as a beacon for any Japanese vessel to aim at. What more could he do? All possible fire hoses had been put to work on it, without much success.

The Dead! Suddenly it came back to him, Millie, and others were still laying wherever they had fallen. Looking around at the darkened and buckled deck plates, there were many bodies, not dead ones, but the living, if one could call them that. The remainder of the crew had taken it upon themselves to fight number one in shifts. While half of them labored with the hoses, the others rested.

And rest indeed, it was more like dying for ten minutes or so before being called back to life, so the others could die. He didn't have the heart to ask them to help bury the dead; instead he went looking for old Pete. Together they would find the ones they could tonight, the rest would have to wait until dawn.

It was well after midnight when Beckler found old Pete already at the task for which he wanted him.

"I was just looking for you," Beckler said as he stepped up behind Pete. "Was gonna ask you to help me do that, guess I should have figured you'd already be at it."

"Least I can do for them" Pete replied flatly.

"Millie's in the forward turret; I'd like to take care of him myself," Beckler sadly stated, remembering his dear friend.

"Thought as much, Captain. I've already seen to the others. Lining them up on the starboard side."

"I picked them for this mission," Beckler softly said as he looked out across the waters with the rain running down his face, hiding the tears that fell. "I'm the reason they were here!"

"Fate's the reason they were here!" Pete corrected. "You ain't God. If they would have been anywhere else, they'd be just as dead. When our time is up, we're all dead!"

Beckler turned and smiled at his old friend, then walked away.

Maybe Pete was right. Maybe people just live so many years, months, days, then they die. Where they are or what they are doing has little, maybe nothing to do with it. God, Beckler hoped Pete was right; it would ease his conscience a lot. It would be the one thing right now that did make sense.

So many things had happened since he had had Millie flown in. He remembered the first time they met. They were both just kids. Millie was about five years younger than Beckler, but they became fast and good friends right from the first day, when Millie went to work for his neighbor on the farm. When Beckler went to sea at the age of eighteen, Millie would always write and ask all about it. Five years later he helped Millie sign on the same ship he was with.

Now, all these years later he would bury his friend at sea, half a world away from Cedarville, Illinois. How would he be able to tell Millie's folks about what happened? He wasn't even sure that this mission was worth the risk it had taken. What if they had made it, would the world be better off? He also remembered Millie not thinking they would even get this far before the war came to an end, and with good reason.

Since the eighth of May, shortly after President Truman announced the surrender of Germany, the U.S. had begun the first "Official Spokesman" broadcast, telling Japan the time had come for peace!

At first, most sailors wrote it off as our own Tokyo Rose, but twelve days later the Japanese replied with their own version of Official Spokesman, showing interest in knowing more about the surrender terms. That had given the men food for thought.

Millie kept saying that the KING would never get to sail; that Japan would throw in the towel before the ship got out of dry dock. But the KING did make it out, and the exchange of broadcasts continued right up until last Tuesday, the twenty-fourth, when Japan's Dr. Inouye said

"If the U.S. will show proof of its sincerity in reference to the Atlantic Charter, peace would be possible."

What the hell was really going on? Where was this peace everyone was talking about? Had Millie and all the others died in vain? Would the fact that they even lived make any difference?

Beckler was beginning to openly sob, not that anyone could have seen it anyway. The rain was still falling steadily, and darkness prevailed within the riddled gun turret; the glow of the fire in number one did little to cast light here.

Millie's body was cold and slick from the rain. Beckler could feel the brittle burnt skin cracking within his hands. The thought of what he was doing repulsed him, so he tried hard not to think of it. Millie was his dearest friend; seeing to it that he received a proper burial was, as Pete would say, "the least he could do."

The hardest part of all was that there were no canvas bags to put the bodies into; they had all been destroyed along with the deckhouse. As Beckler carried Millie's body aft to bury with those of his eternal shipmates, he had to stop twice to pick the body back up, the skin upon which he had gripped would peel off under the pressure, causing him to drop the body. Each time Beckler would apologize to his dead friend, and pick the body back up and go on.

Gene watched in silence as Beckler slowly walked past, he saw the body fall, and had started to go to the Captain's aid, only to stop when he heard what Beckler was saying. He understood, he knew to stay back. It was something Beckler had to deal with alone.

As Beckler laid the body down, he noticed that Pete was wiring broken chunks of wreckage to each body. Upon noticing the Captain staring at him, old Pete replied, "Can't have them just floatin' on the surface can I?"

Beckler didn't reply, just simply took a piece of broken steel and secured it around Millie.

Beckler then stood up and looked out over the forward part of his ship. Half of what remained of his crew were busy fighting the fuel oil fire in number one. The other half laid spread out over the rain soaked steel deck, trying to regain enough strength to relieve the others when the time came. Despair started to set in. What was he going to do? There was no food to feed these men, and damn little drinking water.

CHAPTER THIRTY-ONE
July 29, 1945
02:00
2:00 AM

Gene had called Beckler away from helping old Pete with preparing the dead. He had a plan for putting the fire in number one to rest. It would be risky at best, but when Beckler weighed the dangers of Gene's plan against the possibilities of what could happen if the fire was allowed to burn uncontrolled all night, he opted for Gene's plan.

The plan called for all the fire hoses to be directed in one tight area of the hold. This would allow them to pass a pump hose down into the deep tanks and hopefully pump some of the fuel oil overboard. If the plan worked, there would be less for the fire to feed on; if not, the hose and the pump could explode in their faces!

It took several tries, but finally the pump hose was lowered into the ruptured top of the forward most tank. The pump was started and after several sputters, sent fuel oil belching over the side. The forward tank was of the greatest concern, since all that separated it from the forward peak tank was a steel bulkhead that by this time should have been melted.

Beckler had sent Scotty about sounding the rest of the KING. What it was that was keeping her afloat he had no idea. Her upper works had for the most part been totally destroyed. Three of her five holds had been gutted by fire, with number four slowly taking on the sea via the gaping hole in the hull just above the water line. All in all, things didn't look too good for the tired old ship. She had been left for dead once before, revived at the last minute only to live long enough to be beaten, raped, and left to fend for herself. To ignore the fighting heart of this ship would be like looking at a pinup of Betty Grable, and noticing only that the seams of her stockings are straight.

Out the corner of one eye, Beckler saw the beam of the flashlight Scotty was holding in his hand. At first it didn't sink in; he simply thought that for some reason or other, the carpenter had decided to inspect the second deck of the superstructure. The oversight was to be expected, for Beckler was just as exhausted as the rest of the crew, maybe even more so, for to him fell all the responsibility. It was his lot to oversee everything that went on. If he wasn't helping one, he would be helping another, or planning the next move and the next. At the moment, his mind was on the fire; it had to be brought under control as soon as possible. So long as it burned brightly, it would serve as a beacon to any enemy vessel, especially a sub!

Then it hit home! The carpenter wasn't a deck above him at all! Instead the ship was out of trim down by the head, with the stern slowly rising! Jumping to his feet and racing over to the open hatch cover to number three, he called for Scotty to bring him his flashlight.

"No need to see it, Captain," Scotty puffed, as he made his way to Beckler. "Forward holds must be floodin', she's down by the head, with a slight list to starboard."

"Doesn't that worry you jus' a little bit, Mister?" Beckler shouted.

"Worry me it does! But I can't be sure what's causing it. Could just be the water you're pumping on that fire. If so, I've had some of the men start to flood number five to bring her back into trim."

"Could be the hull is buckled!" Beckler warned.

"Aye, that it could, Captain," Scotty agreed. "But either way, ballast in number five will help the situation."

"Didn't you think I might want to know about it?"

"Well, sure, Captain, but what could you have done that I hadn't done already, if you had known?"

Beckler didn't answer; he knew Scotty was right. Beckler had always held the highest regard for this big old Scot and his simplistic logic. Nobody argued with Scotty, not that at one time or another they didn't want to. It just never seemed to do any good. To have a difference of opinion with Scotty was an open invitation for him to quietly and frankly show you just how much of a fool you were. Here was a man who had indeed missed his true calling. Why he chose to be a sailor instead of a politician, no one knew.

The fire was the biggest threat at the moment. Even if the hull was giving way, there was nothing for them to do. There was no way of radioing for help. No lifeboats for them to take to. Nothing could be done that wasn't already being done, except of course, relieve those poor bastards manning the hoses.

There was no longer any time for the ones not manning the hoses to rest. Water was already being rationed. Instead of allowing them to rest on the deck, Beckler put them to finding anything that would catch rain water.

Beckler and Scotty inspected number three hold and found that the bomb had blown a hole through the bottom of the hold into the double bottom, which now was slowly seeping water. The smell of the charred hold gave both men the creeps. There was nothing left of the precious cargo that it had once held, or the men that had guarded it. The intense fire from the blast had rendered anything that remained unrecognizable.

"Makes a man wonder about what his purpose is in life," Beckler sadly stated, knowing that the reason for their being there, and the reason for all the men of his crew who had died, was now destroyed. It had been for nothing.

"Aye, Captain," Scotty agreed, "destiny awaits all of us somewhere. If you hadn't brought us here, someone else would have. All one can do is make the best of what we have, while we've got it. Besides, Captain, we shouldn't really take life so seriously. Ain't none of us gettin' out of it alive anyway."

"Just what is that supposed to mean?"

"Simply put, don't go a blamin' yourself fer the dead, it won't do them a bit of good. Worry about the ones alive. They're the ones you can help the most."

Danielson had wondered about the men Beckler had chosen, but then he didn't know them. If he had, he would have picked them himself.

Just as they stepped over the coaming, old Pete greeted them.

"Three more ready for burial," he sadly stated.

"Who are they?" Beckler asked, dreading the answer.

"Jimmy, Ace, and Jones."

"How's Louey?" Beckler asked.

"About the same. Still bravin' all that pain, and talking about his home back in Alabama."

"Do what you can for him," Beckler said. "We'll bury the dead as soon as the fire in one is no longer a threat."

"Aye, Captain," Pete replied as he turned aft to offer what comfort he could to Louey. Louey was the only black crew member on the KING. He was a large man, about six foot tall, weighing two hundred and fifty pounds. Despite his size, he had a mild manner and soft voice, except for a booming laugh. He was well-liked by all that knew him. He never complained or said a bad word about anybody.

Louey's condition was a source of real concern for Zimmerman, the head Naval gunner. Louey was one of his boys. They had worked the same gun; number one, stern. The fact that Zimmerman was uninjured was the result of Louey seeing what was about to happen, and throwing himself on top of his commander, taking the wrath of the strafing Zero himself.

Pete did what he could to make Louey comfortable, but under the conditions it was of little help. Nevertheless, Louey remained in good spirits, talking about what he was going to do when he returned to his beloved Alabama, and thanking Pete for taking care of him.

At last Gene's idea was paying off. The deep tanks were almost empty, and the fire was beginning to die down. Enough so that Beckler decided now was the time to bury their dead. Gene, Boss, and Irish volunteered to man the fire hoses, while the others performed the solemn task.

Again, Beckler found himself standing over the remains of the dead members of his crew. With each he would say a few words, nod, and listen to the body slide down the board and splash into the waiting sea. This time it was more difficult. The bodies were not enclosed in canvas. He looked upon their rain soaked features as he spoke, remembering each as they were.

Then came Millie. It was all he could do to control himself. Millie had been so much more than just a First Mate. He had been his life long friend and confidante. Why hadn't he listened to Millie when he wanted to turn back? Would it have made a difference? Would Millie and some of these others still be alive? He nodded, and the board was slowly lifted; Millie's body glistened from the rain as it slid down and off the side of the ship, then splashed into the sea.

With the dead buried, and the fire in one almost out, Beckler sent the Engineering Department back down into their domain with orders to get ready to be underway in twenty minutes. Gene was called aft to man the stern auxiliary helm.

It seemed as though it had been an eternity since the KING was slicing through the swell under her own steam. It started slowly at first then started to build. Like an old friend, the feel of a vibrating deck returned beneath Beckler's feet.

Beckler took a quick check of the forward holds to be certain that the wind from the ship headway wouldn't rekindle the fires. Then he headed aft towards the aft-deck wheel.

"Where we headed?" Gene asked, as if it didn't matter.

"The truth?" Beckler smiled for the first time in twenty-four hours.

"No way of really knowing, is there?"

"Not really."

"So long as we're moving," Gene grinned.

"So long as we're moving," Beckler repeated.

The KING had just gotten underway, when the Japanese I-class sub broke the rough surface of the sea. It had been six long days of searching and finding nothing. The first break came when the sub received word that the target had been spotted in this general area by Imperial aircraft.

The sub's Captain was becoming worried that the target might have slipped away yet another time. How could a worn-out old freighter, as he was led to believe the KING was, be so damn hard to kill?

Twice, he had received reports that the target had been engaged, and twice he was ordered to intercept. How could the KING withstand that kind of assault?

"Target bearing 2-8-2!" the navigator shouted.

Quickly, the sub's captain spun around and started screwing the adjustment on his binoculars until he could faintly make out a dark blur. Since the possible enemy ship was so far out, a range finding would have to wait until he could get his sub into position closer to the target.

"Kaitens, stand by!" the Japanese captain bellowed, after issuing a flurry of commands that sent the sub racing across the surface in hopes of getting set up to lay in wait for the KING to cross her deadly six forward torpedo tubes.

The captain knew that if the enemy ship out there had radar, he was at this moment risking the entire boat and crew by racing on the surface. Due to the darkness, he had totally misjudged the KING's speed. He could have easily moved ahead and gotten into position submerged. Then there was something else about the stranger that bothered him. He wasn't yet sure what it was, but something didn't appear right.

Only 2500 yards separated the Japanese submarine from the URSHEL KING, when at long last, the Japanese captain was able to assess the range and be sure just what type of ship it was that he was about to send to the bottom. The targets length and general hull design matched what he had been hoping for. But where was the superstructure? He couldn't see any! He also noticed a small tongue of flame that would occasionally raise its head over the coaming in the forward part of the ship.

At last he realized what it was that appeared peculiar, besides there not being any superstructure. The KING wasn't steering a zig-zag course, and yet she wasn't holding a steady course either. He had no way of knowing that Gene was doing the best he could without any navigational aids at all. The best shot the sub had at getting a sure hit would cost the lives of the last two Kaiten pilots the boat had on board.

"Arm the Kaitens!" he bellowed, which sent young Japanese sailors scurrying up ladders and through sealed hatchways leading to the human-torpedoes.

While the suicidal pilots scrambled into their steel death traps, the Captain ordered the sub to the proper submerged depth for launching of the kaitens, never once taking his eyes off the vision in the night periscope. The glory of sinking the URSHEL KING would be his!

Patiently the sub's Captain waited. Waited for the range between his boat and the KING to narrow to the point where the Kaitens couldn't miss.

"Fire One and Two!" the Japanese captain ordered, followed closely by the launching of the two kaitens from the sub's back.

At first the kaitens steered for the slight flicker of flame in the distance. But course was slightly altered as the silhouette of the rest of the ship's hull became visible the nearer they got to it.

On the mother sub, the captain watched and waited, holding his breath. He could not make out the kaitens, but the KING's hull was quite plain at this distance.

In an instant a brilliant flash of light exploded, followed by a second. Then came the rumbling a split second later. They had found their mark!

Deep within the bowels of the KING's engine room, Patty, Fritz, Lucky, Bobby, and Stub would never know what hit them. The two kaitens impacted the KING amidship, less than forty feet apart, the devastation was complete. The KING's starboard outer hull, amidship, disintegrated in the onslaught, sending tons of water and debris crashing inward.

For those on deck, the explosion sent the ship reeling to port almost fifteen degrees, sending several of them over the rail and into the sea. Those who remained had been thrown as well, but the cold steel deck was no less forgiving than the sea. Beckler had been slammed against a buckled bulkhead, Gene was able to hang on to the auxiliary stern wheel and keep himself from injury.

The tired but proud ship fought to recover from the deadly list to port; slowly she started to right herself. First to ten degrees, five, even keel, then she started taking a tell-tale list to starboard. She was going to turn turtle! Beckler knew the end of the KING was near as he shouted for those on deck to throw liferings, kapok jackets and anything else that was left overboard to those already in the water.

A raging inferno was rapidly consuming the midship area once occupied by the deckhouse. The engine room was directly below it. Gene abandoned the wheel and joined Beckler in passing the word.

"Abandon ship! Abandon ship!"

Through the rain and smoke men ran across the tilted deck. The slope of which was ever increasing. It would only be a matter of minutes before the KING would take her death roll. Already the sounds of bulkheads giving way, loose machinery tumbling free and colliding with whatever bulkheads remained, rumbled through the hull.

With all that remained of the URSHEL KING's crew, Beckler and Gene stepped over the port railing onto the side of the hull. Luckily, one of the floater nets had survived the living hell of the past two days. Easing closer to the edge of the hull, Beckler could make out the keel, now serving as a waterline. In a burst of strength, Beckler and Gene tossed the floater net free of the wreckage.

"Okay men, once in the water," Beckler shouted. "Make for that net. And watch where you jump! I've lost enough good men for one day!"

Gene stood next to Beckler as they watched the men slide to the edge of the hull and ease themselves into the water.

"After you, Captain," Gene smiled.

"I'll be the last to leave," Beckler smiled back. "I'll thank you to get your ass in that water."

Gene only smiled as he casually walked off the edge of the hull, that was now slanting towards the bow into the water, followed closely by Beckler. Both men swam a short distance before turning to watch the KING take its death slide to the bottom.

"Wonder what Mr. King would think if he could see his namesake now?" Gene questioned.

"He'd be damn proud of her," Beckler replied. "For an old tramp steamer, the KING did swell."

"I wonder if Millie ever found out who Urshel King, the man, was," Gene thought out loud.

"You mean, is," Beckler corrected.

"Is?"

"Yeah, Urshel King is not that old." Beckler continued, "The son of Alvan King, of West Frankfurt, Illinois. Seems Alvan worked in the coal mines there. The URSHEL KING hauled coal. The ship owner named her after this Alvan's son as some sort of tribute to the father."

The two men tried to talk as if nothing was happening. Their ship was sinking by the bow, her bronze propeller had now risen high out of the water until the ship stood almost on beam's end. Then, slowly at first, gathering speed as she went, The URSHEL KING slipped beneath the waves to join that part of her crew that had so shortly ago preceded her.

"We're on our own now," Beckler sighed as the ship disappeared from sight.

CHAPTER THIRTY-TWO
July 29, 1945
04:00
4:00 AM

Abandoning a sinking ship can be a deadly task itself, especially when there are no lifeboats or rafts. All that remained on the KING was the floater net and the kapok life jackets. The real danger in 'jumping ship' is what one might land on. Beckler had seen able body sailors leap from the decks of their ship to their deaths by landing on some jagged piece of wreckage below. He had also seen men panic and leave their kapok jackets behind, or freeze with fear and either have to be thrown over or die with the ship.

There was no panic this time, possibly because the men had been through hell, and were too exhausted to be frightened by death. Regardless, this was one fire they didn't have to fight; the sea had done it for them.

Both Beckler and Gene decided that it would be best to swim away from where the KING had gone down. The sub responsible might come up for a closer look. They looked around as best they could but couldn't hear or see anybody.

"Let's go and try to round the survivors up," Beckler said as he rolled onto his chest and started moving away.

The KING had belched up tons of bunker fuel and oil that now coated everything in the area.

At a safe distance away from where the URSHEL KING, had sunk, he stopped and rested, laying into the buoyancy of the kapok jacket. He was rising and falling in the running swell. Fuel oil coated his skin and plugged his nostrils. He had done his best not to swallow any, but to no avail. With the sea being as choppy as it was, swallowing some had been unavoidable. The heavily toxic substance made his stomach wretch as it tried to cleanse itself. After vomiting several times, he began to feel slightly better.

"You all right, Skipper?" Gene asked in a concerned tone, knowing full well what had happened.

"I'll be okay in a minute or two," Beckler hoarsely stated.

He hadn't heard them before, but now that the KING was gone, Beckler started to hear the voices of his crew. Calling out and telling them to swim towards him, he tried to swim towards the nearest sounding voices. As all of the bobbing heads were completely covered in a thick black coating of oil, there was no way to know who he had found until they spoke.

The first crew member he found was the wounded Louey, with old Pete still by his side. Then, one by one, Beckler was slowly able to get the group of survivors together. Gene had seen to it that the floater net had been properly opened when Beckler caught up to him. He had already gathered Boss, Scotty, Zimmerman, Irish, and Sammy into it. Beckler had been able to locate O'Dell, the last of Gene's men, along with Willy, Joe, Naval gunners Minnow, Martin, Louey, and old Pete.

Of the entire complement of men that sailed from San Francisco, these fourteen were all that remained. Six of these were wounded; Sammy, O'Dell, Minnow, Martin, Willy, and the severely wounded Louey.

As Beckler and Gene helped Louey inside the floater net, they looked at each other, knowing full well what the oil and salt water would do to his wounds. It would be only a matter of time, and yet Louey was his somewhat cheerful self. If ever a human possessed a truly saintly disposition, Louey was it.

Now that the task of gathering everyone up was over, Beckler called Gene off to one side and was about to propose a game plan, when someone shouted that they saw the sub surfacing.

"Where?" Beckler quickly asked.

"Over there, about 200 yards out!" Sammy yelled.

"All right, all right," Beckler calmed him. "Try and keep your voices down."

Quickly, swimming over to that side of the net, both Beckler and Gene stared at the rising form of the huge Japanese I-class submarine as it broke the surface.

Seconds after it settled on the rough surface of the ocean, it turned on its search light and began panning the area. The first two times that the beam of light passed their way, the Americans were lucky. The sea had hidden them into a trough of a swell. Soon a Japanese officer, in surprising good English, started calling out to them.

"Why do you hide from the safety of our vessel? We will find you, you cannot escape. Come forward and surrender now."

"He may have a point, Captain," Pete quietly stated. "What choice do we have? Our wounded will die unless we can get them out of the water."

"They'll use their deck gun on us, as soon as they see us!" Boss sharply warned.

"We'll do nothing just yet," Beckler whispered.

"If I had my choice," Louey quietly said, "I'd take the sea any day to them guys."

Beckler patted Louey on the arm and smiled. He knew why Louey had said that. Louey knew that the others were thinking of surrendering to the enemy just to get him out of the water. He couldn't let them do that, even though staying in the sea would surely kill him.

"I'll do fine, Captain!" Louey persisted, "I surely will."

The Japanese continued to search, as the sub slowly made its way through the wreckage that floated free of the KING. At regular intervals, the English-speaking Japanese would call out to them. The sub was stubborn, it changed course several times in a vain search, its spotlights swinging to and fro in the effort. Then it turned back towards the direction where Beckler and the men were trying to swim away.

"Why do you continue to resist?" the Japanese called out to them. "If you don't surrender, the sharks will have you for breakfast."

Beckler kept trying to think. The war would be over soon. It would be better to end the war as a prisoner of war, than not to see the end at all. Especially the wounded; they didn't stand a chance if left at sea. And with no way of getting off an S.O.S., they could be in the water for a very long time.

"How about it? Will you surrender and accept the warmth and dryness of our vessel?" the Japanese continued.

Beckler was about to reply, when the bright beam of the search light landed on them. Instantly, the Japanese spoke again.

"You, there in the net, swim towards us and surrender now!"

"What are they going to do, Captain?" Willy asked in a quivering voice.

"Come at once, or we shoot!" the voice from the sub warned, sounding like an actor in a cheap western movie.

"Sounds like Tex has us covered," Beckler resigned. "Best do as he asks! It's better to live as a prisoner of war than not live at all!"

Carefully, leaving the floater net behind, something to go back to if they did start shooting, Beckler and his men started swimming towards the enemy submarine. Martin was the first to reach the sub's side. As he climbed up the rounded belly of its hull, several Japanese sailors reached down and hauled him onto the deck. After one of them roughly pushed him towards the forward part of the deck, Martin turned and pushed back. A burst of gun fire rang out, and Martin's limp form fell overboard.

Joe instinctively started to swim away, only to have the 20mm gun, on the top of the sub's conning tower, open up and tear his body to bits.

"Do not resist! We shoot those who resist!" The Jap shouted.

The men in the water had stopped cold. The horror of what they had seen filled them with inertia. To continue towards the sub probably meant death. To make a break for it most probably meant the same thing. Beckler decided that the best chance was still with peaceful surrender.

"Do not resist in any way!" Beckler ordered his men as he started towards the sub again.

Reaching the side of the sub, Beckler could tell that it had been at sea a long time by the growth of barnacles on its cold steel skin, making the climb up the fat, rounded belly of the sub, painful and slow.

The Japanese had thrown ropes down, but they were no help to Louey, and Minnow, who were too injured to make the climb. The Japs showed no mercy; when Minnow failed the first attempt to climb the rope, he was shot and killed before his ship mates could help him. Beckler and old Pete wrestled Louey up the sides of the sub, thereby saving his life.

Once on deck, the Japanese stole everything the Americans had; watches, rings, identification bracelets, kapok jackets, everything. Then they carefully bound each man's hands behind them with heavy wire, so tightly it cut off circulation.

Beckler kept a close eye on how they were handling Louey. From the way the Japanese looked at this giant black American, Beckler could see a certain fear. Then, he noticed the thin smile on Louey's face, and the burning glow of pure hatred in his dark eyes. The search light that was mounted high on the conning tower of the sub, was pointed directly at Louey. Beckler had grown fond of this gentle giant, and had never seen this type of facial expression on any man, much less the easy going Louey.

Then, they were led to the forward deck of the sub and forced to sit cross-legged, and stare only straight ahead.

"What was the name of your ship?" the short Jap, who spoke English asked, as he stood before the group, with what appeared to be the sub's Captain slightly behind him.

No answer.

"The ship's NAME?" he insisted.

"URSHEL KING," Beckler spoke up, knowing it would be fruitless to refuse.

"And her Captain?"

"Dead!" Gene quickly replied, "Along with all her officers. They all died when one of your planes crashed into the bridge yesterday."

The Jap seemed pleased by that answer. He turned and translated it to the Japanese captain behind him, who also seemed pleased with Gene's reply. That answered many things; why the ship had no superstructure, why it was sailing so erratically.

Beckler was unable to hear most of what that was being said, except for the occasional name URSHEL KING. When the officer that Beckler had taken to be the Captain of this sub, heard the name URSHEL KING, his face broke into a broad smile. Beckler didn't understand it, but he had the strangest feeling. It was as if the Japanese Captain took great pride in knowing that he had sunk the KING. Judging from his reaction, one would think that the Jap had just sunk the carrier HORNET.

Gene must have noticed it as well. He turned his face far enough around for Beckler to see the questioning expression on it.

"What was your cargo?"

"Aircraft fuel, and ammunition," Boss stated.

"What else?"

"Combat boots!" Scotty snapped.

"What else?" the Japanese interpreter persisted.

"That's it. The rest of what ever the cargo was, was dropped off at Midway," Beckler replied, hoping to end this questioning.

"Destination?"

"With the officers all being dead, we can't be too sure, but we think Formosa," Beckler answered.

"But Formosa is held by the Empire!" The Japanese officer quickly replied. "Why would you be heading there?"

"How should we know?" Willy flatly stated. "Maybe you won't have it much longer."

The Japanese officer gave Willy a cold, hard stare, but accepted that reply, and turned and repeated it for his captain. The captain said something back to the English-speaking officer, who in turn bowed. Then the two of them stepped aft and out of sight, while three other Japs stepped up to watch over them with automatic weapons.

Beckler and his men were seated two abreast, with Beckler being in the third row, port side. What seemed to be an eternity passed before someone from the back row was lifted to his feet and led astern. The slap of the waves against the hull and the wind and rain covered most of any sounds coming from the aft side of the conning tower. Beckler cocked his head slightly as to be able to hear what was going on behind him, without those in front of him shooting him for disobeying. It wasn't much help. He thought he heard a scuffle, followed by a splash. But since he hadn't heard gun shots, he passed it off.

Soon, they returned, and started to take the next guy, when the Japanese officer returned and told them to take Willy.

Again Beckler listened, hearing the same sounds, again unable to distinguish what it was he was hearing. This time, however, when the Japanese returned, they noticed that Beckler was trying to listen. So, instead of taking the next man, they took him.

As they neared the base of the conning tower, a gag was shoved into his mouth so forcefully and far that he immediately started to gag on it. Then something was quickly tied around his face to hold it in place. The cloth tied around his face covered his mouth and nose, but for some reason they intentionally made sure that it didn't cover his eyes.

He tried to see what the sub's number was as he passed the side of the conning tower, but the legend had been replaced with some sort of flag. However, the sub's legend had been only covered with a single layer of paint, and was slightly visible. The only thing he could be sure of, was that it was I-something between one and nine, as it could only be one number.

Rounding the corner of the conning tower, Beckler saw two rows of Japanese sailors standing, armed with clubs and bayonets. The deck between the two rows was stained with fresh blood, and lots of it. Beckler stood still, staring at the evil faces staring back at him. His eyes shifted back to the deck, and the blood. He followed the trail of blood over the side; it left little doubt of what was about to happen.

There was no doubt about why they had not covered his eyes. They must take great pleasure in seeing the terror in their victim's eyes just before they severely beat then gutted them.

One of the Japs behind him pushed him forward towards the two rows that eagerly awaited the chance to beat and gut him. Knowing he had nothing left to lose, he swung his body sideways and leaped into the sea. He couldn't be sure of how far he had gone down, it seemed like a hundred feet. His lungs felt like they were going to burst before he broke to the surface, and rolled onto his back. The wire around his wrists was beginning to cut in, the cloth around his face had slid upward in the dive and now covered his eyes. He knew that if he were going to survive at all, that had to come off first. Beckler arched his body and forced his head back beneath the waves and thrashed around until the cloth slipped free and floated off.

He also knew that he would have to get that wire off if he wanted any chance at surviving. He first tried to wiggle his hands free, hoping that the water would help make his skin more slippery, but to no avail. Then, he tried to feel for the end of the wire with his fingers, in hopes of being able to loosen the wires grip, again no luck.

The more he tried, the more strain he felt on his shoulders. At times it felt as though he was going to dislocate a shoulder trying to free his hands. Panic started to set in, he would not be able to stay afloat, he was going to die!

Beckler fought to gain control of himself again, he took as deep a breath as he could under the circumstances. The first thing that would kill him was himself. He had to think things out. He slowly kicked his legs, not enough to drain his strength, just enough to stay afloat.

Back on board the sub, something was going on, the prisoners could only guess at what it was, for suddenly all the Japanese ran back to the hatches and dropped below. The cluster lights went out, followed by what Gene knew was a diving alarm.

"Jump for it, men!" he shouted. "The bastards are going to dive with us on their deck!"

The men tried to get to their feet as fast as they could with their hands tied behind them, and their feet numb from sitting cramped for so long. Most were able to make it, luckily the others were swept over board as the sub submerged, all except Zimmerman. Somehow he became entangled on something attached to the deck and was pulled below with the sub. Zimmerman struggled to dislodge himself from what ever held him. He was caught from the back, he felt the pressure of the water depth against his lungs. His mind started to blur, he struggled on. His strength was quickly sapping. He fought back the darkness closing in. Still the sub dropped through the water. The pressure against his ribs increased, and finally death reached out and cradled him into its waiting arms.

Gathering the group together, Gene made an accounting of who was still alive. Of the eleven men that had been captured, four were missing, Beckler, Zimmerman, Sammy, and Willy. They, too, faced the same problem Beckler had, the wire that bound their hands. Working behind his back, Gene was able to undo the binding on Pete's hands, Pete in turn did Gene's, then both went to help the others. To worsen matters, O'Dell couldn't swim. Boss and Scotty were doing their best to keep him up. Gene quickly stripped out of his pants and tied the legs shut. Swinging the pants over his head, he filled them with air and tied the top opening shut, thereby creating a buoyant cushion for O'Dell to float on.

Gene knew it would be of no use to look for the floater net, the sub had been moving, and with the sea running as it was, the net could be miles away. He also figured that with Beckler now being gone, he would have to assume command of what remained of the crew. A job he would rather not have, but there was little choice.

No one said anything. There was little point really. Each was deep in his own thoughts. Not one among them had any idea of what tomorrow would hold. Hope was nonexistent. They were adrift in a stormy ocean; no food or water, no life jackets, and, worse than all the others, only the Japanese knew they were there.

At least the sub had carried them away from the oil slick caused by the sinking of the KING. Gene was trying hard to keep his wits about him, but the nagging urge to sleep was becoming stronger. If they were to stand any chance of living, rest would have to take place, but how? The only thing that was standing between them and certain death was the floaters that they had made of their pants. They offered little security, since they had to be reinflated every hour or so.

Gene finally worked out a way that half of them could sleep, while the others kept watch, to be sure the one sleeping would not succumb to the sea. Each would take turns of two hours watching, then two hours sleeping, as best they could, considering the pants would need to be reinflated.

Gene took watch over O'Dell himself. Since O'Dell couldn't swim, he would have to be watched closely. Also, O'Dell was the last of the dock workers that he had brought with him aboard the KING, and the only member of the survivors to be wounded—other than Louey, and Pete was keeping a close eye on Louey. O'Dell's wounds had been slight, but it wouldn't take the sea long to turn them into salt blisters.

The morning sun was breaking as the first of the two hour rest periods was coming to an end. At last Gene would get the chance to sleep himself. O'Dell was little or no help, Gene found himself unable to sleep; concern for the welfare of the others, and himself, kept him awake, no matter how hard he tried to find rest.

During his two hour rest period, he had dozed off once, only to have his pants deflate. O'Dell wasn't able to do anything to help, as self-pity and fear controlled him.

CHAPTER THIRTY-THREE
July 29, 1945
08:00
8:00 AM

Beckler was fighting to retain his sanity. It had taken more than two hours for him to clear his mouth of the rag that had been shoved down it by the Japanese. During that time he expelled far more energy than he could afford. With the waves running as they were, hands secured behind his back, and choking on a filthy rag, it was all he could do just to breathe. The first round of his prize fight was completed, the rag was dislodged. At last he could breathe easier.

There was still the matter of that wire around his wrists. No matter which way he tried to twist it, to relieve the tension, it seemed to get tighter. He would have to remain patient and keep his wits about himself. To panic now would invite disaster. The only hope he had was to slowly work the wire back and forth until it snapped. It would be slow going and very painful. The Japanese had made sure it was taunt.

Floating as best he could on his back, he kept up with the slow pace of twisting the wire to the right as far as it would go, then turning it back to the left. To add to his problems, his wrists had swollen and become intensely painful. Each bend of the wire sent jolts of excruciating pain through him. Nevertheless, he had to continue.

The sub was nowhere to be seen, as the morning sun began to climb into the sky. He could only wonder about where his crew might be. Knowing that at the moment there was nothing he could do for them, he concentrated on his own problems. He had to free himself of that wire before the sun rose too high into the sky. He would not survive a day of floating on his back, staring into a blinding sun directly overhead.

"Think of pleasant things!" he told himself, as he felt a rising tide of self-pity within. His thoughts instantly turned back to San Francisco, and Becky. For a moment he could hear her sweet voice and smell her enticing perfume. God, how he longed to be with her; hold her close, kiss her lips. Suddenly, the pity returned. It came the moment he realized that Becky was only a desire; being shipwrecked in the middle of the North Pacific Ocean's war zone, with his hands tied, his strength ebbing, was reality. At the moment it was beginning to feel like the two, reality and desire, would never meet.

If only one thing could go right and ease Beckler's situation, it did. The sea was starting to die down a bit. Of course that meant that the sun would be unmerciful in a few hours due to a clearing sky.

Beckler decided to tackle one problem at a time for the moment. And his biggest problem right now was that damn wire!

With every bend of the wire, it seemed to tighten its grip around Beckler's wrists. He fought fatigue, thirst, hunger, and panic with every ounce of courage he had. He didn't want to die here; not now, not after all he had been through. To give up now would be senseless. Still, his mind kept telling his body how easy it would be for him to simply stop fighting it, and just slide beneath the waves that were constantly slashing over his face.

The wire had stripped his wrists of any skin. Blood was slowly mixing with the water around him. Great, he thought, now I'm becoming shark-bait. The swelling and pain continued to increase due to the influx of saltwater into the wounds. How long could this wire hold? For that matter, how long could he?

Finally, the strand of wire snapped. He was free! A wave of self-satisfaction swept over him. Sure, he was still a lone swimmer in the North Pacific, somewhere near where it meets the Philippine Sea, but at least now he had the use of his hands. He now at least had the means of some mobility.

Since he had decided to confront one problem at a time, and his first problem had been conquered, he rested and considered his priorities. He still was faced with exhaustion, thirst, hunger, and the fact that he was alone. He could do nothing about his hunger, or thirst, and if he gave in to exhaustion now, he would die. That left only one choice; he would try and find any survivors of his crew. He reasoned that if he had made it off that sub, then others might have as well. The only question was how would he go about trying to find them?

He slowly paddled around in a circle, surveying all around himself. The sun was coming up in the east, and with the break in the clouds, started to shine through. He had his directions down, he also guessed that he had drifted far from where the KING sank. He tried to remember which direction the sub was traveling when they first saw it come to the surface.

"Did it turn when it came to pick us up?" He questioned himself out loud. "Did it turn again once we were on its deck? How long were we on its deck? And how fast was the sub traveling while we were?"

Try as he might, he couldn't come up with any positive answers, only educated guesses. From the way the spray off the sub's bow had washed over the deck, as they sat on it, he guessed the sub to be heading north, by northeast, towards Japan, at about six knots. He also guessed that they had spent somewhat less than thirty minutes on board. If they hadn't traveled too far north, he should still be in the vicinity of the Northeast Trade Winds, which would be blowing towards the Japanese homeland. That is of course if he hadn't floated into the North Pacific Wind Drift, which is an easterly current, flowing from Japan toward the United States.

He had no stationary objects on which to take a sighting. He looked up towards the heavens and watched several large cloud formations; they seemed to be floating westerly, or following the trade winds. But then he could be floating east in the current.

He decided to conserve his energy as best he could, but slowly swim towards the west, knowing that the enemy could be that way. As he saw it, he didn't have a choice. If he allowed himself to float to the east, he would be carried far out into the vastness of the North Pacific. He could only hope that some of his crew had survived, and were at this moment floating, as he was, somewhere to the west of himself. Or if it was not to be the case, then at least he might find a small island to swim to, before falling into enemy hands. The fact that he might not make it never entered into his mind at this moment.

Beckler had been right about one thing at least. What remained of his crew were indeed floating much like he was, five miles to the northwest. But, for now all he could do was hope and wonder.

Gene, on the other hand, was too busy to even think about Beckler. He had written him off as dead, and now concentrated on the problems before him. O'Dell was starting to complain constantly. At times he even seemed to be losing control of his sanity. Pete seemed to be holding up fine. He spent all his energy on helping Louey. Gene couldn't help but admire both of them—Louey, for his tremendous amount of courage in the face of what must be excruciating pain, with the saltwater entering his wounds and all. Pete, for his undying selflessness. Gene couldn't believe that Pete was holding up so well. Where was he getting all his strength from?

Boss, Scotty, and Irish seemed to sense that it was their duty to keep everyone else inside a circle, as they slowly swam on the outside. When Pete and Louey started floating away from the group, they went after them and brought them back.

Boss must have seen how beat Gene was, and came over and offered to keep an eye on O'Dell. Gene thanked him before moving a slight distance away, reinflating his pants, and falling asleep.

O'Dell was becoming a basket case. One moment he would babble incoherently about some nonsense, then he would begin talking in philosophic terms that seemed almost poetic. Boss kept his tender vigil over O'Dell, ever thinking that the end for the poor soul might be at hand.

Irish noticed the air trapped inside Gene's pants was almost gone. The sergeant's head almost rested in the water. Due to Gene's death-like sleep, he hadn't noticed and slept on.

Motioning for Scotty to lend a hand, Irish made his way over to Gene. While one man held Gene, the other reinflated the pants, then carefully placed them under Gene's head. During the delicate operation, Gene hadn't stirred once. Satisfied with their handiwork, the two men smiled and moved off towards Pete and Louey, who once again had strayed a ways from the rest of the group.

It was sometime after noon when Scotty caught something out of the corner of his eye. He quickly spun around as terror filled his being.

"Shark!" he screamed, finally finding his voice, as the sixteen foot monster swam to within twenty yards of the small group before starting to circle around.

Gene had been asleep for several hours when the alarm was sounded. It took several seconds for his sluggish mind to register what was going on.

"Close up ranks!" Gene shouted. "Form a tight group, with Pete, Louey and O'Dell to the center!"

The men did as they were told. Gene, Scotty, Irish, and Boss closely formed a ring with Pete and the two wounded men to the center, behind their backs.

"I heard that if you play dead, they will leave you alone," Boss offered.

"The problem with that," Irish countered, "is if you play that game too long, an' it ain't so, you will be!"

"Aye!" Scotty agreed. "I don't much like the thought of bein' that bastard's dinner! He ain't gonna have me without a fight, that's fer sure!"

"Shut up! All of you!" Gene ordered. "If it comes in closer, I agree with Scotty. I want you to try and kick it in the nose or eye. Maybe we can make it go away, if we don't make ourselves too easy a meal for it. But, don't make any motions until you have to; I don't want to draw it in. I repeat, only kick if it comes in close!"

The shark kept circling, occasionally swirling around to circle in the other direction. As the monster swam around the small group, it kept its cold, staring eye fixed on them. As if it were deciding which tender morsel would be dinner.

Then, after about ten minutes of that, it seemed to turn and swim away. The men sighed a breath of relief, and were about to break their circle, when Irish shouted that it was coming back again. This time however, it was coming faster, and straight for them!

As the monster raced for them, the circle of men became tighter. As it seemed that collision was inevitable, Irish prepared himself to fend the creature off. As it was about to crash into the group, with its open jaws of death, Irish was able to land a powerful blow to its nose, which caused it to quickly turn its head away and violently smash its body into the group, sending men crashing into one another, and thereby dispersing the group.

The shark had made several other attempts at getting a meal, now that the men were rather wide spread, each turning as to constantly keep the monster in their sights. Now, it was coming back for yet another try. This time however, it seemed to have zeroed in on Louey for its target.

Even with all his injuries and pain, Louey showed no signs of fear. The nearer the shark came, the more ready for it Louey appeared to be. He had laid himself out across the water, belly down, his huge black legs and feet towards the other men, his large powerful arms and fists out in front of him towards the incoming killing machine.

With all the determination fitting of a dying man, Louey pressed his lips tightly together and braced himself for a fight to the death. All the others could see was a spray of water as man and beast collided, then a couple of swirls in the water, and both were gone.

Seconds passed slowly, then suddenly the shark burst to the surface with Louey attached. Not in its jaws, but with one enormous black arm around its head, and the other was appearing to be clawing at its eye. It was happening so fast. The shark, with Louey locked to its back, quickly swam past the others, as if it was trying to rid itself of that black beast upon its back.

Once again the shark dove for the depths. But not in time to save its left eye. Louey had been able, through sheer strength, to force his fingers through the tough outer protective skin covering the eye, and rip the ball from the socket. When the pressure of the water became too great to hang on, Louey released his grip and floated towards the surface, carefully exhaling as he rose to prevent damage to his own lungs.

As he broke the surface, he proudly held the bloody eye ball in his hand for the others to see, but he had been carried too far away from the others. All they could see was that he was waving his arm.

A loud cheer rang out, as they were surprised to see Louey at all, let alone alive. All, including Gene, thought for certain that he was a goner. Now, it appeared that he had killed the shark! How? No one could venture to guess.

The only thing that mattered was getting the group back together again. Once the surprise wore off, they started swimming towards the triumphant Louey. Gene couldn't believe what he had just seen.

Through all the danger and hell that Gene had endured, the wish that he had stayed back at Mare Island, never crossed his mind. He had grown to admire, even love this rag-tag bunch of big-hearted sailors.

Beckler had just turned back over onto his stomach, after resting while floating on his back for a time, when he noticed a fin break the water's surface and race quickly by him. He didn't have the chance to experience fear, as it was gone before he realized it was a shark. He did find it curious that the shark had apparently been wounded quite recently, judging from the trail of blood it left behind. Beckler guessed that the injury was probably from fighting with another shark over some carcass.

Then, it dawned on him what that carcass might have been; one of his men. Maybe they were all dead, then maybe not. He would swim in the direction from which the shark had come in hopes of finding out. Although he knew that he risked the chance of running into the shark, or perhaps a school of sharks, that had fought with this one.

He looked in the direction from where the shark had come, but could see nothing. He had only his hopes to go on. There had to be some of the crew alive yet, and he had to find them.

CHAPTER THIRTY-FOUR
July 29, 1945
22:30
10:30 PM

The U.S.S. Indianapolis was sailing across the Philippine Sea at sixteen knots, having left San Francisco and made stops at Pearl Harbor and Tinian. There she had dropped off a classified cargo, which had created considerable gossip amongst the Indy's crew as to its content. Whatever suspicions the crew might have had, they were heightened when the Indy dropped anchor just off the beach of Tinian. The ship was boarded by a throng of officials who carefully watched as the cargo was hoisted down to a waiting barge.

The crew didn't know what the cargo was, and shortly after it had been removed, didn't care. For the most part they looked forward to getting in some gunnery practice in Leyte. Leaving Tinian, the INDY proceeded to Guam, where she was to receive sailing instructions and drop off some official passengers.

The Indy was instructed to follow 'Convoy Route Peddie', this came as no surprise to Captain McVay, as 'Route Peddie' was the official shipping lane from Guam to Leyte. At first, the routing officer had planned on the INDY leaving Apra Harbor on Saturday morning, July 28, and arriving at Leyte on Monday, July 30, sometime around sunrise.

Captain McVay quickly pointed out that the Indy had just made a long hard run from San Francisco; in fact, his ship now held the speed record for the San Francisco—Pearl Harbor run at 74.5 hours, beating the previous record holder, the OMAHA, by almost an hour.

For his aging cruiser to arrive on Monday, it would have to average almost twenty-five knots. Since McVay wished to arrive at early light, to get in some anti-aircraft gunnery practice, it was decided that by reducing the speed to around sixteen knots, the ship could arrive early Tuesday morning.

Upon her arrival in Leyte Gulf, the INDY was to report to Rear Admiral McCormick, on the U.S.S. IDAHO, for two weeks of refresher training, due to the large number of relatively untrained personnel she was carrying.

Captain McVay signed the night orders, then retired to his cabin, while nine miles away to the west, the Japanese Submarine I-58 was sailing eastward in search of prey. The I-58 was the fourth and last of the Tamon Group to put to sea.

The original plan for Tamon was to put six of the I-class submarines over a large area, namely from 130 degrees to 150 degrees west and 15 degrees to 35 degrees north. Using intelligence information, the four submarines fanned out across this area looking for one vessel in particular. While the Japanese had wanted six I-boats for Tamon, a shortage of sea-worthy boats forced them to commit only four.

The I-58 broke to the surface; as it did so, commander Captain Hashimoto, ordered the signalman, the navigator and the watchman up to the bridge, while he himself checked his surroundings with the night periscope. Suddenly, the navigator shouted down to Hashimoto,

"Bearing red-nine-zero degrees. Possible enemy ship!"

Hashimoto rushed up to the bridge and grabbed a pair of high-powered binoculars. Fate had played into his hands, as several of the clouds overhead had parted and allowed him the opportunity to see the silhouette of the INDY. He quickly ordered his sub into a dive to avoid being detected by the other ship's radar. He knew that he had sighted a big ship, but had no idea just how big, or that it was a heavy cruiser.

Hashimoto remained with his face pressed tightly against the periscope, as he ordered his boat into action. At first, he guessed the speed of the opponent to be twenty knots. He quickly got his sub in a position directly ahead of the oncoming vessel. He could feel the anxiety building within himself as the vessel approached. He ordered all tubes to be made ready, and for the kaitens to stand by!

At a range of four miles, Hashimoto began to sense a trap. He quickly panned the entire surrounding area, and found it to be empty. By now he was elated to see that the approaching ship was a man-o-war. He quickly referred to his book of silhouettes, and rightly guessed the enemy to be a heavy cruiser of the Baltimore class.

Jess had found his bunk in the forward part of the ship to be too hot and stuffy to sleep. Grabbing his pillow and a blanket to lay on, he made his way to the open air of the fantail and settled down for the night near the base of the flagstaff.

"We've got her!" Hashimoto told his men, with his eyes still pressed to the periscope. His kaiten pilots anxiously waited to be ordered into their tubes of death.

Hashimoto turned towards them for an instant and told them that they would not be needed, unless conventional torpedoes failed to fell this giant.

It was slightly overcast as the watch changed at midnight. Most of the crew, including Captain McVay, believed that the weather conditions would hide them from any enemy, and therefore the ship was steaming straight ahead, following a westerly course.

Still the American ship steamed on. No offensive, or evasive action had been taken; they had no knowledge of the sub being there.

Captain Hashimoto had corrected his guess of what the enemy's speed was from twenty knots to twelve, at three thousand yards and closing. He intended to wait until the target was within a mile of his boat. The torpedoes were set to travel at a depth of twelve feet and race through the water at forty-eight knots.

As soon as the American ship was fifteen hundred yards away, Hashimoto gave the order.

"Stand by . . . Fire!"

The torpedoes shot out from the sub and raced for the unexpecting INDY at two second intervals and a spread of three degrees each; all six tubes were fired.

Hashimoto glanced up at the clock affixed to the bulkhead, it was 00:04.

Now they waited. They had turned the sub away from the collision course and were now running parallel. The seconds ticked by; they all held their breath, until almost a full minute had passed. Then suddenly there were several enormous concussions. Their fish had found their mark; the U.S.S. INDIANAPOLIS was mortally wounded.

The INDY shuddered from the first explosion, while the second shattering blast lifted the heavy cruiser's forward section and completely severed the first forty feet off the bow. Although considered by many to be dangerously top heavy, the proud old cruiser settled back down in the water almost on even keel. But, within the first two minutes, the ship had taken a slight two degree list to starboard.

Captain McVay had been asleep in his bunk when the first explosion threw him sprawling onto the cabin floor. Having been sleeping in the nude, he immediately ran to the bridge naked.

Arriving on the bridge, McVay found it to be filled with heavy smoke; he called for the damage control officer. Getting no reply, he shouted for the officer on deck. Lieutenant Orr quickly responded.

McVay was informed that Lt. Commander Moore had already gone below to assess the damage. All communications to and from the bridge were out, including the engine room telegraph. Lt. Orr was very concerned that he could not get the engine room to respond, as the engines continued to push the INDY forward at seventeen knots.

Captain McVay quickly stepped over to the Starboard bridge wing and tried to assess the damage from there. Due to the darkness, the smoke, and the slight list, he felt that the damage was controllable, although he as yet did not comprehend the extent of the damage to his command.

Until he had a damage report, there was little Captain McVay could do, so he returned to his cabin and retrieved some clothing before returning to the bridge. By the time he arrived there, roughly five minutes after the first explosion, the INDY had taken on a list of twelve degrees. That was 3.3 degrees of list per minute since he had last been on the bridge. Still, the Captain's faith in his ship was unfaltering.

Just as the Captain was buttoning his shirt, the damage control officer appeared. Orr was blackened and dirty, and gasping for breath. He reported that the ship was extensively damaged and that it might be in order to prepare to abandon ship.

Captain McVay was amazed by what he had heard, and couldn't bring himself to believe it. He requested Orr to take another check. He couldn't just abandon ship because it was severely damaged, the damn thing had to be going down for certain before he could take such a drastic measure. After all, he was ultimately responsible for this ship, and accountable for it to the United States Navy.

With no other means, a messenger was sent from the bridge to verbally order the engines stopped. Tragically, the messenger never made it, lost somewhere within the dying ship, after a bulkhead burst from heat and pressure just as he was passing it. He never knew what hit him. Not that his making it to the engine room would have made any difference in the long run. The most that could have come of it, is that the inevitable would have taken slightly longer, and possibly more lives might have been saved.

Captain McVay inquired whether the radio room was sending out any distress signals yet. Not getting any sure answers from the officer on deck, the Captain sent Commander Janney down there to see to it. Then he turned to the bugler and asked him to check the inclinometer located in the chartroom.

"Eighteen degrees to starboard, Sir!" the bugler reported.

McVay was stunned. It had only been two minutes since he had last checked it at twelve degrees! The ship was steadily listing to starboard at the rate of three degrees per minute. Unless something could be done soon, the ship would capsize!

At that moment, second in command, Commander Flynn, appeared on the bridge and conveyed his belief that the INDY was doomed, and he suggested that the order to abandon be given.

McVay slowly looked up to his executive officer and told him to pass the word. It was one of the hardest things he had ever had to do. He remembered how badly the INDY had been damaged at Okinawa, yet she survived. In fact, she limped half the way around the world to San Francisco. He had fallen in love with the old gal; to leave her in her dying moments was difficult.

Jess had just dozed off when the explosions took place. From where he was, the concussion was slight, but he heard it and instinctively jumped to his feet and tried to figure out what had happened, as did the men around him. Being at the very stern of the vessel, they could see very little. They could smell the smoke and on occasion see a tongue of flame shoot up from somewhere forward.

Since the vibration of the screws directly below them remained constant, Jess and the others thought whatever the damage was, and whatever had caused it, was minor, especially since there was no general quarters called. So they remained where they were, and actually laid back down.

The forward fire control pumps had been rendered useless so only the inrushing sea water could fight the fiercely burning aviation fuel that was stored below deck. With the bow missing and the enormous hole in the starboard side, directly beneath the bridge, and the ship still charging through the sea at 17 knots, thousands of tons of water was pouring through the forward section of the ship, dragging that section ever lower into the sea.

An effort was made to send an S.O.S. by means of the auxiliary radio set, as it was powered by battery. If the message ever got out, it was never heard.

Jess had almost made it back to sleep when the sounds of excited voices grew louder. With almost 1200 men aboard the ship, one could always hear voices, no matter where one was and no matter what time of day it was. However, with the exception of the wardroom, or the galley, usually the voices were toned down. This was not the case now. The voices were loud and growing louder and carried an uncommon sense of urgency.

Jess sat up and tried to look around. The moon had ducked behind another cloud, restricting what little light there was. All Jess could see of the superstructure was the darkened shape of it against the just slightly lighter sky. The shadowy shape of the superstructure stood before him, but yet something seemed out of wack. It took almost a full minute before he realized that he was looking down towards the bow instead of straight ahead. Also the sea off the starboard side seemed closer than the almost hard to see sea off the port side.

Jess suddenly jumped to his feet and realized that the ship was dangerously down by the head and listing to starboard heavily. Now, there were hundreds of his shipmates gathering on the fantail with him.

"What's going on?" Jess asked of anyone who might know.

Finally, one sailor turned and shouted Jess's worst fears, "We're going down, you stupid shit! The Japanese bastards blew the bow off with torpedoes!"

Within minutes the cruiser had rolled over onto her side, and started its final plunge to the bottom over two miles below. While the ship was rolling over, Jess and many of the others quickly scrambled over the railing and stepped onto the side of the hull. Their only thought was to get away from the stern before jumping into the water, as the forward motion of the ship and the still revolving propellers would most likely suck them in and tear their bodies to bits.

Reaching a point amidship, Jess took a deep breath and jumped into the oily swell. On hitting the water, he kicked with all his might to put as much distance between himself and the dying cruiser.

In much the same manner as the KING had done, the Indy's stern rose high up out of the water, with the screws still turning, then quickly slipped beneath the waves.

Of her full compliment of 1,199 men, almost four hundred of them were trapped inside, and would die with the ship. Of the 800 or so men who had made it to the water, many were seriously injured.

There was to be another sad bit of fate played out before this tragedy would end. It would play an important role in the fate of both the crew of the KING, and of the INDY. In war, there is an enormous amount of paperwork, with all the reporting of troop movements, ship movements, and so on. Shortly before this, every departure of a vessel had to be reported, as did every arrival, with hundreds of ships coming and going all the time, this made for tons of reports. In order to stem the flow of paperwork, an aid to Admiral Nimitz decided that, if a ship had arrived, there was no need to report it, thereby reducing the amount of paper work. His intentions were good, but as it turned out, Harbor Masters also took it to mean that non-arrivals could also go unreported, something that would deal a great blow to the men now in the water.

Aboard the I-58, Hashimoto had the six tubes reloaded with torpedoes. With that completed, he brought his vessel back to the surface. After taking a quick look around and finding nothing except pitch darkness, he ordered his boat to alter course and head northeast. Finding nothing assured him of the kill. With the extent of damage that had been done, the other vessel would have had to speed away at thirty knots to have escaped the area this soon, and since that could not have been the case, the American battleship must have sunk. He ordered the radio to dispatch a message for command.

Although pleased with his kill, that cruiser was not what he had been hunting for.

CHAPTER THIRTY-FIVE
July 31, 1945
00:30
12:30 AM

Just over eight hundred men had made it off the sinking INDIANAPOLIS. Of this number, about one hundred of these men were badly burned and injured. Some had burns to hands and face, others had fractured bones and severely deep gashes to their flesh.

The first night in the water had been a night of torment and torture for the injured. Jess was part of the largest group of survivors, roughly four hundred men comprised this group of bobbing heads. Doctor Haynes, of Manistee, Michigan, seemed to be in charge, although he spent all of his time doing the best he could to help the injured.

The biggest problem confronting the good doctor was the fact that the first aid kits had been broken open in the sinking and for the most part were useless. Of the contents of the first aid kits, only the items sealed in tubes were of any use. These ointments were of little help to the burn victims, as the saltwater continually washed the ointment away.

Jess spent that first night simply floating in his kapok jacket. He had heard someone say that an S.O.S. had gotten out, and that help should arrive by no later than the next morning. The sea was rough, and Jess was constantly getting batted around by oil-covered waves.

After being in the water for about three hours, Jess was asked to help hold one of the badly injured up out of the water, in an effort to ease the poor soul's pain.

The sailor was held up by roughly six men for the next hour and a half. As Jess looked around himself, he found that this exercise was being repeated all around him. The night was filled with moans and cries of anguish. By daybreak, the sounds of pain had for the most part died away, as many of the severely injured had died.

As with the others, the man Jess was helping to hold died. His kapok jacket was removed and his body was allowed to drift away.

The biggest fear at first, was that the Japanese sub would surface and spray the survivors with bullets. After several hours had gone by, with no sub sighting, this fear subsided.

Captain McVay had been somewhat luckier. He spent the first hour after the sinking holding on to a potato crate, before a couple of empty life rafts floated by. McVay quickly swam over to the life rafts, and hauled himself into one of them.

With the other raft securely tied to the first, Captain McVay set out to pick up other survivors. One by one, the Captain was able to herd together a number of men. The rafts contained two paddles, a star shell kit and shell gun, a mirror for signaling, cigarettes, fishing gear, and a worthless first-aid kit and matches.

After some time, those in the rafts came upon a small group of men clinging to a snarled floater net. Two of the men were busily working with knives to untangle the net. The second raft was released from the first and secured to the floater net. The plan was to use the net as a sort of base. The first raft would go out and round up survivors and return them to the net and second raft.

Two other rafts were spotted, one a little over a thousand feet away, the other more like three thousand feet away. The closer of the two rafts appeared to have one injured man, who continually pleaded for help, while the farther raft held a small number of men who appeared to be quite fit.

But as McVay and the others around him were exhausted, they decided not to try for the other rafts until morning light. After first light, Captain McVay and one other man rowed their raft over to the nearest, and found the lone occupant to be in good health, suffering only from fear and loneliness.

Another concern surfaced that first day for the Captain and those men around him. It came in the shape of a twelve foot shark. The shark made a nuisance of himself, but seemed content to only harass the men. A number of times it swam so close to the rafts that the men were able to beat it off with the paddles. After each beating, the shark took off, only to return a few minutes later to start the entire cycle all over again.

Some distance from the other two large groups of survivors, a third group struggled with rounding up stragglers as well. This group was led by Lt. Richard Redmayne. Like the Captain's group, this group of survivors also had the benefits of rafts and floater nets.

Amongst these rafts were a number of fresh water casks. Unfortunately most of the casks had seam leaks, which allowed saltwater to enter and contaminate the precious drinking water. All told, this group was comprised of roughly one hundred and forty-five men. There were three rafts and two floater nets. The wounded were given first berth in the rafts. The floater nets were brought into a circle around the rafts, thereby effectively keeping the group together. Each raft contained approximately twenty men, others clung to the floater nets, or simply floated in the water held up by the kapok jackets.

Each kapok jacket had an expected buoyancy of about forty-eight hours. Surely this should be enough time, so most of the men thought, for rescue to happen.

Jess felt a strong admiration for Doctor Haynes. He had served with the doctor aboard the NEW MEXICO. As long as the Doctor was in charge of the group, Jess felt like everything was going to be all right.

To occupy time during those first hours in the water, Jess thought of home, friends and family. He thought of his friend Milton Lambert with envy. He bet that Millie was at this moment safely snug in his bunk enjoying a good dream of pre-war days. The truth, if he could have anyway of knowing, would only have served to deepen his state of depression. For almost one thousand miles to the north-northeast, Millie's remains already rested on the sea floor, while his shipmates struggled for their lives as well.

During the daylight hours, two planes were spotted flying overhead. The first appeared about 9:30 am. The large group Jess and the Doctor belonged to, could do little in the way of signaling the high flying bomber enroute toward Leyte.

When Jess first heard the drone of aircraft engines, he felt sure an attempt of rescue was being enacted. He searched the heavens for any glimpse of the oncoming planes. At last, he could faintly make out the dark spot in the sky. He flailed his arms and shouted as much as his parched throat would allow. The Ventura bomber flew directly over their heads at about seventeen hundred feet. Jess could clearly see the plane, he could even see the sun reflecting off the bomber's windows.

Someone in the group had a packet of green marker dye in his jacket. As the bomber approached, the dye packet was hastenly opened and the bright green dye quickly spread out over the water's surface around this large group of survivors.

The pilot of the bomber was having problems seeing anything due to the blinding reflection of the sun off the water. Even if he had looked straight down, it would be highly unlikely that he could have seen the tiny oil covered heads bobbing in the swell far below.

As the plane flew out of sight, morale amongst the men in the water soared. Both Captain McVay's group and Lt. Redmayne's group made use of the signaling mirrors. All groups were certain that they had been seen. The bomber had to have been flying a search mission looking for them. Why else would he have been flying so low?

The pilot had been simply trying to get decent visibility for his antisubmarine patrol. How he happened to miss the enormous oil slick the survivors were floating in, no one will ever know. For, by now the slick was roughly ten miles long and growing. But the pilot was looking for the fine lines of a surfaced submarine, the tell-tale wake, not an oil slick. He had no reason for searching for shipwreck survivors, as no sinking had yet been reported, at least by American authorities.

However, the Americans had intercepted a message sent out by the I-58, reporting the sinking of a Idaho class battleship. Both Pearl Harbor and Washington had the same intercepted message, and yet neither did anything.

There was another aircraft sighting that day. The second plane offered very little hope, as it appeared to be flying extremely high. By night fall, the swimmers were cursing 'those blind flying bastards!'.

After the baking hot sun, the evening darkness brought a refreshing coolness to Jess. But as the night wore on he felt chilled to the bone. This night marked a full twenty-four hours in the water. It was painfully clear that the bomber had not seen them. The new day brought with it new hopes. The INDY had been scheduled to arrive at Leyte Gulf at ten hundred hours this morning. Surely the fact that she failed to show should send someone looking for her.

The Doctor was constantly moving among the men, consoling the injured, cheering up the depressed, encouraging the rest. As Jess watched the doctor making his way towards him, he decided that he was not about to have the doctor waste any concern over him. The very sight of the brave doctor casting personal concern aside for the sake of others bolstered not only Jess's resolve but the resolve of many of the others in the group as well.

It will never be known, but the number of lives saved by Doctor Haynes, simply by his example, was substantial. If the doctor could be so brave in the face of these odds, then so could they. Of course the doctor knew that there was precious little to sustain life, other than raw courage. If any of these men were going to survive, it would take an act of God, and a boatload of courage.

This second day in the water was more than some men could stand. Each of the three groups would grow smaller before the merciless sun would settle in the west. This day brought a large number of sharks to the surface.

Many of the sharks fed on bodies of the dead, others would charge into small pockets of men chewing and tearing flesh as they went. Still others would single out the weak and bring about a horrifying end to the misery.

The group Jess was with seemed to bear the brunt of the shark attacks. Jess had lost count, but seemed sure that at least twenty live men were eaten by sharks that afternoon. The more the fuel oil from the ship dissipated, the more aggressive the sharks became.

Another plane flew directly over head about 1:00 am. Jess didn't make the slightest effort to attract attention, it wouldn't have done any good. How could the pilot see him, when all he could see of the plane was a dark outline and its navigational lights.

Captain McVay did manage to fire off a star shell, as did Redmayne's group. For some unknown reason, not only did the plane not see the shell, but neither did any of the other groups of survivors see the shell of another group.

Frustration and depression were taking a firm grip on many of the men in the water. The biggest question they kept asking themselves was, "how could a capital battleship of the United States Navy go so long, not being missed by somebody?"

Another serious threat was beginning to build, a threat that as much or more than any of the others could spell doom for many of the struggling survivors. This threat was the inevitable sapping of strength and will of the courageous leaders; leaders like Doctor Haynes, Lt. Redmayne, and Captain McVay.

Many of those in the water owed the fact that they were still alive to the foresight and courage of these men. But as they weakened, their ability to retain calm and order was diminishing.

CHAPTER THIRTY-SIX
August 1, 1945
05:00
5:00 AM

Beckler held his feeble arm up to the light of the early morning sky. He had almost given up on the idea of surviving this ordeal sometime yesterday. As it was now 05:00, he had been in the water three full days. Somewhere between the tropical heat of the day, the blinding sun, and the cool of the night, he calculated that he had really died, only his soul forgot to mention it to his body.

He was beginning to make a game of it, guessing when he would actually die. He would guess one time, and keep rechecking his watch to see just how long he had left. When that time would slowly pass, he would make another guess and wait for it to come.

In the last seventy-two hours he had experienced all the emotional mood swings—guilt for having brought his men here, especially Millie, knowing for sure that they must surely all be dead, deep sorrow for having lost his best friend, and all the others, self-pity and grave loneliness, as he felt that there wasn't anyone in the entire world that knew he was out here slowly dying; and for never being able to see Becky again.

He had also known fear, plenty of it, but fear didn't bother him anymore. It was as though fear didn't waste its time on worthless causes, for as soon as Beckler had given up on life, fear deserted him.

Then there was the pain that hung with him no matter what. Even the smallest cuts and scrapes he had had when he leaped from the sub, had now become large open sores known as salt-water ulcers. His wrists had swollen and started seeping pus, as did all the other small breaks in his flesh.

Added to that torment was a severe case of sunburn, as he was swimming with no shirt, no hat, and even his pants had been lost to a close brush with a shark. The only protection he had were his shorts, which, during the brightest parts of the day, he would soak before placing them over his head.

The shark must not have been very hungry. It had spent the better part of an hour just swimming around Beckler in a lazy circle. Once in a while it cut in close, just enough to keep Beckler in terror. Finally it must have grown tired of the game and with a sudden splash of its tail, it darted directly towards him. Beckler waited until the last moment to do anything. Then just as the shark came upon him, he rolled off the pants to safety. The shark took the pants in its razor-sharp teeth and quickly headed towards the ocean depths. Beckler found himself alive, for that he was grateful, but now he found himself without any kind of floatation device. He was truly alone upon a vast ocean.

The thing he feared the most was losing his eyesight from the burning of the retina, caused by the bright sun being reflected off the water directly into his eyes. Closing his eyes during most of the day, did little to help prevent this, as the reflection was so bright as to actually be able to blind a person even with the eyes closed.

Luckily for him, he had never cared for having his underwear tight, and his shorts now proved large enough to shield both his head and his eyes at the same time.

By now he lacked enough saliva to even swallow. The urge to drink of the sea water he was floating in was great, but somehoe his common sense had thus far prevailed. Drinking salt water would mean certain doom.

The morning sun was slowly climbing back into the sky. With it came the torment of roasting underneath its burning rays. Gene and the others were doing as much as they could for both Louey and O'Dell, but since they themselves were also suffering from exhaustion, thirst, hunger, and exposure, their help was precious little.

O'Dell had started to become delirious the first day, now after three days in the water, he was becoming more than anyone could handle. He had started ignoring their warning about drinking the water. At one moment he would be telling them about a fresh water stream just below the surface, or that the KING was right below them, and that he had gone down to it and had several large glasses of ice water, or ice cream from its cooler. The men knew he was going insane, but they were dying of thirst, and it did sound so tempting; still, they refrained from following suit. The next moment he would be vomiting violently. Gene realized that it was only a matter of time before O'Dell would be dead.

Beckler spotted a dorsal fin in the distance; suddenly his will to live returned. Cautiously, he began to swim away from it, being ever so careful to not make any more motion than was absolutely necessary to propel himself away from it. Then another fin appeared, and another. Soon there were many, and they appeared to be rapidly gaining on him. He could feel his heart pounding up in his throat as the adrenaline coursed through his veins.

One of the sharks turned sharply, giving Beckler a profile view of its curved, hook fin. They weren't sharks after all, rather a school of dolphins! Playfully they raced along side of Beckler, as he reached out his hand and felt their satiny wet skin. It was as if they sensed his need of help, as they playfully darted in and out around him. Several slowly came up to him and nudged him with their snout. Then as if to say, "hang on," one came up along side, stopped for a moment, long enough for Beckler to take a grip of the dorsal fin, before it raced off through the shimmering water of the Pacific.

Beckler had no idea of how fast he was traveling, only that he seemed to be constantly swallowing water as it splashed over the back of the dolphin and into his face. He could feel the water slapping against his body as he skied along the surface on his belly, but he felt no pain, only the exuberant sensation of enjoying a very special bonding beteween a man and one of God's most marvelous creations.

When the dolphin decided that it had had enough it slowed down, almost to a stop, before plunging downward. Beckler sensed what it seemed to be saying, as it slowed, he released it, and watched it dive away from him, only to break the surface and sail twice its entire body length into the air before splashing back down and racing away.

"Thanks for the lift!" Beckler called out after it, feeling sorry to see it go, but grateful for the moment it shared.

Then it, and the others, were gone. Everything was as before, as if the dolphins had never been. Beckler was sure he was losing his mind. Had he really hitched a ride from a dolphin, or was his mind losing a grip on reality? Suddenly he wasn't sure.

He slowly turned in a circle, and once again surveyed the enormous expanse of ocean all around him. He was alone again; maybe he had always been? If this is how it's going to be going insane, is it all that bad? Whether the dolphins were real or imagined, he had enjoyed the feeling. Possibly going mad was not all that bad!

Beckler hadn't heard it at first, then as the drone of an aircraft engine grew louder, he began to search the blazing sky in search of the source of that sound.

As the sound grew nearer, he panned the heavens with growing panic. There it was, high above him! No way to know if it was American or Japanese. At the moment, he didn't care! It was indeed a plane! The first sign of another human being he had seen in three days!

He shouted as best he could with parched mouth, flailed his arms, but to no avail. The plane was far too high up to see him, even if the pilot was looking right at him!

A tidal wave of self-pity engulfed him. It had taken three days for any chance at rescue to come even this close to him; his chances were dying out along with the sound of the plane!

He followed the tiny speck as it grew smaller. When it was gone his eyes fell to the sea in the direction it had flown. What was that?! There was something in the water just ahead! He couldn't be sure; it looked like a ball, or a head! Suddenly he saw another, then several; maybe his crew was alive after all!

Gene was doing everything he could think of to try and save O'Dell from himself. For a fleeting moment there seemed to be hope as the plane flew overhead, and now that it was gone, the only thing the men felt was more despair. With tired eyes, Gene looked away from the group, his mind filled with anguish, more for the others than himself. This was an awful way to die.

Then, he saw what appeared to be a man swimming towards them! He thought that he was hallucinating; how could a man be swimming towards them out here, in the middle of an ocean? He blinked his eyes, the man was still there!

"Hey, guys, you see something out there?" he asked in a choked voice.

"Where?" Boss, Irish, and Scotty asked in unison.

"Right there!" Gene replied, pointing towards Beckler, who by now was close enough to faintly pick out their features.

"Sweet mother of Jesus," Scotty sighed. "if that don't beat it all."

"It's the Captain!" Boss shouted as he and Scotty started to swim out to meet Beckler.

Beckler seemed to find a renewed source of strength in being with what remained of his crew. He told of his ordeal, and listened to theirs. He had little effect on O'Dell, but Louey was grateful to see him. Pete looked to be far older now than when Beckler had last seen him, but he refused to take leave of caring for his black friend.

"He'd have taken care of me, if the roles were reversed!" Pete replied, when Beckler told him to take a breather.

No one doubted that the large strong black and the small, frail looking Jew were of kindred souls, both tender and caring, held together with the strong twine of the highest moral character. Two saintly beings cast together in the pits of hell.

Shortly before sundown, another shark appeared. This one didn't spend much time circling. After two or three passes, it turned and came straight for the group. Beckler and Scotty tried to fend it off. It turned sharply and headed straight for Louey and Pete. Before Louey could react, Pete pushed him out of the monsters way and attempted to kick at the beast. Suddenly Pete was jerked below the water. He popped back to the surface, not realizing at first, as he was in a state of shock, that the shark had taken off his left leg, just below the knee. Soon there was a sea of red bloody water all around Pete.

O'Dell's mind had snapped. Upon seeing the blood, he quickly turned and started to swim with all his might away from the others, splashing and kicking as he went. He had only gone a short distance when the shark returned to surface and raced after him.

"Help. Please God. Help me!" he cried out in anguish when he saw the monster coming after him. The shark's head raised slightly up out of the water, so as to line its open jaws with the water's surface. O'Dell could see the several rows of teeth that lined the outer edges of the upper jaw as the shark closed in. Then in one terrifying instant, there was an ear-shattering scream, a violent splash, as the monster took its meal to the depths, chewing and tearing as it went.

On the surface, air bubbles broke to the surface mixed with blood and bits and pieces of O'Dell's flesh, as if a boiling, bloody stew was brewing in a witch's caldron.

Beckler and the others watched in silent terror as Louey seemed to sense how badly Pete now needed him. While the others had turned away for that moment, Louey reached out to offer help to his dear friend. The blood was swirling around them in the swell, and Louey knew he would have to stop the bleeding. Having little else with which to fashion a tourniquet, Louey reached down and ripped the elastic waistband from his shorts, tightly wrapping it around the leg just above the knee. Inspecting the damage, Louey's heart sank. The crude tourniquet was doing the job for the moment. Prior to its application, blood was spurting out of the torn veins that dangled from the severed leg. Now the flow of blood was halted, not completely, but enough to give Pete a few more hours of life. If rescue came soon, he might have a chance; if not, well, maybe none of them would survive.

As the others turned their attention back towards Pete, it was the first time they realized how badly he had been hurt. It had happened so fast. All realized how slim the chance of Pete surviving. If the blood didn't attract other sharks, he would probably die of blood loss—but attract other sharks it did.

True to form, Pete was not going to be the reason for his friends being attacked by sharks. He silently waited, bearing the terrible pain that burned at his leg. The only way he kept from screaming out was by biting his lip, which he did until it drew blood.

As the others kept a close eye on the sharks, Pete slowly started to let himself drift away from the others, until Louey spotted him, already some distance away.

"Ah man, what you doin'?" Louey called out. "Don't do it!"

Beckler quickly turned around, and one look into old Pete's eyes told him what he was planning to do.

"Don't come after me," Pete calmly warned. "The way I'm bleeding, they'll never leave you alone! Now slowly start to move away. I'll keep their attention. Now please go!"

There was nothing they could do, the sharks had already started to swim in circles around Pete, ignoring the others. For some unknown reason, it took some time for the sharks to finally move in for the kill. When one started to go for Pete, they all did. Not one scream, or even the slightest uttering, was heard from Pete. He faced his death with all the dignity and honor that he had lived by.

The others turned away, unable to witness the carnage of the feeding frenzy the sharks were making of their dear, brave friend. The final six survivors of the URSHEL KING slowly swam away unmolested; the sharks seemed content with what they had. Pete's sacrificing his life had spared theirs.

CHAPTER THIRTY-SEVEN
August 1, 1945
23:40
11:40 PM

Jess had never been so scared in his entire life. It seemed so long ago, the INDIANAPOLIS, the States, everything. There had been hope, that first day in the water. Surely the Navy would be looking for them, but there was no sign of rescue yet.

To make matters worse, several planes had been spotted, flying directly over their heads, and yet, here they were.

He was bitter, frustrated, hungry, thirsty, and scared. He wasn't afraid of dying, that would be the easy part. He was afraid of being eaten by sharks, afraid of slowly dying out here floating in this god-damn ocean. He was afraid of going to sleep. He was afraid of not going to sleep.

Sleep offered the only release of the torment, the hunger and thirst, and yes, the only release from the fear. But sleep was filled with nightmares, as it would only come in small doses. Every time he would doze off, something happened.

He had dozed off for only a short time, when someone tapped him on the face. Jess bolted out of his sleep just as he was tapped again. It had not been a shipmate, at least not a shipmate he could recognize.

There was no way of telling how many sharks had fed off the corpse. For some reason, they had not eaten that much of it. One arm, one leg and much of the torso had been roughly chewed away. What remained was a hideously deformed, bloating specter.

During Jess's sleep, the corpse had drifted over and bumped into him. The first thing Jess saw when he snapped awake was the torn and whitish face of the corpse, with its lone remaining eye floating out of the hollow socket, just inches from his own face.

Another time he was trying to sleep when suddenly a shrill scream pierced the darkness, soon joined by other screams and cries of anguish. Moments later all was quiet again.

This would be repeated often in a night. Jess was never really sure of what was taking place, as there were many terrifying things that happened at night, only one of which, was the sharks. Sometimes, half-crazed men would suddenly become convinced that there were Japanese among the survivors. These men would lash out and strike death upon their own shipmates.

Sometime during the day before, Jess had seen a friend of his from the INDY swimming by himself away from the large group of men. Jess had been afraid that Don was about to do something foolish like dive beneath the waves in hopes of reaching the INDY and drinking from her fountain. Many men had claimed that the ship was just below the surface, and that they had been there and had had their fill of water and even iced tea from the galley before returning to the surface again.

Jess realized that these men had probably been drinking seawater and would soon die from it.

After swimming out towards Don, Jess was puzzled by the way his friend kept swimming away from him.

"Are you okay, Don?" Jess called out to him.

"I'm doing alright," the hoarse voice of his friend slowly replied. "Just keep your distance."

"What's wrong with you?"

"I want to live!"

"So do I," Jess confirmed, perplexed by Don's actions.

"You been down to the ship?" Don questioned.

"No, have you?" Jess suddenly became a little leery of his friend's condition.

"Hell no!" Don snapped back. "But a bunch of those stupid asses are tryin' it. The sea, the sharks, and the sun are driving them mad, I tell you. They'll kill themselves and you if you don't watch 'em!"

"What do you mean they'll kill me?"

"They'll think you're a Jap," Don flatly stated. "They'll think you're a Jap spy, and tear you to pieces. I've seen it happen!"

"What did you see?" Jess questioned, not believing what he was hearing.

"Last night, I saw one poor bastard beat and cut to shreds by a bunch of our own shipmates. They had gone mad, and someone said he was a Japanese spy. That was all it took. They attacked him quicker than any shark could have!"

"Are you sure?"

"Damn right, I'm sure!" Don quickly snapped back. "Why do you think I'm keeping my distance? I'm not going to let them bastards slaughter me!"

"But aren't you afraid of sharks, out here by yourself?" Jess asked.

"Some," Don pondered. "But out here, all I have to worry about is sharks. With them I have sharks and them to worry about!"

Jess had floated along near Don most of the day, deciding that what he said made sense. Slowly, they had drifted apart, and Jess could no longer be sure which bobbing head was that of Don's, if any.

There had been almost two thousand men aboard the INDY, now from what Jess could see, maybe only a hundred or so remained. Jess tried to remember faces, voices, laughs, anything that would remind him of his friends from the ship. He tried, but nothing came. It was as if his friends had never existed. It was as though the ship had never existed. At times it was as though he was on the outside looking in. Removed from this time and place, existing, yet not existing.

These thoughts served to pass time, take his mind off his pain and torment. But the thoughts also scared the hell out of him. Was he going mad like those others? Would he soon visit the INDY? Would he soon go from one statistic to another, from a survivor to a victim? Would any of the living ever be rescued?

Another high flying aircraft droned on across the heavens. Its navigational lights were either off, or it was flying too high for them to be seen.

"If only I had a flare gun," Jess thought out loud, knowing full well that the plane was probably too high to even see a flare, unless the pilot was looking down at that moment.

It seemed so ironic; rescue was only two miles or so away, straight up! Meanwhile, a great number of American fighting men were dying, not by enemy hands, but by neglect. The thought infuriated him.

"Why haven't we been missed? Where do they think a capital ship could have gone? Why doesn't somebody do something?" Jess cried towards the starry sky.

The only reply was the continued glow of the stars' light. Everything was going on without the INDY or her crew. That cold fact alone made death seem so near.

The only comfort one could find in the night was the absence of the burning sun.

The time of day meant little to the sharks; they attacked, withdrew, and attacked again, day or night. The fear of being attacked and devoured by those monsters was constant. Jess could remember a time when seeing a fin while swimming in the water, no matter how far away, would have filled him with panic. Now he could see a dorsal fin almost all the time. Luckily they were from some distance, and all he felt was pity for the poor soul that would die soon.

The first rays of dawn started filling the sky with light. The distance between Jess and the large group had become greater than he wanted it to become. He had to stay close enough to be able to reach them quickly if they were spotted and rescued. Yet he wanted to remain alone, away from the danger of being attacked by the group.

Looking out over the span of ocean between himself and the group, Jess was horrified by what he saw. It reminded him of when his mother used to make home-made chicken soup. The surface of the water was littered with bits and pieces of flesh that floated in a thin layer of what appeared to be animal grease.

Not wanting to swim through it, but having little choice, Jess slowly made his way through the sickening swells. Twice, some caring soul would swim out to him and offer to bring him into the fold. Twice, Jess politely declined. He was careful not to offend them, but assured them that he could do it on his own.

Jess had suffered no injuries getting off the stricken INDY. But the relentless sun had blistered his neck and shoulders. Those sores were now becoming infected by the seawater. Saltwater blisters; a painful infliction, but one that could be endured. At least he wasn't covered with burns like so many of the others.

He watched members of the large group continue to take turns at holding the more badly burned victims that miraculously remained alive up out of the water as much as they could. But the ones doing the holding were exhausted.

Within himself, Jess felt a twang of guilt for not joining them in their efforts. He wanted to, yet the words of advice from Don filled him with doubts.

As each day wore on, there were consistently fewer to hold up. Injuries, sharks, and attrition were taking their tolls on both the ones being held aloft, and those doing the holding.

As each would succumb to the torment and die, those holding them would release them and allow the body to float away, until some shark devoured the remains.

Like the day before, and the day before that, the sun was steadily climbing as hot as ever. As he had spent the night hoping for daylight, Jess would spend the day hoping for nightfall. It was the only way he knew how to survive. If he could live to see nightfall, maybe rescue would come. At night he lived for daylight that might bring his deliverance.

CHAPTER THIRTY-EIGHT
August 2, 1945
03:00
3:00 AM

Losing Pete had proven too much for Louey. Shortly after midnight, he had lost consciousness. First Beckler took a turn at towing him along, then Gene. They did not know where they were going, only that they were going somewhere hopefully away from where the sharks were.

Each man was keeping his thoughts to himself for the most part. Occasionally someone would shout that they saw a fin, only to have it turn out to be a swell in the water rolling to a crest, then breaking over into a white cap.

Each, in their own mind, at one time or another, envied Louey. He was beyond caring. Death no longer frightened him, not that it had scared him much before, but if it came to him now, he wouldn't even be aware of it. That was truly what each man was secretly longing for. It was rapidly becoming not a question of 'if', but of 'when' they would die, and each wished for the easiest death possible for himself, desperately trying to forget the awful way Pete met his.

As the hours passed, Beckler looked at his watch. The bright fingers of light reached out over the darkened sea to pave the way for the sun to follow. It was 05:30. They had been in the water for ninety-six and one half hours! Louey started to come back around, but unlike his usual self, he was quite talkative

193

and jovial. The change in character alarmed the men. They sensed his death was imminent.

As the night gave way to morning, Louey was beginning to slip. At times Louey would put up a slight struggle to be let go, to drift, due however to his depleted condition, his gestures were weak, and he finally resigned himself to being towed along. By seven he grew quiet.

Louey made several more attempts to speak but was unable. He finally closed his eyes and tried to rest. Speech among the others was also kept to a minimum. It was simply too painful to do otherwise.

By nine, the sun was bright and seemed hotter than ever before, each man dreading another day of baking heat and blinding light. Whatever shreds of clothing they had left were used to cover their heads, and shield their eyes.

It didn't really matter that they were swimming along blindfolded; they had no idea of where they were or where they were going anyway. It seemed the wiser choice to protect their eyes from the blinding glare of the sun off the water than to look out into infinity at nothing but expanse of ocean.

On rare occasions, Beckler would lift the edge of his shorts long enough to sneak a quick glance ahead. Usually finding nothing, he replaced the cover and swam on. This time that was not to be the case. A small speck on the distant horizon, filled him with hope and excitement.

"A SHIP! A GODDAMN SHIP!" He attempted to scream, only to have it come out as a hoarse raspy squeak.

Instantly, every single man uncovered their face and peered into the distance. It was there. No one could tell what it was, but there was indeed something out there. Maybe, just maybe, they would be rescued after all, but they weren't aboard it yet. The ship, island, or whatever it was, was still a great distance away.

"What if they don't see us?" Boss asked.

"What if they do, and they're Japanese?" Scotty added.

"Does it matter?" Beckler countered. "If they don't see us, we're dead. If they are Japanese, they might throw us into a prisoner-of-war camp, or worse they might shoot us, in which case we're no worse off than if they hadn't seen us."

"They could be American," Irish stated.

"Not with our luck," Gene quipped.

"Look," Beckler continued. "if we stay in the water another day, we'll probably all be dead. If they shoot us, what the hell, all they can take from us is a few damn hours of misery. I say that no matter what kind of vessel it is, we have to do our best to get its attention."

"Could be an island," Gene said flatly.

"That it could," Beckler argreed. "I guess time will tell. I just hope that it is a ship, cause if it's an island, it could be two days away from here! Those prospects don't appeal to me at all!"

An hour passed before they were sure that the object was indeed a ship. As it appeared to be moving towards them, it took longer for them to be able to make out the configuration of its upper decks. It appeared to be a coastal patrol boat. Their fears confirmed, the small destroyer heading towards them was definitely JAPANESE!

As the ship came close enough for the men in the water to see the sailors working on the ship's deck, Beckler took a deep breath and turned to the others.
"Well men it's now or never."
"Aye, Captain!" Scotty agreed, as the others nodded. Everyone except Louey started waving their arms and trying their best to scream towards the ship.
They knew that their efforts had been successful when they saw a sailor working on the forepeak of the vessel stop what he was doing, stare out at them for a moment, before shouting and pointing in their direction. Soon an alarm was sounded aboard the ship, and it appeared to be losing way.
Japanese sailors ran to the deck railing and started pointing and shouting. Soon others appeared, armed with rifles aimed towards Beckler and his men, while, towards the stern of the ship, a lifeboat was being readied for lowering.
"Well Dad," Gene calmly said, "how would you like to call this one? Will they send that boat for us? Or will they shoot us?"
"Too close to call," Beckler replied. "They seem to be preparing to do both. Let's just hope that both parties are acting on orders. If they are, I'd say that so long as we don't do something stupid, like try to attack their ship with our bare hands or something, the ones in the boat will get us—if we do, the ones with the rifles get us."
"Could be," Scotty quipped, "that those bastards are pretty poor shots and they aim to get a wee bit closer before they waste any bullets on the likes of us."
"Oh shit," Gene sighed, shaking his head.
"There's a thought that you could have kept to yourself," Beckler said, while forcing a tight lipped smile.

The boat was finally in the water. Its motor coughed to a smokey start, then roared to life as the boat turned in a sweeping arc and curved in towards them. Standing in the bow on the boat, two sailors armed with their rifles aimed directly at the men.
"Captain, you don't suppose . . . ?" Irish started to say.
"No, I don't suppose!" Beckler quickly replied. "Just don't do anything to give them cause. They won't shoot unless they feel threatened."
One of the Japanese towards the rear of the boat, started to yell something at them. Beckler only caught part of what the Japanese were trying to tell them. Frustrated by the inaction on the part of the Americans, the Japanese standing

the rear of the boat started gesturing with his hand, that he wanted them to swim over to the boat.

"I'll go first," Beckler whispered, as he moved towards the boat with Louey in tow, as the others followed cautiously.

Beckler neared the side of the boat, turned slightly as to bring Louey alongside first. The Japanese sailor bent over the edge and looked down at the unconscious black American. He turned and looked over towards the ship for a moment before shouting some orders out in Japanese.

Beckler wasn't sure what had just taken place, but he guessed that the man in the boat had been ordered to return with any and all persons in the water. Upon seeing Louey, he had second thoughts about carrying out those orders. Beckler further guessed that the purpose for looking back towards the ship was to see if the Captain would be able to see what was going on. There was little doubt that Louey would have been left for dead if the man in the boat had his way.

Follow the orders the small fat man in the boat, who appeared to be in charge, had shouted; several sailors reached out and roughly hauled Louey's huge form over the gunwale, and laid him in the bottom of the boat, followed closely by Beckler and the others, one by one.

As soon as the last man was pulled aboard, the boat turned and sped back towards the mother ship, where it slowed to a halt underneath the swaying falls of the davits from where it had come. Soon, the cables were attached and the boat was hauled up even with the deck, where the Americans were taken off and led forward. Louey was placed on a litter and carried forward as well.

At the base of the ship's superstructure, amidship, they were put in line, with Louey laid on the deck next to them. Several minutes went by before the Japanese captain strode up in his neatly pressed uniform, burdened with an impressive number of ribbons and medals.

The Japanese captain was a small framed man of about five feet, six inches, and somewhere around one hundred and forty-five pounds. He had a stern but somehow friendly-looking face. He didn't speak at first. Instead, he slowly paced back and forth in front of the Americans, as if to study them. Then he turned to the short fat one from the boat and barked an order to summon the ship's doctor. The fat one stiffened, bowed, then hurried away. Next he turned to the Japanese officer and quietly said in Japanese that the black one needed attention right away, while pointing towards Louey.

The second officer bowed then, pointing to Louey, said something to the two sailors that had been carrying the litter. They picked it up and started to carry it away.

"Where are you taking him?" Beckler questioned, which made the Japanese captain's eye brows lift.

"So you are the captain of these men?" the Japanese Captain asked, sounding more like a statement than a question, in surprisingly proper English.

"No," Gene quickly interrupted, as he had done before, "we just want to know what is to become of our friend."

"We will do all we can for your friend, I assure you, we are only taking him to our ship's hospital," the captain replied. "Are you the captain then?"

"Naw, I'm just a misplaced mechanic," Gene calmly replied. "All the officers died when our ship's bridge was hit by one of your kamikazi pilots."

"I see," the Captain said, as he continued pacing back and forth in front of them, studying their faces for anything that could answer his questions, "What was the name of your ship?"

"The KING." Scotty answered.

"The URSHEL KING?" the Japanese Captain questioned.

"Aye, that be the one," Scotty surrendered.

"Ah, so the KING was sunk?!" The Captain said, as if the KING had been the largest threat to the Empire.

The way that he had said it, and the fact that he knew the ship's name, had caused an uneasy feeling in Beckler. He remembered that night on the sub; they too seemed pleased to hear that the name of the ship that they had sunk was the KING. Something was afoul. Why would the name of an old tramp steamer mean anything to the Japanese?

The look of frustration was showing on Beckler's face, the Japanese Captain noticed it, but said nothing. Instead, he went on with his line of questioning.

"When and how was your ship sunk?"

"She was finally done in by one of your I-class subs." Scotty answered.

"Four days ago." Gene added.

"Then you have been in the water for four days?" The Captain seemed shocked.

"That's right." Gene said.

"How many of you got off the ship? And where are the others?" The Japanese Captain asked showing genuine concern.

"There are no others," Beckler stated angrily. "Only fourteen men made it off the KING, six were killed by the crew on the sub, two others were killed by sharks while in the water."

"I see," the Captain said, before giving some orders in Japanese to the Japanese sailors standing guard over the Americans. "These men will see to your needs; while on this vessel of the Imperial Navy, you will not be mistreated. However, I should caution you, that you are prisoners of war, and will be treated as such. Do as you are told, when you are told, and nothing will happen to you. Is that clear?"

The Americans nodded, then were led below.

CHAPTER THIRTY-NINE
August 2, 1945
08:00
8:00 AM

Loneliness and desperation filled Jess's very being. Thirst, hunger, and pain from saltwater ulcers tormented his frail body to no end. He had given up all hope; no one was going to rescue them from their living hell. Half of the men that had survived the sinking of the INDY, were now dead. With each passing hour that death toll rose. The only thing that had subsided was fear. Jess no longer felt fear.

Jess watched in detached indifference as sharks fed on his friends. He felt nothing as a human body part floated past, just inches from him. Even the good doctor was now exhauted. One by one, they would all die. It no longer mattered. Death was no longer something one would fight, you only waited your turn.

There was no longer a large group; without the doctor's energy and others like him to keep the men together, they soon dispersed and, like Don and Jess, found themselves floating more or less by themselves.

Jess had stayed off by himself since he had talked with Don, but always managed to stay within range of Doctor Haynes' group. At least until the doctor collapsed from exhaustion. Now he drifted farther and farther away, not that it mattered.

Twice since sun up, sharks had passed within twenty feet of Jess, and yet not one made any attempt to feed on him. The only reason Jess could think of, was that with there being so many dead floating around, the sharks had plenty to eat without bothering the living. Whatever the reason, even the sharks had no interest in him.

Three hundred miles to the south-east, another Ventura bomber lifted off the runway and made for its assigned search and destroy sector. The bomber's mission was simple and direct. Search out enemy submarines, report them first, then attack.

The pilot of this bomber was a cocky young flyer by the name of Wilbur Gwinn. Gwinn had a stroke of bad luck in the take-off. The dead weight attached to the metal antenna sticking out the aft of the plane had been dislodged and fell off. The purpose of this antenna was to enable the flight crew to affix their position by means of radio signals. Without this weight, the antenna whipped in the wind so much as to be rendered useless.

Instead of returning to base for repairs, Gwinn decided to fly by the seat of his pants. So long as visibility remained good, he should be able to find his way home again.

After having been in the air for almost two hours and not having sighted anything, Gwinn decided to try and fix the antenna. After crawling through the fuselage to the rear of the plane, Gwinn studied the antenna and tried to think of ways to anchor it down. For some reason, his eyes were drawn downward towards the sea, some three thousand feet below.

"Jackpot," Gwinn smiled, as he noticed a thin trail of oil on the water. For the moment, he forgot about the antenna and quickly returned to his forward seat. After pointing the slick out to his crew, Gwinn took the twin engine bomber down to nine hundred feet and started to follow the trail. The longer the trail went on, the more he got a gut feeling that this was no submarine he was trailing. There had to have been a major ship sunk in this area. No sub carries this much oil, to create a slick of this size.

Jess could faintly hear the approach of the Ventura, but it didn't register. He simply floated on, his hands over his face in an effort to protect his eyes from the painful glare of the sun. The flesh on the back side of his hands was severely sunburned and blistered. Luckily his shoulders and the top of his head had avoided the same problem, due to the layer of oil that coated him and shielded the flesh from the burning rays of the merciless sun. As for his hands, they felt numb. It was becoming progressively harder to flex his fingers as the skin grew tighter and tighter. Even in all that water, the sun was effectively evaporating all the fluids from his hands.

The drone grew to the point where it was now a steady roar. Slowly, Jess took his hands from his eyes and blankly watched the American bomber fly by. Again, Jess made no effort to signal it. This time however, it was not because it wouldn't have done any good; he simply didn't have the strength to do so.

As quickly as the bomber had come, it was gone. It mattered not. It was becoming difficult for Jess to define reality. He could not be certain that a bomber had just flown by. He could no longer be certain of anything, much less care.

Gwinn could not believe his eyes; he had just seen thirty odd men in the water, covered with oil! Who were they? Where did they come from? Why hadn't there been any reports of a vessel sinking in this area?

The Message was quickly sent back to base:
>Have THIRTY MEN in water
>Doing what I can
>Location . . .

After getting an affirmative reply from base, Gwinn decided to continue following the oil slick. After flying for more than twenty more miles, Gwinn estimated that the number of men in the water was over one hundred and fifty.

Whatever ship had gone down, it was a major vessel. He had to get a rescue ship enroute as soon as possible. It was the broken antenna's turn to come back to haunt him. The first location reported was done by dead reckoning, and could be as much as fifty miles off course. The antenna had to be repaired, and repaired now!

Gwinn turned the controls over to his co-pilot and returned to the tail of the Ventura in an effort to repair the whipping metal shaft. Finding little else to use, he affixed a section of rubber hose to the end of the shaft, then fed it back out the rear of the plane. Calling out for the navigator to check it, while he himself prayed that it would work. His prayers were answered; it worked like a charm!

There was no time to waste; Gwinn was now certain that the men in the water were American sailors! The second message was sent back to base one and a half hour after the first:
>SEND HELP
>have counted 1-5-0 men
>in water.
>Need surface vessel ASAP
>location . . .

After a short pause, the radio sprang back to life with the base's response:
>STAY put
>PBY on way

Should arrive on scene
Fifteen hundred

Many of the men in the water waved and splashed their arms in hopes of getting this pilot's attention. When the bomber flew on, they lost all hope. They knew with all certainty that they would die within hours. Being spotted by that plane was their last hope.

There had been many back at Command that treated the sighting with little more than casual interest. It was believed that the survivors spotted in the water must surely belong to a Japanese submarine, so why rush? Why rush rescue teams out into the area for a handful of enemy sailors? It could be a trap.

As soon as the second message was received, all hell broke loose! How could there be one hundred and fifty men in the water? Who were they? There were no reports of destroyed enemy craft large enough to crew that many! Then the cold fingers of reality began to settle in. It had to be one of ours! But which one?

Quickly, orders were dispatched, sending rescue vessels enroute to the scene. A destroyer escort had already been rerouted toward the area, now two destroyers were also dispatched. Sadly, it would take until midnight for the escort to make it and until 03:00 for one of the destroyers, with the other destroyer not arriving until 04:00.

After scouting the area, Gwinn returned and passed over the men a second time. For those who had an hour ago given up all hope, this gesture was a godsend. For most, it gave them the strength and will to survive a little while longer. They had been seen, rescue would, this time, be not far behind.

The second pass of the Ventura bomber had little effect on Jess. With swollen eyes, and feeble breathing, he simply watched a blurry vision of the plane as it passed overhead. Time for Jess was quickly running out.

Gwinn's commanding officer had tried to get the Dumbo in the air sooner, but after a phone call failed to get the proper response, he personally drove over there and kicked the right tails to get the blasted thing in the air.

After returning to his base, the commanding officer, George Atteberry, fitted up, and took off in a Ventura himself towards the last radioed position. Gwinn's fuel supply was running low. Atteberry knew this. Yet he didn't want to leave those poor devils in the water without the moral support of a spotter plane over their heads.

In the interim, an enormous transport seaplane, known as a PBM, who had been flying in that direction, decided to lend a hand with supplies and moral support. After the PBM dropped all the supplies it could spare, it hung around until it too, had just enough fuel to reach its destination. By this time Atteberry had arrived on the scene and relieved Gwinn and the PBM.

For the survivors of Doctor Haynes group, life had just gotten a lot better. Gwinn had tossed everything that would float down to them. Along with the rubber rafts, was fresh water, which the good doctor carefully meted out to ensure each man would at least get a small dose of the life-giving substance. Also, emergency medical supplies, and of all things, a sunbonnet of sorts. It was these bonnets that seemed to be the most highly prized, next to the fresh water of course. The bonnets gave protection from the deadly sun.

For the first time in four days, many of the survivors from this large group were able to get out of the water. Small ten-man rafts suddenly had thirty or more men packed into them.

Like the PBM and Gwinn before him had done, Atteberry dropped all the emergency supplies he had to the survivors below as soon as he arrived. Doctor Haynes group had been the unfortunate ones, they lacked even a floater net for protection until Gwinn spotted them. Now they had become the fortunate group; they were the recipients of the windfall from the sky.

As each group was certain that it and it alone were the only survivors of the INDY, the other two groups, Captain McVay's and Redmayne's, became confused and irritated by the sight of the planes keeping well to the south.

"What are those idiots doing?" one man croaked through parched lips, echoing the sentiments of all.

As more planes arrived on the scene, Redmayne's group, which was considerably larger than McVay's, was also spotted. Supplies and first-aid were accordingly dropped to this group as well.

Jess could faintly hear the joyous voices of his shipmates, but it all seemed so far away, so unreal. His vision was completely blurred, so he was unable to comprehend what was happening. His mind had become muddled with pain and exhaustion. He didn't become afraid, thinking that they had started killing each other again. He didn't think that rescue was finally at hand. In fact, he didn't think anything...nothing. It was as though his mind had reached the point of no return. The madness of it all, the long and agonizing torment, the hopelessness had worked against him for so long. His only release was for his mind to shut it out, to turn off, and that it had seemingly done quite efficiently. Salvation was at hand, and Jess couldn't even sense it!

At last the first Dumbo had arrived, and landed in the water. Shortly thereafter the second Dumbo appeared and also landed. The first Dumbo had been quite efficient in scooping up survivors, the second was not having the same luck. The task of maneuvering through the survivors without runnng over them had been difficult enough during the day, but as darkness fell it became almost impossible.

Finally around 20:00 hours, the searchlight of the escort could be seen as it had been directed towards the heavens to signal those in the water that help was near.

After ninety-six hours in the water, the first survivor of the INDIANAPOLIS was pulled aboard the Destroyer Escort DOYLE, at roughly thirty minutes past midnight.

Although Jesse had been keeping rather close to the group led by Doctor Haynes, he remained in the water while others all around him were being pulled to safety. Not that it mattered to Jess; unconsciousness had freed him from the agony.

CHAPTER FORTY
August 4, 1945
18:45
6:45 PM

Becky looked so beautiful as she strolled along with the evening sun reflecting off her auburn hair. Beckler couldn't believe his good fortune. He had always loved Krape Park as a kid growing up in Freeport. Now here he was again, sitting on the banks of Yellow Creek fishing for catfish. And watching the woman he loved walk along the river in search of the perfect stones that would skip out across the water as she tossed them.

Twice, he had thought of informing her that that would scare away any fish. But decided that he enjoyed watching her more than he really wanted to fish anyway, so he let her go.

After growing tired of tossing stones, she came to his side and gently seated herself next to him. Wrapping her long slender arms around his shoulders she kissed his neck. He turned and was about to be the recipient of one of her sweet tender kisses, when something nudged him in the side. He tried to swat it away, only to have it happen again. This time it had worked. Beckler quickly sat upright, and tried to clear his mind.

As both his eyes and mind slowly started to focus, he realized that he was still aboard the Japanese destroyer. A feeling of loneliness crept up from a deep hole within him. He was bone tired, and had no idea of what time it was. He had been sleeping most of the last two days. He knew that much at least, because he had been awakened several times just long enough to eat some rice dish and drink water or tea, and notice how the sun was shining through the porthole.

Twice, the captain of this ship had come to visit with him. However, finding Beckler too tired to be of much company, he politely left, allowing Beckler to resume his sleeping.

"Captain Andrew Beckler, are you awake?" the soft voice asked.

"Yeah, yeah, I'm awake."

"You are Captain Beckler?"

"Yeah, I'm . . . " Beckler started before he realized that he had been tricked. "How did you know my name?"

"Why don't we talk about that over some tea in my cabin?" The Japanese captain offered, in a bow, while motioning with his hand towards the door.

Beckler didn't argue. He rose to his feet and followed the Captain out into the corridor and down the passageway, stopping at a door, then entering into the Captain's cabin.

"Please, be seated, Captain Beckler." The Japanese captain offered pointing to a small chair next to his desk, while he himself took a seat behind the desk.

"I do hope you like tea." He said as a steward entered with a tray containing a pot and two small cups.

"Yes, thank you. Tea is fine," Beckler replied, trying to return the kindness. "You speak better English than some of my crew did."

"I studied in the States, before the war."

"Oh, really? Where 'bouts?"

"The University of Wisconsin, at Madison."

"Really?" Beckler asked in surprise. "That's only sixty miles from where I grew up!"

"It's a small world, Captain." The Japanese officer said with a warm smile.

"Look, Captain, you know who I am. Who are you? Other than the captain of this ship?" Beckler asked.

"I'm Captain Ito Fujiamino," came the friendly reply. "I tell you what. While we're in private, just call me Ito."

"Ito, I'm Andy," Beckler replied, while offering his hand to his captor.

Ito didn't hesitate for a moment. He cupped Beckler's slightly larger hand within his own and smiled. Seeing how readily Ito had taken his hand, confirmed, in Beckler's mind, that Ito had indeed spent time in the States, as most orientals Beckler had met in the past were rather unaccustomed to shaking hands.

"Not that I don't enjoy the friendliness of the moment," Beckler started slowly, measuring his words, "but what was it you wished to see me about, and how did you learn my name and rank?"

"We learned of you from the Imperial Intelligence, and while you were asleep, we tested my theory of you being the captain, by calling you by your name. I didn't mean to trick you, but I wanted to be sure that my hunch was correct."

"I see."

"As for why I wished to see you, there are several reasons, the first of which, I fear, is rather sad news."

"Louey has died." Beckler guessed.

"Yes," Ito replied, carefully studying the emotional reaction of Beckler to the news. "I am truly sorry for your friend. There were so many injuries, internally, we just couldn't do enough on this ship. Our medical supplies are so few, and mostly outdated by American standards. Please believe me that we did our best; regretfully, it simply was not enough."

"I do believe you," Beckler quietly said. "I didn't think he had a chance of lasting as long as he did."

Ito said nothing.

"Living as long as he did showed what strong fiber he was made of."

Again Ito said nothing, only nodded his agreement.

"What will happen to his body?" Beckler questioned.

"What do you want me to do with it?"

"An honorable burial would be nice, but I suppose that would be too much to ask of the Imperial Navy."

"I believe I can arrange something for you." Ito surprisingly answered.

"Would tonight be too soon?"

"No," Beckler started, in an unmasked state of shock. "Tonight would be fine . . . Why are you doing this?"

"Why? Should I not because we are enemies?" Ito calmly replied. "You and I, Andy, are not true samurai, we lack the knowledge of hatred. We are just two men of different countries, each fighting a war we don't belong in. I am a simple fisherman, who, due to my experience and the extreme shortage of capable men, suddenly found myself in officer's training. Next thing I know I'm captain of this vessel. I'm simply a misplaced fisherman, who is saddened by any death, and who believes that any life is deserving of proper respect in the form of a honorable burial."

"I agree," Beckler said. "And as for your integrity, I thank you. You said that there were several things you wished to discuss, what was the second?"

Ito hesitated for a moment, as if to arrange the words in a less than direct manner, but after a few seconds went straight to the point.

"Why would the Americans use an old ship like the KING, to transport a shipment of V-2's?" Ito inquired.

"V-2's?" Beckler asked in surprise.

"Yes, German V-2 rockets. Was that not what you were carrying?"

"Why would we be carrying V-2's?" Beckler questioned.

"To allow you to utterly destroy our homeland as your country's propaganda statements have said," Ito reasoned.

"Look," Beckler flatly stated. "I don't know what it was that we were carrying, but it sure as hell wasn't any V-2 rockets!"

"If not rockets, what then?"

"You've got me there. Before I even got close enough to take a look, whatever it was, or wasn't, had been obliterated by some of your bombs, along with the men who were guarding it!"

"Men guarding it?" Ito questioned.

"Yeah, some Marines were sent along to look after whatever it was." Beckler replied.

"Then it was a secret cargo."

"It was secret all right, but I have no idea what it was."

"I believe you, Andy," Ito assured, while appearing to have been relieved by the information that the KING had indeed been carrying a secret cargo.

"What I don't understand," Beckler questioned, "is why the Japanese threw so much fire power at the KING? Was it due to that cargo? And how did you know about it?"

"Intelligence told us that whatever you were carrying was going to be used to destroy our homeland! The KING had to be stopped at all costs!" Ito excitably explained. "Sink the KING and have our homes and families!"

"Do you believe that?"

"In part, yes."

"What do you mean in part?"

"I believe that whatever you were carrying would indeed be used to destroy my homeland. Now that it is destroyed, maybe there will be something for us to go home to after this war is over. And it will end soon, won't it?" Ito questioned in a defeated tone of voice.

Beckler didn't know what to say, or what Ito expected him to say.

"I know my country has lost the war," Ito continued. "We are a broken society, our women weep for their lost sons. So many have died that there is little left but tears."

Beckler was about to say something when someone rapped on the door. Ito said it was open, and the door opened. Several Japanese officers stepped into the office and started rattling off in Japanese to Ito. Beckler acted as though he didn't understand what was being said. No point in giving everything up just yet.

As soon as he heard the words 'killed the American,' he bolted from the chair and turned to face those who were speaking.

The short fat man from the boat was there, with bright red blood stains all over the front of his uniform.

Upon seeing Beckler quickly stand up and spin around, two of the Japanese grabbed for their pistols. Ito held his right hand up and stopped everything at once.

"Am I to understand that you speak Japanese?" Ito asked Beckler, in Japanese.

"Yes, of course I do." Beckler brushed the question off. "Who killed one of my men, and which one? You assured me no harm would befall us."

"It is a very unfortunate event," Ito consoled. "I assure you, it was not intended."

"What happened?!" Beckler demanded.

Ito put up his hand to his officers, then turned towards Beckler, "Please explain what has happened."

The fat one stepped forward, and very nervously began speaking. "One of the Americans became enraged when he was told of the black one's death. He attacked me. In the struggle, he was killed."

Most of the U.S. Naval ships that had arrived on the scene in search of survivors had since departed. Of the nearly two thousand men that had been on board the U.S.S. INDIANAPOLIS when she was hit, only three hundred and twenty were rescued. Of the bodies being pulled from the sea for identification, eight out of ten were either too badly decomposed, or had been so mutilated by sharks as to make proper identification impossible.

Each ship taking part in the gruesome task of identifying victims had to post guards with rifles to drive off sharks feasting on floating corpses.

Powerboats sent out from the mother ships would attempt to retrieve personal effects from the bodies in an attempt to make identification. Where name tags could not be found, skin was carefully removed from the fingers, in the hopes that it could be dried and some form of print could be taken.

For many, all efforts were fruitless. Sharks had rendered a large portion of the bodies unidentifiable. What sharks hadn't done, the sea had done for them. Bodies that still had fingers attached to them, had decomposed to the point that the flesh had started to fall off, removing any trace of prints.

It had taken almost a dozen rounds of rifle bullets to drive two very determined sharks away from one body that showed very little signs of decomposing. The fresh-like state of what remained of the body, told those in the powerboat that this sailor had died only a short time ago.

Sadly however, the sharks had made what would have been an easy job of identification, impossible. So like all the others, the body was weighted with three 5" shells tied securely with two inch rope. After a few kind words, the body was rolled off the side of the powerboat and dropped into the depths of the ocean.

The men in the powerboat couldn't help feeling a true sense of grieving the young sailor whose body they had just committed to the deep. He had such a youthful looking face, at least what was left of it. The hardest part of all was the fact that he must have just died, the body was fresh, lacking any signs of bloating. If only they could have reached him sooner! How could a capital ship of the United States Navy go missing for so long?

The answers no longer mattered for the hundreds of bodies floating around them, waiting for some form of burial. It sure didn't matter to the young sailor they had just committed to the deep. Jess Tasman was gone.

CHAPTER FORTY-ONE
August 6, 1945
08:00
8:00 AM

It was a bright clear day as the ship neared its home port of Kure. Beckler was a bit uneasy about what might be in store for him and his men when they were put ashore. Ito had treated them well, and had done what he had said he would, in regards to proper burials for Louey, and Irish. He had even investigated the incident that left Irish dead. The fat officer had incited the scuffle by laughing when another Japanese officer translated into English the news of Louey's death. Ito was apologetic, but also pointed out that there was nothing he could do, since no rules had been broken by his officers.

Ito had sent for Beckler this morning, and now the two of them were standing on the forward part of the open bridge, enjoying their last few minutes together. They had grown to enjoy each other's company and respect. Having a prisoner-of-war on the bridge was not something that was generally accepted, but since the war was almost over, and the prisoners would soon be the victors, Ito only thought it in his best interest to be accommodating.

The city of Kure was now in plain view. Beckler would soon have to go below, to keep Ito from getting into trouble with his superiors, as Kure was one of Japan's prime naval bases.

High above the ship Beckler heard the steady roar of B-29s. Ito glanced up with a sullen face, Beckler could sense the pain and frustration going through this mild man.

"Could be reconnaissance," Beckler spoke softly, as if to ease the pain.

"The B-san could be President Truman making a social visit," Ito sadly replied.

Beckler didn't reply. The B-29s had been bombing Japan at will. There seemed very little the Japanese could do to stem the flow of American bombers over their cities.

Beckler was about to be returned below, when suddenly, an enormous cloud appeared in the distance, somewhere beyond the city.

Both men stepped closer to the foreward rail, as the cloud rapidly grew in size, climbing higher and higher, before it started to fall back to earth forming a titanic mushroom, then came the sound of a distant boom, followed by a sudden wind blowing in from the sea towards the cloud.

Ito shouted something in Japanese.

"What the hell?" Beckler wondered out loud.

The ship quickly started to alter course and come about, bringing her nose into the wind and head back out to sea.

Ito shouted more commands out in Japanese, as a young officer came running up and handed a apiece of paper to his captain.

"What's going on?" Beckler asked.

"Hiroshima is being bombed! Imperial Command feel Kure is next. We're going back out to sea! Now go below!"

Beckler took one last glance over his shoulder at the large sinister dark cloud, before dropping below.

Hours had passed before Ito had Beckler sent back up to his cabin. As he entered, Ito was seated behind his desk, slouched over, resting his head in his hands leering at the reports on the desk. His face appeared ashen. His eyes were swollen and reddish as if he had been crying.

"You sent for me, Captain?" Beckler asked, using Ito's rank for the benefit of the officer who had brought him up.

"Yes, be seated." Ito replied, as he waved the officer off. "I have something I wish you to see."

"What is it?" Beckler inquired, as he leaned over the desk, trying to make sense of the Japanese writing before him.

"Your country has just wiped out an entire city with a single bomb." Ito said flatly. "Hiroshima is no more."

"Oh my God," Beckler sighed, suddenly realizing what it was that he had witnessed earlier, and that the KING had been a decoy for the real carrier of the secret super-bomb.

Both men were in a state of shock. It took some time before either man spoke.

"I was set up. I was a pigeon for you to shoot at while the real bomb was carried by someone else! Those fuckin' bastards!" Beckler shouted.

Ito stepped over to a bureau and retrieved a couple bottles of sake, handing one of them to Beckler and keeping the other for himself. As they drank, they talked, and drank some more, it wasn't intended but Beckler could barely remember being helped back to his room.

Over the next three days, Beckler and Ito kept pretty much to themselves, each trying to figure out where the world was heading. Beckler could not bring himself to tell Scotty, Boss, and Gene what he had come to realize about their mission. Finally, one night after a short visit with Ito, Beckler was resting on his mat.

"Somethin' been a troubling me, Captain," Scotty said. "If they dropped a super-bomb on Japan, where did it come from?"

"I don't know."

"I mean, what the dickens were we carryin'? If it wasn't that bomb?" Scotty continued.

"I don't know."

"I don't mean to be rude, Captain, but don't you suppose that just maybe we wasn't carryin' a blasted thing down in that hold?"

Beckler didn't answer. He didn't have to. Scotty could tell by his look that he had indeed been thinking that very thought.

"I never did think much of that little one," Scotty signed. "What's his name?"

"Delair."

"Aye, Captain, that's the one!"

Eight days had passed since Hiroshima had been hit. Three days later Nagasaki had also been destroyed. After the second bomb had fallen, the Americans were left in their cabins. The only time the Japanese were seen was at meal times.

Then, shortly after the evening meal of rice, Ito came to Beckler's and Scotty's cabin. As the door was opened, he, and the officers next to him, bowed. Beckler and Scotty looked at each other, then returned the bow. The Japanese bowed again. Ito calmly looked Beckler in the eyes and surrendered the ship to him.

"What?" Beckler asked in surprise.

"The Imperial Empire has formally surrendered. I now do likewise to you. Becklerkun, you are now in command of this vessel. I have instructed my crew to follow your orders, and to release your men. We are now your prisoners."

"You are no such thing!" Becker snapped back. "As you said before, we are not samurai! The war is over. We are once again just two plain men. However, I do want the fat one held for killing Irish."

"As you wish," Ito bowed, before translating it into Japanese, and sending two of his men after the fat officer.

"Can I send a telegraph from this ship?" Beckler questioned.

"Yes, I will take you to the radio room," Ito replied.

Delair was busy filing some papers into his briefcase. The war had been long and hard for him. He had done things he would never forget, although he found some comfort in telling himself that the war had been shortened by the bomb, and maybe the sacrifice was worth it. Danielson had kept telling him so, but still he just wished that the KING could have made it through. As he placed the final papers into the case, a WAV entered his office and placed a sealed envelope on the desk.

"A telegram for you, Lieutenant," she said.

Delair tapped the edge of the envelope on the deck before tearing the end of it open and sliding the telegram out and unfolding it.

> TO LIEUTENANT RICHARD DELAIR:
> YOU OWE ME . . . BRING LT. HEWITT TO KURE . . . DOCKING THERE ON 19TH . . . ABOARD CAPTURED JAP DESTROYER . . . STOP SIGNED . . . DECOY.

Delair was stunned! Not only had that bastard survived, but somehow managed to capture an enemy destroyer! He didn't know how to feel, he was elated that Beckler had made it, but a sense of foreboding, and shame flashed through him as he now knew that Beckler had figured it all out. He quickly tucked the telegram into his pocket and rushed out across the base towards Danielson's office.

Beckler treated Ito and his other Japanese captives with all the respect that they had offered him. They were free to roam the ship almost at will. As for the fat one that had killed Irish, he was no longer Beckler's concern. Shortly after learning that the war was over, and that he was now a prisoner of war himself, he had committed suicide. Scotty had gone looking for him, finding him in a pool of blood with a dagger skewered into his bowels.

Beckler had also had the time, as they sailed back towards Kure, to visit with his new friend Ito about his plans after the war.

"If it pleases the Americans, I would like to return to my fishing boat and take my rightful place as a fisherman."

"Then why did you attend college in the States, if a fisherman is all you wanted to be?" Beckler asked.

"I had wanted more out of life at one time. But now I wish for nothing more. I've had enough excitement. The sea is so peaceful and beautiful. I can live out my life in the harmony of nature. What more could one ask?" Ito replied with a smile.

Beckler didn't argue, it did make sense and sounded so tempting.

As the ship neared the pier, Beckler could see two people standing off by themselves. He raised the binoculars to his eyes and adjusted the focus. His heart sank.

"Those rotten bastards!" Beckler pounded his fist down on the console.

"What is it?" Ito, who was standing next to Beckler asked.

"See those two American officers standing on the pier?" Beckler asked, as he handed the binoculars to Ito.

"Yes, I see them," Ito replied.

"Those are the slime responsible for the KING even being a part of this war!" Beckler said. "They were suppose to bring me something. I see they didn't bother."

As soon as the gangway was lowered, Danielson and Delair marched up and asked directions to the bridge. Gene removed the cigar from his mouth and spit on the deck next to their feet, before motioning with his thumb towards the bridge.

Beckler didn't mince words as he told the two of them just what he thought of them. They didn't put up much of a fight, instead they tried to explain how he and the crew of the KING had done a great service for their country. How they were heroic and might have saved thousands of American lives.

"Tell that to their families!" Beckler shot back.

"The official record shows that the KING was carrying regular military supplies," Danielson replied. "I'm sorry, but that is how it must be."

"I figured as much," Beckler snapped.

"What about this ship?" Danielson questioned. "How did you capture a destroyer?"

"Things are not always as they appear," Beckler testily shot back. "You of all people should understand that. They captured us, treated us well, then surrendered to us when the end of the war was announced. I want them to be treated with honor and released to go back to their homes as soon as possible."

"They're just a bunch of Japs! They don't get special . . . " Danielson started to say before Beckler landed a strong right cross to the admiral's jaw, which sent the admiral smashing into the engineroom telegraph before crashing onto the floor.

"Do you realize what you just did?" Delair shouted. "You hit a superior officer."

"It's all right," Danielson said, somewhat in a daze. "He was right in doing so. I'll do what I can, Captain."

Beckler leered down at the Admiral, then turned to leave, suddenly stopping and quickly turning back around to lay Delair out across the deck with another right.

"That's for Millie!" He said. "And for not doing as you were asked."

"Asked? What do you mean asked?" Delair puzzled.

"Lt. Hewitt. Where is she?"

"Stationed at Great Lakes," Delair started to defend himself. "But she is gone on leave. Don't really know where. That's why we didn't bring her along."

"I'll find her," Beckler sharply replied. "and remember you haven't got my bill for services yet."

"We'll take care of you," Danielson offered.

"To settle the score, see to it that Ito, that's the Japanese Captain of this vessel, gets treated real fair. Then set him up with a steel hull fishing trawler."

"How do we go about getting a boat like that?" Danielson asked.

"You found the KING didn't you?" Beckler shot back before stepping out of the bridge, slamming the door behind himself.

Beckler noticed a military guard leading Ito away.

"Hey, hold up there!" He shouted to the guards, as he ran up and faced his new found friend.

"Need a silent partner for that fishing boat of yours?"

"I would be very honored to be partner with you, Captain Andrew Beckler." Ito replied with a broad smile as he bowed, then was led away.

CHAPTER FORTY-TWO
August 30, 1945
13:00
1:00 PM

Beckler rose from his seat in the guard shack at the main gate to Great Lakes Naval Training Station as soon as he saw the taxi pull up. Beckler ran through the steady downpour of rain and quickly threw himself into the cab's back seat.

"LaSalle Street Station, driver," Beckler said as he wiped the rain from his brow.

The driver nodded and set the taxi in motion. Beckler relaxed into the thick seat and watched as rain drops ran down the side windows. As the scenery whisked by, Beckler remembered a time long ago. The time of his youth. His father had brought him to Chicago. The memories came flooding back, after all these years. The windy city had filled him with excitement. He remembered the first time he had ever seen Lake Michigan. He was sure that it was larger than any ocean could be.

Now, as he looked out the left side window, the deep blue, magnificent, fresh water lake was getting farther and farther away.

"Hey, buddy," Beckler called out. "Why not take the scenic route, along the lake."

"As long as you're paying the bill," the cabby shrugged. "I'll take any route you wish."

"The lake shore it is then," Beckler smiled.

"How far would you like me to go along the lake?" The cabby asked.

"At least to Michigan Avenue," Beckler quickly replied. "Then we'll finish our little trip off with a trip down the 'magnificent mile'."

The cabby didn't bother with a reply, simply nodded and drove on. They turned off U.S. 41 onto Old Elm Road, then on down to Sheridan Road which brought the lake back into full view. After passing through Evanston, Sheridan Road (after several changes in name), runs into Lake Shore Drive, certainly one of the most beautiful streets in the world.

A couple of blocks past Lincoln Park Zoo, Lake Shore Drive swings off to the east and continues following the lake, while Michigan Avenue shoots straight south towards the heart and soul of the city.

The trip seemed all too short, for soon the cab was turning right onto West Congress, with LaSalle Street only seven blocks from Michigan Avenue.

"Here you are buddy, LaSalle Street Station," the cabby said without turning around.

"Thank for the tour," Beckler smiled as he paid the fare. "I really enjoyed it."

"All in a day's work. Have a nice trip."

Beckler didn't waste any time waiting in line for a ticket, there wasn't a line. There were hundreds of people milling about. But luckily, few were in need of a ticket.

"Where to?" An over-weight, middle-aged lady with a pleasant face asked.

"Marshall, Michigan, please," Beckler replied.

"Oh, dear!" the ticket lady frowned.

"What is it?"

"I'm sorry, sir. But you're either very early or slightly late."

"How's that?"

The Detroit bound train," she apologeticly sighed, "which makes a stop in Marshall, just left."

"Well, don't worry," Beckler soothed. Suddenly realizing that he was feeling sorry for her. "I'll just catch the next one. When will that be?"

"Not for another two hours, I'm afraid."

"Two hours is just fine," Beckler assured her. "I'll take a ticket for it."

"Very good, sir."

"By the way," Beckler asked as if he just thought of something else. "Will you still be working then?"

"Why yes, why?" She perked up and nudged her hair with her hand.

"Well, I'm rather tired," Beckler replied. "And I thought I might sit right over there," pointing towards a row of wooden benches. "And take a little nap. Would you be so kind as to be sure I'm awake for that train?"

"Yes, I'll be sure," she quietly replied.

Beckler was half the way towards the benches when he realized that her tone of voice reflected that she must have thought his request was going to be something else.

"Mr. Beckler," the soft and pleasant voice called to him, as the ticket lady gently nudged him. "Mr. Beckler, the train for Detroit is now boarding."

Slowly, shaking off the drug-like sleep from his mind, Beckler looked into her soft brown eyes and smiled. "You're a gem. Thank you."

She smiled, nodded, then returned to her ticket counter that now had a line in front of it.

Beckler settled into a window seat, reclined it, then resumed his sleep. He felt the train begin moving, slowly building speed with every yard of track traveled.

"Kalamazoo!" A conductor sang out. "Next stop Kalamazoo!"

Beckler had slept almost all the way there. Marshall was only two stops away from Kalamazoo. He wiped the sleep from his eyes and looked out across the now-darkened Michigan countryside. The train roared around a bend as the lights of Kalamazoo city limits streaked by the window. Soon, the train started to slow until it pulled along the depot and stopped. After several minutes, it was going again.

"Battle Creek!" sang the conductor, as he strolled down the aisle. "Next stop Battle Creek in ten minutes!"

The process was repeated in Battle Creek, and as soon as the train was moving again, the conductor was again moving through the cars calling out the next stop.

"Marshall! The next stop is Marshall!"

Beckler felt his stomach tighten. God, he hoped that she was here. What if she had already left for Chicago? After only a few minutes of racing through the darkened countryside, the train began to slow down until it finally stopped.

"Marshall!" called the conductor. "All passengers for Marshall may now depart from the left side of the train."

Beckler rose from his seat, grabbed his duffle bag and stepped from the train.

He moved over to one of the other passengers that had gotten off the train, and asked where one might find a room for the night.

"I suggest the National House," the man replied. "It is located just three blocks west and three blocks north."

"Thanks," Beckler said, as he turned and made for the inn.

The National House Inn, was the oldest operating inn between Chicago and Detroit. It was built of brick and had a limited number of tastefully decorated rooms to offer. Beckler's room for the evening was the Ketchum room, so named for the town's founding father.

The sun outside his window was warm and bright, as Beckler awoke. Looking at his watch, he couldn't believe that it was already almost eleven-thirty. After a quick shower and shave, Beckler left the inn.

He had devised a game plan for finding Becky. The key to it lay in finding a drug store. The one person in any small town that would know everybody was the druggist. He was standing on the north side of the National House Inn, on Michigan Avenue. Across the street was an unusual house. It reminded him of similar structures he had seen on the Hawaiian Islands. To the right, east, layed the downtown business district. Beckler decided that his best shot was in that direction.

Beckler crossed over to the north side of the street and headed east, passing Grant Street, the Inter-Urban Railway station, then Eagle Street. About midway through the next block, he found what he was looking for, a Rexall Drug® store, it's huge orange sign proclaimed it as Hemmingsen's Drug.

Stepping through the door, Beckler's eyes quickly surveyed the entire store. To the left, the druggist's counter, and the usual shelves filled with health and beauty aids. To the right, the lunch counter area. The entire place appeared spotless and shiny. The floor was a soft blue linoleum, the walls a crisp white.

The hollowness inside his stomach made Beckler step over to the lunch counter and take the end stool. As soon as he had taken his seat, a stream of people began flowing through the door for lunch.

"This place is as popular as Mama's!" Beckler smiled.

"How's that?" someone asked.

Beckler turned and faced a gentle-looking man of about five foot six inches tall, medium build, with slicked back hair and wire frame spectacles.

"I just said that this place is as popular here as a place I know of in San Francisco."

"I see," the man said. "We serve over two hundred meals here during lunch. We have a deal worked out with State Farm Insurance®. We have food made up in advance so that the office personnel from there can get a hot meal in twelve to fifteen minutes."

"I'm impressed," Beckler said.

"How about you?" The man asked. "What can I get for you?"

"How about a shaved ham sandwich, and a cherry coke."

"Shaved ham and cherry coke it is."

As the man returned with the order, Beckler asked if he could talk to the druggist.

"You are," the man grinned. "I'm Chet Hemmingson. I do a little of everything around here. Between prescriptions, I give the girls at the counter a hand during lunch."

"Please to meet you, Chet," Beckler smiled as he offered his hand. "I'm Andrew Beckler."

"Andrew," Chet said, as he took Beckler's hand. "What else is on your mind?"

"I'm looking for someone, and I figured that the local druggist might be the one person that knows most people in town."

"Know most of them anyway," Chet beamed. "Who are you looking for?"

"The Hewitts's. Rebecca Hewitt in particular."

"Becky?"

"Yes!"

"Oh sure, I know them. The father's name is Gerald. Live up on North Madison. Second or third place past Oaklawn Hospital. Big white house trimmed in blue."

"That's great!" Beckler said as he polished off his sandwich and took his last swallow of coke. "Where's Madison?"

"Madison is two blocks east of here. The hospital is one block north, on the corner of Mansion and Madison."

"Great." Beckler said while he shook Chet's hand. "What do I owe you?"

"Thirty cents."

Beckler threw a dollar on the counter and thanked Chet again, then made for the door.

"Nice to have met you Andrew," Chet called after him. "You come back again."

"You bet." Beckler said before stepping back into the sunshine.

Marshall was everything Becky had said it was. The perfect home town. Tree lined streets, manicured lawns, well kept stately homes. But the thing that struck Beckler the most was the open and friendly townspeople. He had never stepped foot in this town before, and yet everyone he met smiled and said something nice.

At last, Beckler was standing in front of the Hewitt home. A large victorian frame home, with a full porch, and high peaked roof. As he climbed the steps of the porch, he could feel his heart pounding in the side of his neck. The love of his life was about to be in his arms again. He stopped in front of the door and paused a moment to rehearse what he was going to say, then knocked on the door. After several seconds passed without a reply, he knocked again, still no reply.

Disappointed at not finding anyone home, he decided to try the back of the house before leaving. Rounding the side of the house, Beckler noticed someone bent over, weeding a beautiful flower garden.

"Excuse me," Beckler began. "Could you tell me if this is the Hewitt residence?"

The lady slowly straightened up, turned and looked at the stranger standing before her. Beckler smiled. He knew from the woman's facial features, that he did indeed have the right place.

"You must be Mrs. Hewitt," he smiled while offering his hand. "You look so much like you daughter, Rebecca."

"Thank you," she returned his smile. "And you are?"

"Andrew Beckler."

"Oh, my," Mrs. Hewitt laughed as she put her hands to her face. "I'm so glad to meet you. Becky has said so many nice things about you. We were worried when we didn't hear from you."

"I wanted to surprise her," Beckler shyly offered.

"And that you will, that you will! But I'm afraid she and her father are downtown at the moment getting the car serviced. But you can come inside and wait for her if you like."

"Would you mind terribly if I went to the garage. It has been a very long time since I've seen her, and I'm quite anxious."

"I understand completely," Mrs. Hewitt sweetly replied. "They are at the Ford garage on Eagle Street. That's only several blocks from here. It's a big fieldstone building."

"Yes I know where Eagle Street is. Thank you."

As Beckler stepped through the open service door into the cavernous garage, illuminated by a dozen or more large skylights in the humped roof, he could see a man and a woman in a paisley floral print dress, standing with their backs to him, watching a mechanic working under the hood.

The closer he got to them, the more he could hear what they were saying. There was no doubt, the voice belonged to his sweet Becky.

Without saying a word, he stopped about ten feet from them and stood silently with his hands tucked into his back trouser pockets. It took several minutes before Becky's father noticed him, and turned to see more clearly who it was, causing Becky to do the same.

At first her expression was blank, as if in total disbelief. Then it slowly melted away as she flushed with excitement. She dropped her purse and ran toward him with open arms, and tears welling in her eyes.

"Surprise," Beckler said, as he took her in his arms and twirled her around. Then hungrily and passionately, he kissed her soft, moist lips.